HELEN CRUMMY

# WHOM DYKES DIVIDE

A STORY OF THE NIDDRIE COALBEARERS

ISBN: 978-0-9546397-4-7

Published by Small and Crummy Publications
4 Whitehill Street
Newcraighall
EH21 8RA
http://www.smallandcrummy.co.uk

Illustrations by Andrew Crummy
Editting by Carmel Daly and Shirley-Anne Murdoch
Book design by Shirley-Anne Murdoch

HELEN CRUMMY

# WHOM
# DYKES
# DIVIDE

A STORY OF THE NIDRRIE COALBEARERS

Whom Dykes Divide is an historical novel tracing the history of two mining families in the Niddrie and Newcraighall area of the Lothian Coalfield in Scotland. The main purpose of the book is to explore and highlight in a way that has not been done before the extreme poverty and the appalling working conditions of Scotland`s collier families and the manner in which they were tied to their pits by deprivation and legalised slavery. The principal characters are fictional (except the landowners) but the social and historical setting is based on fact. An authentic backcloth for the events described in the book has been provided by the author's research into the history and development of the Niddrie and Newcraighall areas over the last six centuries. This book is dedicated to the memory of Agnes Moffat, a ten year old coalbearer.

*Ah! Freedom is a noble thing*
*Freedom makes man to have liking*
*Freedom all solace to man gives*
*He lives at ease that freely gives*
*A noble hert may have nane ease*
*Nae ellys nocht that may him please*
*Gif Freedom fail: for free liking*
*Is yornit owre as ither thing.*
*Na! He that aye has livit free*
*May nocht knaw weill the propertie.*
*The anger, nae the wretchit doom*
*That it couplit tae foul thirldom*
*But gif he had asssay it*
*Then all perquer he suld it wyt*
*And suld think Freedom nair the prize*
*Then as the gowd in warld that is.*

**JOHN BARBOUR** (1316 -1384)

*A! Freedom is a noble thing!*

# CONTENTS

## CHAPTER 1 **WONDER AND DECEPTION**

A raging gale blew Edinburgh's lightweight lawyers, gentry and dandies hither and thither, hindering the boy as he hurried down the Royal Mile. Hindered, but didn't stop, Lachie Macgraw: eighteen years old, freckled faced, sturdy and impatient.

He was in a hurry. He was on the last lap of his long journey from the west of Scotland to the Port of Leith, where, with all the optimism of youth, he saw himself board a tall ship, which would carry him to adventures on the high seas.

Pushing through an excited mob milling around the mercet cross he found himself suddenly unable to move. Now, Lachie had an aversion to mercet crosses: his father having been hung on one in his native village. Determined to keep going, he roughly elbowed his way through, only to find himself wedged between two men. One was a small, red nosed, shabby, genteel-looking gentleman, reeking of stale ale, the other a fierce looking individual whose pugilistic bearing warned, *"Dont meddle wi' me!"* Lachie was trapped.

Just then a fanfare of trumpets brought a resounding cheer from the crowd. This was followed by a hushed silence and an air of expectancy. All eyes were raised to the cross where a procession was filing in. A second fanfare followed; then the voice of the Herald boomed out, *"Hear ye! Hear ye!"* The next words were lost, carried away on a gust of wind, which simultaneously filled the nostrils of the crowd with the stench of the open drains. Between gusts the herald cried, *"In the year of our Lord, 1606, an act of the Scottish Parliament declares that from this day, no person within this realm shall, hire or conduce any collier, or coalbearer, without a sufficient testimonial of their master, whom they last served. And the said collier and coalbearer are to be esteemed repute and held as thieves and punished in their bodies for stealing themselves from their masters."*

The rest of the proclamation was inaudible, carried away on the gale and leaving in it's wake another strong whiff of the unforgettable High Street stink. A hush had come over the crowd: many seemed stunned as a voice from it's midst cried out in despair, *"My God! What next in this accursed land! Slavery in Scotland! Wha wid hae believed it! Shurily it went oot wi' feudalism!"*

At a loss to understand what was happening, Lachie sought an explanation from an old woman standing nearby. Before she had time to reply, he was answered by the cultured voice of one of the gentlemen hemming him in. *"It means simply that the law of Scotland enslaves the collier and his family to the pits for life. From the cradle to the grave he and his family will be serfs, the property of the coal owner, to be bought and sold as his goods and chattel."*

*"But guid news fir the coal-owners- is it no Duncan?"* his companion answered gleefully as he caught his eye and winked. Observing the look he bestowed on the young Lachie as he spoke, the old woman shuddered. She recognised the two men as well-known Edinburgh rogues, whom, tavern gossip had it, were now in the body snatching business. Quickly pulling her plaid over her head, she shuffled away as fast as her creaking joints could carry her, muttering to herself, *"Puir chiel! He's some mither's son! God help him, that's a' I can say!"*

Meanwhile Lachie, in all innocence, was enquiring of the rough-necked man who colliers were. He had never heard of a coal-pit. Where he came from, people used peat in their fires. *"Oh them- they're the broon folk!"* was the curt reply. *"They howk coal. Decent folk like us hae naething tae dae wi' that kind- Dinna waste yer sympathy on the likes o' them!"* Quickly changing the subject, the friend intervened saying, *"Tell me laddie, why are you in such a hurry and where are ye bound for?"*

*"Oh I'm on my wey to the Port of Leith- I maun get there afore dark!"* replied Lachie, making a determined effort to go. *"Well, yer luck's in laddie,"* smiled the small man gripping his arm. "Just by chance we are travelling that way and know a quick and safe course- you can't be too careful these days laddie, with so many rogues and robbers on the roads!" Lachie thought for a moment then politely refused the offer. But the wheedling voice persisted, *"Oh come laddie! The day is still young and, as I gather this is your first visit to Scotland's capital. We would be honoured to show a fellow Scot the sights as we go."*

Lachie felt it would be ungracious to refuse such an offer and, after being given an assurance that he would reach his destination before dark, he agreed. *"First let's introduce ourselves,"* said the little man. *"I am Duncan Rumble, one time clerk to Lawyer Linton. At present I'm suffering temporary- only temporary - embarrassment and harassment and debarred from employment because of scurrilous lies being spread abroad about me. But don't you believe a word of it laddie. I am an honourable gentleman- son of a Scottish Earl no less!"*

*"Aye,"* snorted his companion under his breath. *"Drunken Duncan- born on the wrang side o' the blanket!"*

Lachie beamed as Duncan turned to him and said, *"Allow me to introduce my business partner, Peerie Pummel esquire. No doubt you will have heard of him…. He is a famous prize fighter, champion of the fayres. He is resting between bouts. We have recently formed a business partnership to raise a few bawbees to help resolve our temporary troubles."* Bowing low with a flourish he smiled and asked *"And whom do we have the honour of addressing sir?"*

Lachie felt flattered, yet at the same time ignorant and clumsy. He had never been addressed by a lawyer's clerk, far less the son of an Earl. *"O…Oh!"* he stammered. *"I…I'm Lachie Macgraw frae the west o' Scotland sir!"*

Suddenly Duncan stepped smartly aside saying, *"Excuse me laddie."* Turning his back, pulling his cloak over his face he fumbled in the folds of his clothing till he found a stoneware bottle, put it to his lips and took a long drink. *"Medicine laddie,"* he explained as he re-adjusted his dress, *"to sustain me on the journey. Come- let's go!"* So off they set walking into the wind. Out of his village for the first time, Lachie allowed the excitement of his adventure to blanket out the warnings instilled into him by his mother about putting his trust in strangers. As they trudged along, with no inhibitions, he answered question after question fired at him by Duncan. He told him that he had been brought up by his widowed mother and that, after her death a few weeks ago, he had been forced to vacate their croft.

*"Oh! so you are homeless and jobless! We are sorry to hear that are we not Peerie?"* said Duncan sadly. *"Aye,"* replied Lachie, *"ye could say that at this time I hae nae job and nae hame, but I'm shair I'll get work on a ship like my Uncle Lankin, wha sailed tae the Indies frae Leith."* Eerie, with a punch-drunk leer nudged Duncan and rubbing his hands together whispered under his breath, *"That's what ye think!"*

As they walked the wind gradually subsided. Lachie, no longer having to struggle against it, was able to look around. For the second time that day a sense of amazement and excitement welled up in him as he beheld the High Street with its tall houses and fine buildings. He was overawed. *"So this is Edinburgh Toon- what a wondrous sight!"* he thought aloud. To himself he muttered, *"Oh Mither- that you could hae lived to see this!"* Never had he seen so many people bustling to and fro. Some were buying wares from the stalls and luckenbooths, others were weaving their way through the milling crowd as they dodged the sedan chairs carrying the capital's gentry. But with one accord, all were intent on one thing… avoiding contact with the stinking filth lying everywhere.

Walking between his two companions, Lachie listened intently, eagerly asking questions. Duncan had already explained that this was the Royal Mile with the Castle at one end and the Royal Palace at the other, with four famous streets- Castle Hill, High Street, Netherbow and Canongate sandwiched between. As they passed St. Giles Cathedral, Duncan pointed out the Scottish Parliament, the Courts and the Tolbooth Jail. Lachie's head was spinning: he could not take it all in. On being told that John Knox had lived in one of the houses, his eyes lit up. *"Oh I hae heard o' him. He wis an evil man!"* The men looked at each other, nodded and said nothing. Leaving the Canongate they came to the Palace. *"Now here,"* said Duncan with a bow *"is the royal palace of Holyrood House!"*

*"Aw, I canna believe it!"* cried Lachie gaping. *"A real palace, guarded by soldiers!"* He could not contain his excitement as he eagerly asked, *"Wull we see his Majesty?"*

*"No"* was the curt reply. *"Since the Union three years ago, when our King became James the First of Great Britain, we rarely see him or his court in Scotland!."* Pointing to the tenement houses beside the Palace, Duncan went on, *"See these fine town houses. That's where many of his court live in style... that's when they're here!"* Lachie, scratching his tousled red head, wondered how people could live in houses built one on top of another. He had never heard of a stair. *"Come on!"* interrupted Peerie impatiently. By now he was bored and showing it. *"We canna tarry if we hae tae get there afore dark! Come on Lachie- he'll catch up!"*

It seemed Duncan needed yet another stop for medicinal reinforcement. Walking briskly the trio headed southeast passing Jock's Lodge, There they followed a rough uphill track, which led through tranquil rural countryside, where men and women could be seen labouring in the fields. Animals grazed around farm steadings and hens scratched outside the small thatched cottages dotted over the landscape. As they passed a country estate at Duddingston, the sea came into view.

Stopping and pointing to the silvery waters of the River Forth, Peerie said, *"Look Lachie! There's the river. We're nearly there!"* But he failed to mention that the harbour in the distance was Musselburgh, not Leith.

As they trudged along a rough track known as the Toll Road, Duncan wanted yet another stop, this time at a traveller's inn. After a whispered word in his ear from Peerie, he grudgingly conceded that they could not spare the time. His partner had reminded him that they had an important business deal to clinch before dark. At this point they were joined by a friendly, deaf old servant who informed them he was on an errand from his master; Sir John Gilmour of Craigmillar Castle. His destination was the Capella de Nudry Mershale Chapel on the banks of Niddrey Burn.

Rudely ignoring the servant the two men left Lachie to trudge along behind with him. Suddenly, his chatter became inaudible, as the afternoon quiet was broken by the fast-approaching clip-clop of horses' hooves. Two stallions thundered up the track pulling a carriage and forcing the men to jump off the track into the ditch. As the carriage passed, with one accord they respectfully doffed their bonnets and bowed their heads. *Ah!"* gabbled the servant, *"that's the new laird o' Niddrey an' his lady on their way to Niddrie Marischal Mansion. His faither, Archibald Wauchope, forfeited the lands when he and the Earl of Bothwell were found guilty o' leading an attack on Holyrood Palace. The King gied the estate to their enemies, the Edmonstone, then to Sir James Sandilands. But noo the King has pardoned the Wauchopes and Francis has married Sir James's dochter!. Yin wey tae get yer estate back eh lad!"*

Nudging Lachie hard in the ribs, with a a mischievous, toothless grin he asked, *"Dae ye think she'll hae heard the rumour aboot a Wauchope being a bedfellow o' the Duke of Lauderdale?"*

Neither the now drunk Duncan nor Peerie were interested in the old man's gossip- they had more important matters on their minds. So just as Lachie was about to learn what a bedfellow was, he found himself being roughly dragged away by Peerie, leaving the old man talking to himself.

By now they had reached the banks of a burn. Upstream surrounded by trees was a picturesque, stone-built, red-tiled chapel. *"Ah!"* thought Lachie, *"this must be the Chapel de Nudrey where the old man is going!"* In stark contrast, downstream beside a mill stood a dilapidated village. *"Surely nobody lives in such hovels,"* he thought, as they crossed the rickety bridge over the burn where he could now see the cluster of thatched hovels at close quarters. The place was deserted, with no sign of life despite the sunny afternoon.

There was also no sign of the sea! For the first time Lachie felt apprehensive and began to wonder if he had been wise to join up with this strange couple. By the scowl on Peerie's face, it was apparent he was angry with Duncan who by now was staggering some distance behind. Without his punch-drunk leer, the ex-boxer looked even more evil. Lachie shuddered. Walking in silence the trio came to a tumble-down shack, where a smith was working at a forge. Nearby a horse was walking round and round pulling a gin. *"Ah life at last!"* thought Lachie as ragged, bare-footed women and children scurried past carrying huge empty baskets on their backs.

Lachie never did remember just what happened next. All he could ever recall was Peerie bending down behind him and then an almighty crash.

## CHAPTER 2 **THE DARKNESS**

A wave of black pain threw Lachie up from his sea of unconsciouness. But was he now conscious of the world or the underworld?

This was a place of black darkness, pervaded by a stinking smell, the like of which he had never encountered before. He shuddered. He sweated. His head, pounded by invisible hammers throbbed and throbbed. The seething pain became unbearable. He passed out again, but not for long. Another wave pitched him back into the black world, to the pain, to the stench and the hammering. *"That stinking smell! What was it? The stench of death? Was this the grave?"*

Flickering funeral lights glimmered eerily in the darkness moving in procession forward then upwards to disappear suddenly into the blackness. Others took their place in a never-ending column. As Lachie's eyes grew accustomed to the darkness, he could not believe what he saw...Lights coming out of the heads of moving animals! Strange, giant, crab-like creatures with mis-shapen shells... or was it humps on their backs? Spindly legs quivered, as bodies struggled under heavy loads, as they moved ever upwards, higher and higher. But how? In the shimmering light he could just discern the outline of a crude ladder fashioned from a tree-trunk. In terror Lachie cried out, *"Mother of God! Where am I?"*

Suddenly, out of the darkness came a groan of pain as two of the creatures came crawling towards him. Petrified with fear, he could only scream as they drew nearer and nearer. He was engulfed in a great wave of uncontrollable terror. His teeth chattered, his heart pounded, and every bone in his body rattled as if his skeleton was no longer clothed in flesh. In anguish he cried out, *"Holy Mother of God, where am I? Hae I fallen doon a stinking pit? Is this Hell? Am I deed? Is this Eternal Damnation? Oh Christ hae mercy on this puir sinner! Oh those hammers! Are they the hammers o' Hell, hurled by the Deil himself? Oh Mither, Mither where are ye? Save yer puir Lachie- save me from those crawling critures!"*

The groaning and panting grew louder and louder as the creatures drew nearer and nearer. In terror Lachie covered his face with his hands. As he did so his fingers touched something furry slithering down his face. It was a rat. Screaming, he fell back into unconsciousness. But the merciless wave once more deposited him back on the black shore. Sobbing bitterly and crying out for his mother, he came round to find himself lying face down in a sea of mud. As he slowly dragged his aching body to a sitting position he remembered the monsterous crawling creatures.

Fearfully covering his face with his hands he peered through his fingers. All he could see was the darkness. He listened. All he could hear was the invisible hammers. Relieved, he relaxed. The creatures had gone. But had they? From the corner of his eye he could see two lights moving away from him. They had passed him by as he lay unconscious. Terrified that they might return, his eyes riveted on the lights, never leaving them as they joined the upward procession. Suddenly one of the creatures stumbled and cried out.

*"My God,"* Lachie cried in amazement, *"they're wemen and wee bairns wi' candles on their heeds, carrying great burdens! But what? Holy Mother of God this must be coal. This Hell Hole must be a coal-pit and the hammers- they're no in my heed- they're pick-axes hewing coal!"* In a flash, it all came flooding back- the Proclamation at the mercet cross, the two men and the journey. *"This must be the 'broon yins' the colliers and coal-bearers made slaves by law this very day."*

*"Oh Christ, hoo did I get here?* he yelled out in anguish. Panic stricken he made to rise, only to be grabbed by the hair, dragged through the mud and dumped at someone's feet. Landing him a kick in the ribs, his assailant shouted, *"Get up Macgraw!"* To the collier at whose feet he lay, the voice barked, *"MacVie, put this vagabond tae work! Caught begging he noo suffers the penalty o' the Law. The money in his pooch wull buy his pick-axe and candles. Show him hoo tae howk the coal and then let him get on wi' it!"* Landing a second kick he yelled *"Macgraw! Ye'll hae tae find yer ain coal-bearers within a week. And dinna try tae run away. The law will find ye, fetch ye back and punish ye in yer body. It could be the jougis or ye could dae the rounds wi' the gin horse - or worse still!"* With a sinister laugh he walked away, shouting over his shoulder, *"MacVie, tell him how we tamed ye, or better still, show him! Haw! Haw!"*

Lachie cried after him, *"Sir, there has been a terrible mistake. I hae ne'er begged in ma life!"* But the overseer kept walking, his vile laugh echoing through the pits.

Collier James MacVie's inscrutable face had never flinched. The only visible sign he gave that he had heard the overseer was when he faltered and missed a stroke with his pick-axe. In a flat voice he told Lachie to start filling the creels. *"Tomorrow when ye buy yer tools and candles, I'll show ye how tae howk the coal- No that I can teach ye how tae become a collier in the time oor Maisters gie us- it takes years tae become a skilled collier. But they dinna care. All they care aboot is getting the coal oot as fast as we can. Never mind oor safety, Life is cheap here in the pits. You'll learn that lad."*

He went on to explain how Lachie would be allocated a 'room' within a week. A room was a section of the coal face between two pillars of coal left to keep up the roof. *"An' dinna worry aboot findin' coal-bearers. Maybe a starving widow wumen will come looking fir work. But mare likely they'll pick up yin beggin' and put her tae work...Jist like they did tae ye, though they'll mare likely use the coorts tae dae it legally!"*

Lachie started to protest his innocence, but James cut him short saying, *"Aye lad! We ken ye're nae vagabond! You were probably tricked into admitting it afore a witness. We a' ken that it is illegal if ye are no' first charged in the coort and then sentenced. But ye try proving yer case! The coorts are run by oor maisters an' their ilk!"*

*"Ye can come hame and stey wi' ma family until ye get fixed up in the village,"* said James wielding his pick-axe at double time to make up for the minutes he had lost talking.

Lachie dragged his sodden and aching limbs to where a women was helping children to load and fasten their creels. No one spoke. As each child struggling under it's heavy load reached the foot of the ladder, he or she would grip the sides, pause, then before starting the long haul up, would turn and smile to a candle burning in one of the rooms. In pain, Lachie helped a woman fill her creel. The effort needed to lift it up on to her back almost ruptured him. *"My God Mistress! Hoo can ye cairry sic a burden? It must be one and a half hundredweight at least!"* The women only grunted. She could not spare the energy to reply- she had to save every scrap of strength for the journey ahead. Permanently bent and dragging her crippled leg, she too paused at the foot of the ladder, turned her face towards the candle and smiled. *"What strange manner o' ritual is this?"* wondered the bemused Lachie. *"Maybe it's fir guid luck on the journey!"*

Peering through the glimmer of the candle he could just make out the faint outline of a tiny head swathed in sacking. Two large eyes stared out of an elfin face, blackened with coal dust. The figure, like a delicate statue sculptured from coal, sat strangely still, as if hypnotised by the steady beat of the pick-axes resounding through the pit.

Suddenly a child's piercing scream rent the foul air. In the next room a collier with a leather strap cursed loudly as he brutally beat a boy of about eight years of age. The child's mother, screaming and shouting, pulled her son away yelling, *"Ye ken better than tae waste time playing at the top when yer creel is empty. He has telt ye often enough he needs every load tae mak up oor wages. There is nae time tae play when ye're at work! Ye are o'er big tae play onyhow!"* When out of his father's earshot, she whispered as she wiped away the boy's tears with her sacking apron, *"Dinna greet Wull. Ye hae only twa mare loads and then it'll be lowsing time."*

*"Thank the Lord!"* thought Lachie. *"Will this day never end?"*

Meanwhile the face behind the candle continued to stare, oblivious of the commotion behind her. Wull, still sobbing bitterly, with his creel now full, struggled to the ladder and like the others before him, paused, turned his tear-stained face towards the candle and bravely gave a wan smile.

In answer, Lachie saw a radiant smile light up the little face behind the candle. *"A wee angel sent by God tae light up this hell hole,"* thought Lachie through a haze of fear, pain and trepidation. He was later to learn that five-year-old Mary MacVie was deaf and dumb. For the past year she had sat holding her father's candle while he hewed coal sixteen hours a day, six days a week.

Finishing time came at last. With tools and creels neatly stored away, Lachie followed the family up the creaking ladder. To him it presented a perilous journey. He dare not look down. The children, free of their burden, scrambled up like monkeys out into the bitterly cold, moonlit night. There, like shadows in the night, they joined other families trudging wearily and silently along the same rough track Lachie had tread that afternoon.

As the exhausted families reached Niddrey village, he recognised it as the wretched assembly of hovels he had passed earlier. Standing in the moonlight, waiting for James to light a candle before entering, the hovel reminded him of his 'cot' in Ayrshire. The walls were a jumble of stones built without mortar, there was no window, and the thatched roof had no chimney, only a hole to let out the smoke.

Bending almost double he followed the family into a low, dingy room, which smelt of damp and smoke reek. In the flickering candlelight he could just make out a rough box bed, two straw pallets, and a crude bench on which lay wooden bowls, horn spoons, a cooking pot and a box containing meal.

In total silence the family went about their daily chores. James kindled a fire on the circular hearth in the middle of the earthen floor, the boys were dispatched to the communal well for water. Martha, James's wife, and their daughters busied themselves preparing the supper of porridge and kail. Lachie gasped and spluttered as the room filled up with smoke, which swirled around before it eventually found its way out through the vent-hole in the roof.

When the meal was ready, Lachie was invited to join the family as they squatted round the fire eating in total silence. Immediately it was finished, the children, making no attempt to play, reluctantly wiped their hands and faces with a piece of wet sacking, removed some of their clothes, crawled on to the pallets and fell fast asleep.

Lachie watching James wash was horrified to see a huge brown weal appear on his brow as the collier wiped away the dirt. Catching his look of horror James said, *"Aye Lachie, yer eyes are nae deceiving ye- it's a brand! When ma brither an' me were young, we thought we could fight tae improve oor lot. He was transported, fir inciting a riot, they said! We were in fact trying tae get colliers to form a combination- a union o' workers- to fight fir better conditions. And me? I was branded! Many o' us tried to keep up the fight after he left an' were punished many times. I hae been flogged, fastened in the iron collar, and harnessed tae a gin in place o' the horse! But in the end the maisters won. They always wull! With a wife an' four bairns tae feed, I canna dae ither than submit- that's what that swine meant this afternoon. An' noo he tells us the law o' Scotland hae made colliers and salters the legal property o' the pit! Then a' I can say is, God help us a!"*

Lachie, convinced by now that he would be better dead, crawled into the damp straw pallet beside the boys. There he spent the night tossing and turning; dreaming of escape, while afraid to face the morrow.

And so Lachie Macgraw became a press-ganged collier in the Niddrey pits. Within a few weeks he acquired a young widow and her four children as his coal-bearers. They had been arrested for begging, tried, and enslaved to the pit for life.

## CHAPTER 3 **A FA'**

About this time the Niddrey pits were rife with rumour. An Act of Parliament[1] had ratified King James's decision to restore the lands of Niddrey to the Wauchopes. Sir Francis, the new laird, was planning sweeping changes on the estate. The mansion, which once had housed a hundred men, had been burnt some years earlier by his father's enemies and was now to be lavishly restored. A new turret and battlement was to be added, a high stane dyke was to be built to replace the ditches encircling the estate, and there was a plan to extend the garden and orchards.

As rumours wafted over the estate ditches to the village beyond, colliers' hopes soared sky high. The community was agog with excitement and expectancy. Only a few voiced doubts that these improvement plans would extend to their hovels or to the coal works.

Meanwhile the pit where Lachie and the MacVies worked was nearing the end of its life. All the coal that could conveniently be reached had been extracted. The flooding was almost unmanageable so the pit was to be abandoned and another opened nearby. This was the practice at the time. Colliers were instructed to retreat, demolishing and extracting the pillars of coal in the worked out rooms as they went. This of course weakened the roof supports. Everyone knew the dangers and worked with all speed to get out.

It was early morning, work had started as usual. Martha MacVie, after helping her children fill and fasten their creels, watched them mount the ladder. She then filled her creel and securing it to the leather strap around her head hobbled to the foot of the ladder, smiled at Mary, and started the ascent. Almost immediately she stopped. An eerie silence had fallen. Pick-axes had ceased and colliers were listening intently to a faint noise. A shudder ran through the pit. Martha's heart missed a beat. She knew the signals only too well. The faint noise became a rumble. Gradually it grew louder and louder, followed by a thunderous crash mingled with human screams. She watched in horror as tons of rock hurtled through the roof, flattening the pillars of coal where her husband worked with little Mary.

Colliers, moved by a common impulse to help their comrades regardless of the danger, raced to the spot, grabbing shovels as they ran and shouting, *"A fa'.... A fa'!"* The terrified woman on the ladder yelled to her children to keep going. Without question or a backward glance, they blindly obeyed. They knew only too well the danger of trying to go back. There were others on the ladder between them and their mother. To falter and drop a piece of coal on the bearer below could mean injury or death. Leaping from the ladder, coal spewing from her creel, Martha raced to the fall. With bare hands and Herculean strength she clawed at the rock and slurry while the men shovelled frantically for what seemed hours. Gradually they uncovered James. He was clinging to little Mary, still with the smile for her mother on her lips. She was dead, but by some miracle James was still alive.

*"Ma bairn! Oh ma bairn!"* cried Martha hysterically as she flung herself on her daughter. Silently, tears mingling with the blood running down his blackened face James clasped his wife and dead child to his bosum.

Minutes later the voice of the overseer thundered down the pit, *"What the hell's gang on doon there? Why hae ye a' stopped?"* On being told that there had been a rock fall and that a child had been killed, he hesitated just for a second then yelled, *"The mither is doon there, is she no! Tell her tae fetch it oot! The rest o' ye start up again! An' MacVie - get yer section cleared!"* James MacVie, grief stricken and with murder in his heart, blindly obeyed. Treated like animals, they had come to respond like well-trained beasts. As if in a trance, he found his shovel and started clearing away the rock and slurry. A broken man. he knew only too well that all he could do was vent his feelings on the rocks, while crying to his God, *"Why hae ye forsaken us?"*

Anger swiftly followed horror making Lachie raise his fists and make to rush after the Overseer, but the branded face of the powerless father stopped him in his tracks *"Gawd! Ye are richt!"* hissed Lachie recalling James's words as he had released him, almost unconscious from the gin horse two months before. As punishment for trying to escape, Lachie had been made to 'do the round' - walk backwards facing the horse as it worked the gin. *"Lachie",*

James had said *"serfs in Scotland canna win! Oor maisters hae it a' tied up! They control Parliament, Kirk, Army and the Coorts. They make the laws to suit them an' their ilk, no us, their serfs. Aye lad! The rich in Scotland help themselves- only God can help the puir! An' where is He?"*

Meanwhile Martha, clutching her lifeless child, shambled to the ladder. As she passed, each collier ceased from his labour, placed his pick-axe at his feet, removed his bonnet and reverently bowed his head. On reaching the foot of the ladder, the mother paused and through her tears smiled down at Mary for the last time. Slowly she started the long ascent through the darkness into the sunlight, to the sun her little daughter had only felt on her face on the Sabbaths of her short life. That night as Lachie tried to comfort the sorrowing family- the family he now felt himself part of- he decided he could stand this life no longer.

Throwing caution to the wind, he bid them good-bye and under cover of darkness stole out of the village and headed for Leith. For a short time James's God was at hand, as the last that was seen of Lachie was of him triumphantly boarding a tallship which sailed on the tide in the morning.

But it sailed without Lachie Macgraw. An hour earlier the law had boarded the vessel, dragged him off and arrested him saying, *"Lachie Macgraw ye are charged under the 1606 Act of the Scottish Parliament of being a thief and stealing yourself from your lawful master- the Laird of Niddrey. In accordance with the said Law you are sentenced to be punished in your body!"*

## CHAPTER 4 **CLARET AND UNREST**

A blizzard had raged all day. In the heavily curtained library, candle light fell on magnificent paintings and gleaming furniture. Reclining before a blazing fire were Andrew Wauchope, Laird of Niddrey and his weekend guests. Surfeited by a sumptuous meal, they had left the ladies to their prattle and were now silently sipping claret from exquisite Venetian glasses. Sprawled in a deep armchair, the eminent lawyer and historian from neighbouring Newhailes estate James Dalrymple seemed in danger of dozing off. On the sofa opposite were two members of Parliament, the Earl of Abercorn from Duddingston, and Sir Charles Gilmour owner of Craigmillar Castle. The fourth guest, Mungo, a coal-owner's son from the Kingdom of Fife, had awkwardly squeezed his ungainly bulk into one of the high-backed chairs drawn into the table that held the decanters.

Earlier, the five had been discussing 'Cora Linn' a recent acquisition by the host. An etching, it was the work of fashionable artist John Clark, son of a fellow coal-owner Sir John Clark of Penicuik. It now hung beside a portrait of the Chevalier, which the Laird had explained with pride, was a personal gift from the Old Pretender himself, in recognition of the House of Wauchope's loyalty to the Jacobite cause. On either side of the fireplace were two other well known portraits... Sir William Wallace and the beautiful, but luckless Mary Queen of Scots, whose cause the Barony had also supported. The topic exhausted, a drowsy silence had fallen over the room. From the depth of his comfortable arm chair, where he was idly sipping his drink and watching flames from the fire dance in unison with the flickering shadows on the book-lined walls, more to himself than the company, Wauchope was murmuring, *"What a wonderful discovery coal has been for the human race. Mined here in Niddrey for nigh on 400 years, it is only now, in the early 1700's, that we're beginning to appreciate it's real value and potential!"*

*"Particularly in this cold climate,"* snapped Dalrymple smugly, sliding deeper into his chair, *"It certainly makes life more bearable for us who live in large houses. Now we can have a fire in every room and heat our greenhouses and vineries!"*

*"And"* added Mungo gleefully, his small beady eyes lighting up as he refilled his glass, *"now that steam power and mechanisation are improving drainage we can go deeper and deeper and get our hands on even more of the black gold!"*

*"And now that Andrew has installed the biggest steam engine in Scotland, this puts the Lothians in the forefront of coal exploitation in the country, does it not?"* asked Gilmour enthusiastically. *"It does indeed Sir Charles!...And gentlemen, it is imperative that we keep this lead- no matter the cost!"* cried Wauchope, thumping the arm of his chair with his free hand and turning red in the face. A servant had noiselessly entered the room and using the heavy brass tongs re-stoked the fire before replenishing the gentlemens' glasses from one of the crystal decanters. *"Thank you Grace, that will be all just now,"* said Wauchope.

Grace Young, a tall thin tight-lipped middle-aged spinster, with a spotty complexion, flat chest and scraggy grey hair well hidden beneath her bob cap, walked as if her feet hurt. It was no wonder..she had been on them since five that morning, when her day had begun by raking out and kindling the library fire. Not that she was required to do such menial tasks. There were young kitchen maids for the rough work but Grace fiercely resented any other servant entering the room she had been given personal responsibility for. The library was the Laird's private sanctum. Here he worked and entertained his gentlemen friends. Apart from the servant, no women were allowed within its hallowed walls. So Grace felt honoured and special... a cut above the other servants! She rewarded her master by devoting her life to looking after his creature comforts and maintaining the high standards of excellence he demanded.

Grace Young had worked in Niddrey Mansion since her brother, a gardener on the estate, had spoken for her some twenty years before. *"Long hours, scant time off and no lads allowed to call,"* were the reasons Grace primly gave for her spinsterhood. But behind her back, fellow servants would snigger as they gave their version, *"Choosy that yin! Sets her sights high! Nane o' us guid enough fir her! Apes the gentry she serves, dis Grace Young!"*

In Grace's private fantasy world, the library was the home she never had, whilst her frustrated mother-love was showered on her brother's only child, Andrew. She skimped and saved from her meagre wages to help pay for the boy's penny classes over at Newton Parish School, where he rewarded her by becoming the star pupil, reading everything he could lay his hands on. So keen was she to advance his studies, that she persuaded the housekeeper to obtain permission from the Laird to let her take discarded newspapers from the library so that she could pass them on to the boy.

After wrestling long and hard with her conscience and at great personal risk, she went so far as to smuggle out books for the sake of Andrew's education. When kneeling at her bedside saying her prayers in the attic she shared with three others, she would dutifully confess her sin qualifying it with, *"But oh Lord, I just borrow them! They are never missed. Nobody in the Laird's family reads them anyway- not like our Andrew does!"* She was so proud of him! Her life was hard, with long hours, scant pay and only one day off a month. But Grace knew her place, quoting from the Bible, *"The Lord maketh the rich and the Lord maketh the poor!"* When worn out and exhausted, young Andrew would tell her she was overworked, underpaid and exploited. On the rare occasions she would wearily agree, she would quickly add, *"I'm lucky te hae a job- a guid job at that- and on the richt side o' the dyke!"*

Satisfied that everything was as it should be and that every desire of her betters had been met, Grace noiselessly hobbled from the room as the Laird was asking Dalrymple, *"As a lawyer and a historian, what do you think history will make of this age James?"* After a long pause and with eyes fixed on the glowing embers, Dalrymple laid down his glass, pulled himself upright in the chair and gripping the lapels of his tunic as if about to address a jury, said, *"Gentlemen, it could be said that we are witnessing the dawn of a new era for Scotland- a golden age for its people. Something is stirring! It is as if the pent-up energies of the Scots has suddenly erupted, freeing their creative spirit to aspire to great achievements."*

*"What with James Watt and with the other brilliant young Scottish engineers inventing those ingenious machines, we are paving the way for a period of rapid and unprecedented progress, the likes of which Scotland has never witnessed in it's history before. And now with the rise of the iron industry and the Treaty of Union opening up new home and overseas markets, the demand for coal could be insatiable...aye insatiable!"*

Looking first at Wauchope, then at Abercorn, raising his shaggy eyebrows his voice changed as he said slowly, *"Well it's certainly a good time for you coal-owners to be alive. Scotland, rich in coal, is sitting on a gold mine- black gold- owned by a lucky few!"* Abercorn, coal-owner as well as member of Parliament, unable to conceal his annoyance, snorted, *"All right! But with one fifth of the Scottish nation in a state of beggary it could not come at a better time for the masses! It could be a boom and a blessing for all of us, could it not?.... Lawyers included!"* Before Dalrymple could reply, Gilmour, who knew these two of old...no love lost there, quickly intervened, *"Gentlemen, Andrew rightly says we must keep the lead- but how?"* Getting no immediate response he answered himself. *"I would say that now, as never before in our history, it is up to us, who by virtue of our noble birth and divine right to rule, should in the interests of Scotland through the offices of*

Parliament, Kirk, Court and Army dutifully play the role God bestowed on us, his humble servants, and guide this coming industrial revolution- because that, gentlemen, is surely what it could be."

"But first, how do we find extra labour to dig out the coal?" piped up Mungo peevishly, gulping down his sixth glass of claret.

"Aye. How! The masses are flocking to the new factories, using the new-fangled machinery, they won't come to work in our pits in spite of the high wages we are forced to pay to get workers!" complained Wauchope.

"Well all I can say is b..beggary can't be that b.. bad!" slurred Mungo, "when those so called b..beggars turn up their noses at honest work in our pits... Anyway, we all know what that kind do with their wages... drink, gamble and fornicate. Most don't want to work anyway! Bu then, they are not made like us - able to appreciate the finer things of life. They certainly don't have - what did you c..call it Sir James? Ah yes, the c..c..creative spirit!" With that, he hastily refilled his glass, flung back his head and tossed back another long drink.

Dalrymple, warming up as the claret loosened his tongue and brought a sparkle to his eyes said provocatively, "Come, coal- owners, admit ye are worried men! Here you are, sitting on a great untapped source of wealth and all you require is skilled labour to extract it... the skilled labour that only those whom Mungo calls 'that kind' can supply! Gentlemen, your chickens have come home to roost. That 'kind' would rather die of starvation than voluntarily don the halter of serfdom to work in your pits. Come on, admit within these four walls that the Act your noble coal-owning forbears pushed through Parliament has well and truly back-fired!"

"All right!" snarled Wauchope, no longer able to curb his anger. "It has left us with an acute labour shortage and forced us to push up wages- much higher than colliers really need or deserve. Mind you, for the life of me, I am at a loss to understand why they are so ungrateful for the long-term security and protection working in our pits undoubtedly provides for them and their families. But be it on their own heads! Much more important for us gentlemen, is, how do we get the Act amended?" Scratching his head, he thought for a moment, then turning to Abercorn, his eyes lit up as he said, "Ah! Could not you and Sir Charles as Members of Parliament, with the help of other coal-owning MPs, get a bill through the House to repeal the 1606 Act!"

Before Abercorn could reply Dalrymple posed the question. "On what grounds gentlemen? In a Christian country it would be fought purely on humanitarian grounds. But we all know that in the British Parliament, only sound economic arguments carry the day. Is it that you'll have to admit to the large profits waiting to be made in the home and overseas markets as well as in the new iron industry!"

"What about compensation for us coal-owners?" slurred Mungo, by now bleary-eyed. "We'll demand it! L..loss of s..serfs is loss of p..property!"

"If you want the Bill through in a hurry," retorted Dalrymple, "then you had better forget that!" Suddenly Wauchope had doubts. "In spite of the severe punishments we mete out we are all plagued with growing unrest... I have more than my share here at Niddrey, I can tell you! So if the Act were repealed, could it not be construed as giving it to colliers' demands'? But Abercorn had an answer *"Have no fear Andrew, Parliament can deal with that. You wait and see. Trust us!"*

*"Then how do we prevent a mass exodus once they are free?"* queried the Laird still not convinced.

*"Easy!"* said Abercorn. *"Stipulate they work a number of years before earning their freedom. And even then, we can make it that they will have to seek it through the Courts- a daunting experience gentlemen when you cannot read nor write!"*

*"Good t..thinking! Just imagine how that'll frighten the living daylights out of that i...ignorant, ...illiterate lot,"* yelled Mungo as he roared with laughter.

And so these gentlemen sat laughing and drinking into the early hours of the morning, planning a bill that would protect every facet of their power and wealth. Two hours after midnight as the Laird and his guests finally rose and prepared for bed, in his snow-covered slave village the day's toil was just beginning.

## CHAPTER 5 **BIG BELL**

One by one doorways were lit up by flickering candlelight and voices could be heard calling sleepy-headed children to rise for work. In answer to her father's call, Nettie, eldest daughter of James and Janet Macgraw, scrambled over her sleeping sisters and out of the straw bed. Her mother was already up. Looking gaunt and weary, having lit the fire in the middle of the earthen floor she was now stooped over it making porridge. As the thick smoke swirled around the room seemingly loathe to find its way out of the hole into the cold and dark, she tried hard not to cough for fear of waking the children.

*"Nettie leave wee Jemmie to the last!"* she whispered *"He is no weel. He has been greetin' a' nicht wi' the pain in his leg an' spittin' up blood."* Shaking the two boys sleeping beside Jemmie, she put her finger to her lips and whispered to them, *"Wheesht! Get up! An' dinna waken Jemmie."*

Sleep was important to Jemmie because three weeks before he had been the victim of a pit accident. The roof in Will Millar's room had collapsed leaving the eight year old, who was already weakened by consumption, with a badly mangled leg and Will gravely injured. In spite of their interrupted night's sleep, the boys rose like larks and, ignoring their mother's plea, like two wild pups started to fight over their clothes. Losing patience, Janet walloped them with the porridge spirtle till they howled in pain.

*"Faither,"* shouted Nettie above the din, *"hae ye forgotten it's ma birthday?"*

*"Naw lass, I have'na. Ye're sixteen taeday!"*

*"Oh Faither! I wish I had ma birthday on the Sabbath, then I widna hae tae gang doon the pit. Oh Faither I hate the pits!"*

*"I ken ye dae lass. I ken!"* muttered James with a sigh.

*"Faither, if it were the Sabbath I'd tak wee Jemmie tae paddle in the burn. He'd like that. He says it maks him feel better. If it were the summer an' it wis sunny, he'd lie in the sun -it's guid fir his consumption, isn't it?"*

She prattled on without waiting for a reply. *"Faither, oor Jemmie is real clever. He reckons I hae worked mare than half ma life in the pits, is that richt? He's guid at the countin'. Yin o' the best pupils in his class the Dominie says. Oh Faither, I wish I were a laddie an' could gang tae school an' learn tae read an' write."* Nettie kept chattering and shivering as she put on her pit clothes- pathetic rags covered with a sacking apron. No wool or flannel to keep her warm and no proper shoes for her feet. As she rattled on, her alert dark eyes kept following her mother. The moment she saw her turn her back, she quickly undid her pleat and shook out the long, dust-filled, tangled hair. With rough tugs she combed it with a crude horn comb then with deft twists, placed a knot on the front of her head and tied it in position with her sacking head-piece. *"Nettie Macgraw!"* yelled her mother over her shoulder. *"Fir God's sake, shut up will ye! Ma heed is splittin'. What wi' oor Jemmie greetin' a' nicht an' ye haeing yin o' yer bloody nightmares, there's nae much sleep fir ony o' us in this hoose!"*

*"Oh Mither! Can wee Jemmie no stey wi' Wull Millar the day? He is sae ill,"* begged Nettie. *"No he canny!"* snapped Janet. *"Jess Miller went into labour at the coals last nicht. Jemmie'll jist hae tae come wi' us an' sleep in a corner. Noo get the ithers up an' keep quiet!"* Sobbing, Nettie turned to her Father, *"Oh Faither! It's nae fair! Jemmie is sae ill! Ither bairns dinna hae tae gang tae work like collier bairns when they're ill. Why? What hae we done?"*

*"Wheesht Nettie! jist dae as ye're telt!"* warned James in a whisper, *"Mither's no feelin' weel this morning ither!"*. Exhausted by lack of sleep and at the end of her tether, Janet turned on her daughter and screamed, *"Why... bloody why? I'm sick tae death o' ye fore'er asking why tae everything. This time ye'll answer ma why fir a change. Why can't ye no be like yer brithers and sisters and accept yer bloody lot? Ye've worked in the pit for eight years noo and afore that I carried ye there in ma creel an' yet ye still go on aboot being feered! We're a' feered, but jist hae tae git on wi' it. What's sae special aboot ye that ye canna accept that yer yoked tae the pit till ye dee? There is nithin' ony o' us can dae aboot it. Sae shut-up an' let me hear nae mare aboot it! Dae ye understand?"*

With eyes flashing she turned to her husband and yelled, *"James Macgraw, it's yer bloody fault onywey! Ye talk tae her like she wis a laddie. Ye fill her heed wi' talk aboot fichtin' fir freedom, aboot* colliers *formin' a combination tae ficht the coal-owners. And if that's nae enough, ye're noo talkin' aboot freedom tae worship in the Kirk. What bloody next? She'll come tae a bad end that yin, mark ma words, an' it wull be yer bloody fault!"*

Without pausing for breath she renewed the attack on her daughter yelling, *"An' a lot o' bloody guid it has done him or us. Fichtin' fir freedom and actin' the martyr while maist o' his cronies sat back an' let him git on wi' it. Aye! an' when he wis jailed in the correction house or near throttled in the jougis, an' there wis nae money coming in an' we starved, wha cared? Naebody! Wha will remember him, or the name Macgraw, when we're deid an' gone! Naebody! Naw! There wull be nae mare bloody martyrs in this family! I'll see tae that ma lass!"* As she finished she stormed up to Nettie and, roughly tearing the piece of sacking from her head shouted, *"An' when I'm at it, get that bloody hair pleated like the rest o' the lassies! God! ye must always be different! Wha dae ye think ye are? Ye'll come tae a bad end, there's nithin' shairer. An' that faither of yer's encourages ye, makin' a comb fir ye when he's got better things tae dae! He never made yin fir me in a' the years I've been married tae him. Vanity! That what I ca' it! Jist what hae ony o' us tae be vain aboot?"*

*"Oh Mither!"* cried Nettie, *"it's jist that I dinna want tae get a bald patch on the front o' ma heed like a lot o' lassies dae! That's a'!"*

Ignoring the explanation Janet ranted on, *"An' anither thing, I've telt ye afore, if ye hate the pits sae much, there is a wey oot. The smith is lookin' fir a second wife tae bring up his wee bairns. That wey ye could work at the pit-heed an' we'd a' get peace frae yer bloody nightmares!"* With that she stamped back to the porridge pot and noisily started filling the bowls. Biting her lip to hold back the tears, Nettie helped Jemmie out of bed and tried to persuade him to eat some porridge.

All through his wife's tirade James had stood open-mouthed. His first reaction had been to belt her across the mouth for daring to talk to him like that. But his hand dropped when he looked into her eyes. Staring back at him was a look of such utter defeat and dejection, the like of which he had never seen before on any human being. *"Aye,"* he thought wearily, *"She's richt...it's a' been in vain. Naethin' has changed! Maybe she is richt when she tells me we shouldna' hae listened to grandfaither telling us we must cairry on the ficht fir justice an' that we owe it to oor ancestor Lachie Macgraw wha was killed o'er a hundred years ago leading yin o' the first riots!"*

In sixteen years of marriage, James had never heard such an outburst from his wife. Never had she spoken to him like that. Who would have thought that his dour submissive wife could harbour such thoughts, far less voice them. His mind went back to the days when she was sixteen and they fell in love. She was young, bonny and strong... all a collier could desire in a wife. In these days she sung like a linty. Come to think of it he had not heard her sing for many a year, far less laugh! Reluctantly James jolted himself back to the present...no time for daydreaming. Such luxury was not for colliers, even though it was free! Going over to where Nettie was helping Jemmie to dress, affectionately he rumpled his son's tousled hair and picking up a handful of coal dust rubbed it into the infected wound. As Jemmie winced he said kindly, "Bite yer lip son an' be a man! This is what the collier does when he gets hurt in the pit. Noo tak Nettie's hand an' she'll help ye along!" With that the family reluctantly left the dying embers to face the blizzard which was showing no sign of let-up. With the snow driving in their faces they struggled through the drifts, often falling or sinking up to their knees. Janet, who was dragging along a boy on each arm, met up with her friend Big Bell.

Big Bell, twice widowed, was until a year ago an agricultural worker at Wanton Wa's. After three bad harvests in a row, she had been caught begging with her four starving children. She was arrested and her punishment was to be put to work in a pit thus making her and her children the property of the coal-owner for the rest of their lives.

"Hoo's Jess?" enquired Janet anxiously, showing no signs of her earlier outburst. "Lost the bairn!" replied Bell with a sigh. "Puir Jess, she's haeing it rough. She hud tae work up tae the last meenute an' then the bairn wis born deid. We've been up a' nicht wi' her."

"Weel, it maun be God's Will- or maybe a blessing in disguise" murmured Janet drawing her sacking shawl tighter round the shivering child she had now lifted. "An' what aboot her man?" she enquired as she bent down to reassure the other child who had stumbled and was in tears.

"Oh Wull, he's gie ill," replied Bell. "They say he'll nae last much longer. What with his black spit and noo this last accident wi' Jemmie, he's no lang fir this life. He kens it, an' he worries what wull become o' Jess an' the bairns." As she spoke Bell glanced behind and saw Nettie and her little sister struggling to help Jemmie along. Pretending to stop to fasten the sacking on her feet, cheerily she greeted Jemmie as they met up with her, "Guid mornin'...An' hoos ma wee Macgraw this snowy mornin'?- a gie drooked craw I'd say! An' lookin' at yer sisters, two lassie drooked craws eh!"

The girls gave wan smiles, but Jemmie, clutching Nettie's hand, kept his head down. But Bell went on, "Come to think o' it Jemmie, I ken a sang aboot three craws. Dae ye think it is ye three Macgraws? And as ye a' ken, Big Bell canna sing, so what aboot some help lassies?" With that she put her arm around the little lad and in a deep voice started to sing as she helped him hobble painfully along.

> Three craws sat upon a wa',
>
> Sat upon a wa', sat upon a wa',
>
> Three craws sat upon a wa'
>
> On a wet an' windy mornin'.

Turning to the girls, she cried, "Richt lassies, noo ye ken the words, belt it oot!"

*Three craws sat upon a wa',*
*Sat upon a wa', sat upon a wa',*
*Three craws sat upon a wa'*
*On a wet an' windy mornin'.*

As they finished she bent down and gently stroking Jemmie's face with her coarse coal-ingrained hand, sang in her tuneless voice,

*Wee Jemmie Mcgraw, couldna walk at a',*
*Couldna walk at a', couldna walk at a',*
*Wee Jemmie Mcgraw, couldna walk at a',*
*Tae work at the coals in the mornin'."*
*"Noo Big Bell, wha didna gie a daw,*
*Didna gie a daw, didna gie a daw,*
*Noo Big Bell, wha didna gie a daw,*
*Cairried him tae the coals in the mornin!*

As she finished, Bell bent down and calling to the girls to start at the beginning, gently eased Jemmie on to her back. Heedless of the driving snow in their faces the girls belted out the song at the top of their voices and for the first time in days they saw their little brother smile as he snuggled into Bell.

Meanwhile James had caught up with his cousin Andy Macgraw and Dave Erskine, a comparative newcomer, who had come to Niddry Pit after being exchanged for a donkey (not an unusual occurrence). Originally from Fife, Dave still had difficulty understanding the local dialect. A thin, sinewy, private man, he preferred to keep his own company. For some reason known only to himself, he had never married. Now in his late thirties, he bore all the hallmarks of a typical collier: a permanent bent spine caused by lying sideways in low seams, blue and black scars all over his body, and a hand left partially disabled by unset broken bones. But now, when his night's rest was disturbed by a racking cough, he worried that this was the beginning of the black spit, the dust-related disease dreaded by all colliers. As the three men trudged along they were overtaken by Big Bell. With Jemmie perched on her back, she was still belting out the song. while behind her trudged an assortment of ragged, snow- covered child coal-bearers singing lustily as they gathered speed in the fast-falling snow.

Andy, standing aside to let them past, turned to Dave and James and said with a grin, *"What a wuman! Jist look at her, the biggest mistress fir miles around! But God she's coorse! She can curse and sweer like ony man an' match ony collier wi' the pick and shovel. Truth to tell, many o' them are feered o' her. But underneath, she has a heart o' corn. Mind ye, she's only been here a year. Gie her anither yin or twa toiling in these hell- holes and she'll look like the rest of the wemen, worn oot an' auld afore their time."* James chimed in, *"Aye, she's got hands like shovels, a voice like a foghorn an' feers naebody. But God help ye if ye cross her. They say the mare she says, the least guid it dis ony! "Noo work that yin oot Dave!"*

Andy, winking at his cousin nudged Dave saying, *"A word in yer ear Dave. She's on the look oot for number three"*! Turning to his cousin he solemnly asked him, *"Have ye noticed James hoo she keeps eying Dave here? Mind ye, I'll say this fir her, she's choosy. An' as we a' ken, what Big Bell wants, Big Bells gets- or taks! So Dave, look oot!"* Dave, getting more agitated by the minute muttered, *"Oh Christ!"*

*"Oh He'd tell ye, ye could dae a lot worse!"* retorted Andy. *"She'd be a guid asset. She's big, strong and willin', an' with four strong bairns intae the bargain, what mare could ye want?"*

*"Come tae think o' it,"* said James nudging Dave in the ribs again, *"there wid no be much coal howked efter a nicht wi her, wid there Andy?"*

Dave, who by this time was visibly shaking, stuttered, *"It's b. . b. .bloody b. . b. .buried I'd be gettin', nae m.. m..married wi' that yin!"* Ignoring Dave's discomfort, Andy with a chuckle went on, *"Yer intentions maun be honourable Dave. Last week she bloody near killed yin o' the lads fir trying his hand wi' her. God she nearly drooned him in a waterhole! It took three o' us tae haul her aff! He'll no go near her again, that yin!"* Wagging his finger in Dave's face he went on, *"Sae ye see Dave, if ye are the lucky man, she'll dae the winchin', the askin' an' the rest nae doobt!"*

By this time, much to Dave's relief they had reached the pit- head. Early morning work had already begun. Silhouetted again the dark sky, the brawny arm of the smith could be seen wielding a huge hammer as he struck a glowing piece of metal on his anvil. Further over, a gin horse was walking in a circle pulling an axle which operated a gearing system raising coal and water from the pit bottom. From a large heap of snow-covered coal, women were filling the horse-drawn carts which would deliver the coal to distribution centres in Edinburgh, or to Musselburgh for shipment overseas.

Having reached the pit-head, Bell shook the snow from the children's clothes as best she could, put three of them into an empty basket and watched as the horses pulled the little ones out of view. With Jemmie still on her back, she lit a candle and led the other children down the ladder to the pit bottom where the women and children collected their creels, straps and chains. They were followed by the colliers who picked up their mattocks, shovels and hammers before making their ways to their respective rooms.

Big Bell and Janet found a worked-out room which was about thirty inches high and gently eased Jemmie into it. There they tried unsuccessfully to dry him, but their aprons were soaking-wet. Nettie pleaded with her father to leave him a candle. *"Oh Faither ye ken hoo*

*feered he is o' rats- they'll smell the blood he's coughing up. Oh please, dinna leave him in the dark!"*
James hesitated before agreeing. Candles were a precious commodity; each collier had to pay for his own and that of his coal-bearers. Nettie went with him to collect one and on her return found Jemmie tossing, turning and coughing on his damp stone bed. Lighting the candle, she paused for a second before climbing into the room. Carefully she placed the light at his head, then gently stroking his feverish brow she wiped the blood from his mouth with her apron.

Kissing him, she made to leave. As she did so, she was suddenly seized by a spasm of fear which engulfed her whole body. Uncontrollable terror gripped her. Trembling from head to foot, with hands shaking she fumbled with her apron, stuffing it into her mouth in an effort to stifle a scream. In a blind panic to get out of the confined space, she made to stand up, only to bang her head on the roof and be flung back into the hole, momentarily knocking herself out. With a superhuman effort, sobbing and shaking somehow she managed to throw herself from the room, landing in a pool of water on the pit bottom. Next minute she was back beside the others filling her creel as if nothing had happened.

Nettie was claustrophobic, not that she knew what that meant. All she knew was that she had these terrifying fits of morbid fear and that they only happened when she was in the pit. She told no one. She was so ashamed, convinced that she brought them on herself, a punishment from God because she was a coward. The fits she could hide in the dark of the pit, but the screaming nightmares were beyond her control. She joined the others as the booming voice of Big Bell was resounding through the pit. She was refusing to let the children use the ladder until a broken rung had been repaired. Her request fell on deaf ears. No collier could spare the time to do it. Time was money and money was only earned hewing coal, not repairing ladders. In exasperation she grabbed a mattock, a piece of wood and some nails. Mounting the ladder, cursing all and sundry at the top of her voice, she noisily replaced the rung. The day's work could now begin for the women and child coal-bearers.

They would now load their cockle-shaped creels with anything up to one and a half hundredweight of coal and carry them from the rooms, along the pit bottom, often knee-deep in water. Painfully pulling themselves up the ladder they would pant for breath in the foul air. Some would make as many as twenty journeys a day- a distance equivalent to the height of St Paul's Cathedral.

As they came back with their empty creels, Janet, Bell and Nettie, making sure they were not seen by the overseer would take it in turn to look at Jemmie. By mid morning his cough and fever seemed to have subsided and he appeared to be sleeping. When it was Nettie's turn, she found her father rubbing more coal dust into his son's wound whilst pressing his ear against the little chest.

*"Oh Faither what's wrang?"* she cried anxiously as she splashed ankle deep through water towards him.

"*He's a'richt lass... the fever has gone. He's sleepin'!*," he replied, his voice lacking conviction.

The morning wore on. The pathetic little body, as thin as a stick, soiled with coal dust and splattered with blood-stains, lay huddled in the hole where he had been hidden. The only sign of life was an occasional faint moan and a movement of his scrawny arm feebly trying to clutch the mangled leg.

The last of the candle spluttered and went out. Water started to seep through the roof above his head. In the eery darkness the drip.... drip.... tapped out a message, "*Come! Come! Please come!*" The drip become a steady trickle then a rushing streamlet screaming, "*For God's sake, come quickly - please come quickly!*"

Big Bell came. It was too late. The little coal bearer was dead, his matted hair buried in the mud, his lifeless eyes wide open in wonder, his face serene, bereft of pain. Easing the little body gently out of the hole, with tears streaming down her face Bell held him close, quietly singing,

> *This day, wee Jemmie couldna walk at a',*
> *Couldna walk at a', couldna walk at a',*
> *His legs hackit sair, his feet red raw,*
> *He deed at the coals in the mornin'.*

## CHAPTER 6 **VENUS AND THE GARDENER**

*"Ta, ta!!"* cried Andrew Young to his parents and Aunt Grace as he left them at the door of Newton Kirk to spend his usual Sabbath afternoon, roaming Niddrey countryside. It was a brisk day with no sign of last week's snow storm. Andrew whistled as he went, his bonnet perched on the back of his head and his hands thrust deep in the pockets of his best breeches. He wondered what the afternoon would bring. Would he catch a glimpse of the early linnets, the yellowhammers or the bullfinches? It was too early for the cuckoo? Maybe he would catch a trout in Niddrey Burn, or even spot the badger which was rumoured to have been seen last year further up stream? He was also hoping to find a sheltered nook where he could read the Thomas Payne's pamphlet he clutched in his pocket.

Picking his way through the tombstones, his alert ears detected a muffled cry coming from over the stone dyke at the far end of the graveyard. It struck a cord in his memory. Years ago he recalled his mother telling him in a hushed voice that paupers and colliers were buried beyond that dyke. Puzzled, he had asked why children were forbidden to walk over the graves in the kirkyard yet were allowed to play on the paupers' graves. The reply was to be dragged quickly past the dyke and told not to ask questions. *"You'll learn soon enough!"*

*"Better late than never,"* he thought impulsively clambering over the dyke, where he found a tattered bundle of humanity, huddled on the ground, sobbing bitterly. As the startled figure momentarily looked up, he caught a fleeting glimpse of a dirty tear-stained face, partially covered with a pair of black hands. The rest of the body was covered in filthy sacking. Only the matted hair, tightly pleated around the head, gave any indication that the apparition might be female.

As he stared down at her, he was overcome by a feeling of revulsion as he heard himself instinctively ask what was wrong. *"It's Jemmie, ma wee brither. He's deid!"* came the distraught reply as she tenderly touched the freshly-dug soil. Lifting her face to the sky, she cried out through her tears, *"Oh God, why did he hae tae go? Oh I ken the guid dee young and that gentle Jeus taks them tae bide wi' the angels in Heaven. An' God I ken I'm a wicked sinner fir questioning yer Will, but I lo'ed him dearly. I wid hae looked efter him fir always. He wis sae bonny an' sae clever! We lo'ed him dearly.. An' God, hoo wull Gentle Jeus ken where tae find ma wee brither when we are nae allowed tae mark his grave, like the graves o' the ither bairns o'er the dyke in the Kirkyard?"*

*"I ken we're nae allowed tae worship in yer Kirk here on earth 'cause we're colliers, but what hae oor wee bairns e'er done that they are barred frae the Kingdom o' Heaven? Tell me Gentle Jeus!"*

Getting no answer from Heaven, she turned to Andrew, *"Sir, dae ye ken why?"*

But Andrew had no answer. Andrew, a gardener in the Wauchope Estate, like his father and grandfather before him, led a hard and frugal life, toiling long hours for poor wages. Having been reared in a tied cottage in the estate, Andrew knew little about life beyond the estate dyke. As a young boy he had been to Edinburgh only once, although unknown to his parents he had found his way there recently. He certainly knew there was a collier's village further down the Niddrey Burn and that the 'broon yins' lived there. That was what his mother had called them when she warned him never to go beyond the dyke. *"Decent folk don't go there! They're no like us. We serve the gentry. We're a different class- never forget that!"* she had told him proudly.

Defying the warning, one day Andrew climbed the dyke and made his way down stream to the village. There he found a wretched assembly of dingy, low-roofed hovels encircled by a stinking midden in a sea of mud. Each cottage had a hole in the roof to let out the smoke and a small unglazed window stuffed with rags to keep out the weather.

Andrew thought of the ragged collier lad who erractically used to attend the Parish evening class. None of the pupils ever spoke to him except to call him 'broonie' and snigger when he dozed off. Perhaps he had come from this village!

Although it was a beautiful summer day the village was deserted. Accompanying the stench a ghostly air of despondency and desolation pervaded everything. Andrew shuddered and muttering *"God-forsaken!"* he hastily left and made for the millpond and Mill upstream.

Andrew's parents could not read or write, but his mother and Aunt Grace laid great store on him getting an education. They scrimped and saved to pay for his penny classes. Nor were their sacrifices in vain, as he quickly developed a love for learning and, driven by a passion for reading, he soon became the star pupil. Thanks to his doting Aunt's willingness to put her job at risk for his education, he had access to books rarely seen by poor lads like himself.

One of the results of his secret visits to Edinburgh was that he became acquainted with Willie Brown, a member of the Friends of the People Society. It was Willie, an apprentice shoe-maker, who first made Andrew aware of the plight of the Scottish poor and that beggary was rampant. The more Andrew read the Society's radical pamphlets, the more he identified with their cause and the more determined to become a member and join in the fight for justice and liberty for all.

Now there he was that Sabbath afternoon, for the first time in his life face to face with abject poverty and, when put to the test, his reaction was revulsion. He felt ashamed and shattered. And even more so, the very foundation of his faith was shaken, when he learnt that not only was the door of his kirk barred to certain members of God's family, but so too was the gate to the Kingdom of Heaven.

His mind was in turmoil. The girl's large pleading eyes stared up at him. He felt uncomfortable and useless as she sat squatting on the ground, patiently waiting for an answer to her question. But he had none. For the first time in his life he found himself completely at a loss for words. Groping frantically around in his mind for an answer, all he could think of was to pray to his God for help and guidance. He did, but none came. He turned back to find her and offer whatever help he could. When he came upon her haunched form he found himself blurting out, *"We're told that God helps them that help themselves. Let's mark the grave ourselves."*

*"Oh naw, we daurna!"* cried the frightened girl. *"We'd be caught an' punished like ma faither wis. We'd be put in the correction hoose an' flogged!"*

*"We won't get caught. Trust me. We'll do it so that only God will understand what it means. Wait there!"* he cried as he vanished over the dyke. Ten minutes later he returned carrying a large root of a wild plant and a broken earthenware pot half-filled with water. Laying them carefully on the ground, he asked the mystified girl for her brother's name.

*"Jemmie Macgraw,"* she replied, anxiously watching him.

On the soft soil of the recently dug grave he traced the letters J and M. Carefully dividing the root into little plants he set them one behind the other in the grooves so as to form the initials. Pressing the soil firmly down, he watered each tiny plant. Taking a step backwards critically he scrutinised his handiwork, added two more tiny plants and then, when satisfied, turned to the gaping girl and tracing each letter with his finger said slowly, *"Look. J for Jemmie and M for Macgraw."*

*"Do you know these are very special flowers? They are wild primroses - God's first roses of spring. When they bloom He will look down from Heaven and see wee Jemmie's initials as plain as if they were carved on marble, like the ither bairns o'er the Kirkyard dyke."*

Staring out of the bundle of rags, two large soft brown eyes, shining with gratitude, met his. Without giving her time to reply, he found himself rashly making a promise that he would keep the primrose plants trimmed in the form of the initials. *"That way,"* he said *"God will be sure to find wee Jemmie and take him to Heaven!"* Rising abruptly he climbed the wall and was gone.

True to his promise Andrew furtively returned every Sabbath to tend and trim the primroses on the ground where Jemmie lay. He knew it was a crime to mark a pauper's grave so he was careful not to disturb the surrounding weeds in case their secret should be discovered. Then one glorious spring morning, climbing the wall he beheld two clusters of gold gleaming in the sunlight- two masses of pale yellow primroses nestling in the weeds, spelling out J and M. Elated he bent down and touched the delicate flowers marvelling at the sheer beauty of each tiny petal. Suddenly a shadow fell over the grave. It was cast by a thin wisp of a girl, whose faded blue dress was being dampened by water dripping from her long auburn hair. Flinging herself at Andrew's feet she cried, *"Oh thank ye kind sir! Noo Jeus can find Jemmie an' tak him tae Heaven tae live wi' the angels."*

Andrew looked down into two unforgettable eyes, this time no longer pleading, but glowing like fires as they restored hope and life to the gaunt sallow face. Slowly sinking to her knees, lifting her joyful face to Heaven she cried,

> *Dear Faither in Heaven wha speaks o' love,*
>
> *Look doon on wee Jemmie frae above,*
>
> *Noo that he's laid tae sleep*
>
> *In that cauld grund, fir ever tae keep,*
>
> *Wrapped only in a canvas sack,*
>
> *Nae fire tae warm him in the cauld an' dark,*
>
> *Wi' primroses yellow an' violets blue,*
>
> *Faither in Heaven, cam doon frae above*
>
> *An' tak ma wee brither wi' care an' love,*
>
> *Keep him safe till mornin' is nigh,*
>
> *And we meet in the sweet bye an' bye.*

Andrew stepped back intending to leave the girl to mourn alone when suddenly, as she lifted her face towards the sun, his heart missed a beat. In a flash he realised that, not only was she the filthy bundle of humanity whose forlorn brown eyes had tugged at his heart's strings and committed him against his better judgment to find an earthly answer to a heavenly question, but she was also another, the Venus of his dreams- the Venus he had by now convinced himself could only be a figment of his imagination.

His mind went back to a Sabbath day last summer when, sitting reading on the banks of Niddrey Burn, the silence had been broken by a tinkling laugh and a voice calling *"Feerdy, Feerdy!"* He could see a child but not the owner of the voice. He tried to continue reading his book but, as if drawn by a magnet, his eyes kept returning to the burn. After a while a ripple spread over the surface and slowly a figure rose out of the water.

It was a girl with long auburn hair falling to her waist. Flinging wide her arms, she turned her face to the sun. *"Like Venus rising from the water,"* thought Andrew recalling an etching he had seen in one of the Laird's books. The young body, emerging into womanhood, sparkled as the sun rays lighted on the silver droplets trickling down her body. His eyes followed their journey. He had never seen the naked body of a young girl. It was beautiful. As the warmth softly licked her body dry, flinging back her head she faced the sun and smiled.

Never had he seen such a look of sheer happiness and joy.

Skipping lightly out of the water, the girl ran to where a faded blue dress was drying in the sun. It was still wet. Shaking it vigorously and pulling it over her head as she ran to where a little boy was basking in the sun. Laughingly she lifted him and carried him to the water's edge, where she washed first his hair and then his body. Within minutes of returning to the bank he was fast asleep. Watching over him she sat quietly first tugging then combing her hair with a crude horn comb. As it dried in the sun it curled and lay like a mantle of burnished gold on her scrawny shoulders. The child wakened. They rose and walked towards the ditch picking daisies and making a chain as they went. They stopped. Solemnly he twisted it into a crown and placed in on her head. They laughed and laughed. Walking hand in hand they clambered over the ditch which fenced the estate and disappeared into sunset, taking their tinkling laughter with them.

Summer that year was long and hot. Six days a week, before the sun rose or the dawn chorus began, the village of Niddrey would disgorge its families into the bowels of the earth. Sixteen hours later they would re-emerge, often to be met by a blood red sky proclaiming 'The shepherds' delight!'...the promise of yet another glorious day. A promise made for the rest of the human race but not for the collier and his family. Their tomorrows had no sun; no seasons; just eternal darkness, and a daily dice with death and danger...except on the Sabbath.

It was thinking of the Sabbath that kept Nettie Macgraw going. As she struggled under the weight of the creel on her back, she deadened the pain by reliving the sunny Sabbath afternoons she spent with Andrew on their secret walks through Niddrey Estate, the place where he as a gardener was free to roam but where she, as a collier-serf serving the same master, was outlawed.

In the dark of the mine, the ladder became the path through the woods, where in the shade of the great oak and beech trees wild violets and bluebells grew. She would feel beneath her bare feet on the rocky pit bottom the carpet of yellow celandine, over which Andrew and she ran. The dank of the pit became the scent from the sweet smelling briar and honeysuckle wafting in the wind, as they lay basking in the sun. The rats were rabbits scurrying through the stately willow herb. While gripping the ladder with her calloused hands, she would smile and feel again the slippery, fish (trout Andrew called it) she had caught with her bare hands.

When in times of deep despondency it was to the light of her candle she would turn…the light that lit up her darkness. Her sun. The sun she yearned for. And oh, how she longed for the Sabbath and the sun. Then she would wash away the pit filth from her body, while the gentle breeze would waft away the fears of the pit from her troubled mind. Then with arms flung wide, she would face the sun, whose life-giving rays would caress her bruised and battered body, joyfully bestowing on it strength and courage to endure.

As Andrew toiled from sunrise to sunset in the sun-drenched gardens of the estate, his thoughts were ever with Nettie and her fellow moles, burrowing for coal deep down beneath his feet. In the night he would dream of rescuing his Venus and carrying her off into the sunset. But always his dream became a nightmare. Followers of the Black God… Bishops, Judges and Knights- would snatch her from him, tear off her mantle of burnished gold and replace it with an iron collar, while the Black God himself solemnly condemned her to eternal damnation, to be chained forever by the neck in the dungeons of Mother Earth. All his life Andrew had sat in the Kirk comfortable and secure in the knowledge that he was one of God's family. Now his mind was filled with questions. Who decided who could worship in the kirk? Was it the Laird, the minister or was it God? Were not the broon yins part of God's family? Why were they banned from their Father's House and from receiving a Christian burial? Was not that punishing them on both sides of the grave? And for what?

Now the leaves had started to fall and soon the summer would become a memory, a beautiful memory to be cherished forever. Kicking the dead leaves, Nettie and Andrew walked with arms entwined that autumn Sabbath afternoon along the banks of Niddrey Burn sharing their hopes and dreams. Their nightmares they left behind. There were in love.

Over the summer Nettie had blossomed almost beyond recognition. Tossing back her auburn hair she would laugh and sing while her gaunt sallow face glowed with an inner radiance. In Andrew's eyes she was beautiful, as beautiful as the Venus in his Laird's book.

She had found a soul-mate, someone to share her innermost thoughts and fears, Someone who would listen and not deride the rhymes which came unsought into her head. They had so much in common- a love of nature, love of wide open spaces and, above all, a love of life in spite of all its misery. Standing beneath a great oak Andrew took his Bible from his pocket and opened it to reveal a red rose pressed between its pages. Looking into her eyes he whispered,

> *The warmth o' the colour,*
>
> *The depth o' the scent,*
>
> *This rose fir ye frae Heaven was sent*
>
> *Keep it nearest an' dearest*
>
> *And ever in yer heart.*
>
> *God be wi' us*
>
> *May we never pairt,*
>
> *Ma dearie, I lo'e ye,*
>
> *Wi' love ever true,*
>
> *As we walk hand in hand*
>
> *I'll cherish ye.*

Closing the Bible he took her hands and wrapping them around it murmured *"Keep this... fir always!"* Grinning widely he took a step back saying, *"Not bad fir ma first attempt- rhyming I mean!"* They started to laugh then abruptly stopped as the clatter of hooves rent the air and a horseman came galloping out of the woods and pulled up before them.

The rider's face was purple with rage and in his hand he held a vicious horse crop. Instinctively Andrew clasped Nettie to him and looking over her shoulder met the gaze of an angry father. His father!

Before Andrew knew what was happening, Drew lashed out at him with the crop yelling, *"Sae this is what ye hae been up tae, ye gormless git! We wondered what wis gittin' intae ye these last weeks. Noo we ken! An' yin of the bloody 'broon yins' at that. God forgee ye! I'll bloody skin ye alive. Gang hame richt noo an' I'll deal wi' ye there. Bring shame on me an' mine wid ye!"* Turning to the terrified Nettie he bawled *"An' as fir ye, ye collier's whore, I'll see ye'll get fir what ye hae done. I hope ye burn in Hell, tarred and feathered. If I ever hear ony mair aboot this, I'll tar an' feather ye masel'. Get back tae yer hole where ye belong, ye brainless, misbegotten coal howker's bastard."* Yelling *"Take that!"* he brought the full force of the whip across Nettie's back. She screamed in pain and fell to the ground clasping the Bible. Grabbing the whip with one hand, with the other Andrew helped Nettie to her feet yelling *"Run Nettie, run. O'er the ditch, quick!"* Still clutching the Bible the terrified girl, sped like the wind, convinced she was pursued by the Devil himself hurling the curses of Hell at her.

*Nettie Macgraw, ye'll get yer ferrin',*

*In Hell they'll roast ye like a heron,*

*If not like a heron, then like a troot,*

*Nettie Macgraw ye'll nae get oot.*

If Andrew's father was furious, his mother was mortified. Her first reaction, typical of her, was to burst dramatically into tears and cry, *"What will the neighbours and our Kirk friends think when they hear of this?"*

Mailey Young, still a handsome woman, had been a servant at the mansion house, when, with spinsterhood looming, she had succumbed to her friend, Grace Young's matchmaking and married her brother. Rough, uncouth Drew, a huge man who prided himself on his brute strength, could not believe his luck when the handsome, genteel Mailey Main consented to be his wife. Even now, after twenty years of marriage, he still could not fathom what went on behind her dark veiled eyes or why she had married him in the first place. One thing he knew for certain, she despised him. In their first year together she made it quite clear that she endured his advances only because it was her wifely duty, all the time making him feel awkward, boorish and sinful. After what she never tired of describing as *" ma close-to-death experience"* … the birth of her son, she made it quite clear that she would never go through that again. If her husband could not resist the pleasures of the flesh, then he had better find them elsewhere, provided the neighbours and her friends at Kirk never found out. He did. They found out, but pretended they hadn't.

Henceforth Mailey devoted her life to raising her son, assisted by her sister-in-law Grace. So Andrew had two mothers. But he also had a down-to-earth Granny on whose knees he learned what life was really about; the toil and struggle that lay ahead and the injustices of their time. It was Mailey who first sensed something was happening to her beloved son, something he was keeping from her and something connected with his Sabbath rambles. So she sent Drew to follow him and now here she was, mortified and dumbfounded at what he had discovered. Such was her blind fury that she failed to notice the fierce weal spreading across Andrew's face, nor the closed swollen eye. Like a demented creature she just kept screaming, *"How can ye do this to us... carrying on wi' a broon yin? Ye ken weel they're no like us. Decent folk like us have nithin' tae dae wi' the likes o' them. Just like animals they are, what with their drunkenness, debauchery and fornication. They've nae morals.. Their carnal goings on in the pits doesn't bear thinking about. They live like rabbits and breed like them.. How can a son o' mine bear to look at yin, far less touch yin?"* Covering her face with her hands she shuddered as she moaned, *"May the guid Lord hae mercy on us!"*

Grace, with her arms round her sister-in-law, hugged her closer, while nodding and shouting *"Aye they're an ignorant lot, nae better than animals. I doobt if they ken how tae behave like human beings. I've watched them crawling oot o' their holes in the glooming and padding along like a pack o' wild beasts, with never as much as a word to say to each other!"*

Andrew, who had stood quietly by as they ranted and raged, shrugged his shoulders saying *"Well if ye believe a' that ye'll believe anything. I may as well tell ye now I intend to marry her. Her name is Nettie, Nettie Macgraw!"*

For a moment there was a deadly silence, then all hell was let loose. Father's face went an even darker shade of purple; he looked as if he would take a fit of apoplexy any minute. *"Merry her?"* he screamed. *"Dae ye ken whit ye are saying? A Young merry a broon yin! I'll kill ye first wi' ma bare hands! Fir Christ's sake, tak her in the ditch if ye must, but ye'll ne'er merry her as lang as I hae breath in ma body! The law o' this land will stop ye. Ye're the yin in this family wha is supposed to be the scholar. Ye should ken that. She's a serf. She's the property o' the Laird."*

*"I'll beat the law,"* retorted Andrew. *"We'll leave Scotland and work oor passage tae America and start a new life there!"*

*"No ye wont! Try it lad. Jist try it! I'll report ye masel' an' see that the law catches ye and brings her back. Even on a ship the law can claim her. An' anither thing, if I catch ye near her again, I'll report her tae the Laird an' hae her clamped in the jougis!"*

Andrew knew he meant it.

All this time Mailey and Grace had kept wailing and moaning, *"Oh the shame o' it! We'd a' be better deed than face sic a scandal!"* Grace, still with her arms around her sister-in-law, shrieked over her shoulder at her nephew, *"Aye! the high hopes we had o' ye! A' the hard earned bawbees we spent gettin' ye an education- the times we went withoot so that one day ye would be head gardener or even the factor here. Fir what? Fir this? Sae that ye'd marry a broon yin? May the guid Lord save us a'!"*

Drew, turning to the two women barked, *"Shut up ye bawlin' bloody bitches!"* Normally he was not allowed to express an opinion far less swear.. *"Shut yer greetin' faces!"* he went on. *"A'tween the twa o' ye, ye've made a bloody ediot o' him. Oh aye, ye wid mak him a scholar, no let him be a Young like his faither and grandfaither afore him. Oh naw, ye widna let me tak ma ain son tae the cockfichtin' or the boxing booths, far less the Inn. An' this is the result. Yer bonny laddie daeing something naebudy on this estate wid daur dae- carrying on wi' a collier-whore!"*

Nobody dared answer him. For the first time he was master in his own house. Poking his finger in his sister's face he bawled, *"An' as fir ye. Ye'll bring nae mare o' these stolen books here! Aye, I ken damn fine that ye dinna get permission frae the Laird tae borrow them. Dae it again an' I'll tell the Laird masel'. See if I'll no!"*

Grace knew he would.

Turning his spleen back on Andrew he shouted, *"An' ye remember this! As lang as ye are under ma roof, ye'll dae as I tell ye! Nae son o' mine, nae Young, will e'er merry a broon yin. I'll see ye in Hell first!"*

There was a long silence and then a quiet voice from the ingle piped up. It was Granny Young. She had sat through all the commotion, seemingly dozing at the fire. She knew better than to take sides. She knew her place. She was beholden to her son Drew and her stuck-up daughter-in-law for a home. So most times, ignored by all except Andrew, she would appear to be deaf. Afterwards she would wink at her grandson and whisper, *"Wide lugs an' a short tongue are best!"*

*"Aye Andrie,"* she was saying quielty and slowly, *"listen tae ye're faither an' always remember ye're a Young! N'er forget that jist like yer faither and yer aunt there, ye're yin o' the lucky Youngs, the 'Big Yins' as folk hae ca'ed this family fir generations. Ma grandfaither ne'er tired o' telling us, hoo his great-grandfaither, a giant o' a man whae was a farm worker at Wanton Wa's, was starving efter the harvest failed. Along came the factor frae Niddrey Estate wi' only yin job on the land tae offer. Mare than a dozen workers were desperate fir it. Looking them o'er as if they were cattle, he picked the strongest and the biggest, the yin he wid git maist work oot. He picked the Big Yin' himsel'- Big Young! Frae among the ithers he took the youngest an' strongest and put them tae work in his coalpit. Nane wanted tae go, but they hud nae choice. The ithers he left tae dee. Years later the law made these colliers serfs. They and generations tae follow were trapped, yoked tae the pit fir life. Aye, Grandfaither ei finished tellin' the story saying, 'Aye! there but fir the grace o' God gang us! Aye, we the Big Yins are special: we're the lucky yins!"* Her voice trailed off. She was asleep. Drew grabbed his bonnet, banged it on his head and without another word made for the Inn and oblivion.

Day in day out, rows raged in the Young household. Andrew was not allowed out of sight. Between bouts of raging, ranting and drinking Drew sulked. Mailey took to her bed while Grace behaved as if there was a death in the house. Throughout it all Andrew remained adamant that he would find a way to marry Nettie. Then one Sabbath, unexpectedly from the pulpit the minister ordered him to leave his pew and stand beside the Repentance Pillar. Once there he lambasted him unmercifully in front of the whole congregation solemnly saying, *"Andrew Young, it has been brought to the notice of our Lord God by dutiful God-fearing members of your family that you have committed a grave and ungodly sin. Namely, after the Kirk on the Sabbath you have been secretly consorting with one Nettie Macgraw: a collier serf, the property of the Laird of Niddrey. Is this true?"*

Taken aback, Andrew could only nod his head.

*"Then in the name of the Lord,"* went on the minister, *"I not only chastise you, but order that this must cease forthwith, or the wrath of the Lord will fall upon you and your family. You must from this day resist the temptation of the Devil and not allow yourself to be caught up with the likes of her, a hapless collier whom the law of Scotland decrees to be a serf- the property of our Laird and Master. Association with the said serf will bring you into disrepute with the law of this land and can only bring trouble and disaster to you and yours. I hereby give you notice that if I hear any more of this sordid affair the Laird himself, who is mercifully absent from this House of God this day, will have to be duly informed and you will suffer the dire consequences. Andrew Young I say to you, repent of your sins before it is too late and you face eternal damnation. Be grateful to your Maker that you are being given the chance to redeem yourself before it is too late. Stand humbly by this Repentance Pillar and beseech the Lord's forgiveness. Amen."*

*"Amen,"* repeated the congregation. This time it was not only Mailey but Grace who was

mortified. Together they had gone to their minister, confiding in him their troubles and asking him to chastise Andrew privately and bring him to his senses. They could not believe their ears. Here was the Man of God, who, without consulting them, was using their confidences to make a public denouncement which would have the effect they dreaded most- Kirk folk and neighbours would now know of their shame. How could they ever lift up their heads again in the parish?

Andrew, unrepentant, held his head high and left the Kirk even more determined than ever to marry Nettie. Exploring every avenue of escape he could think of, always he was stymied by the fact that the law would win every time. Slowly it dawned on him there was only one solution- he began to think the unthinkable.

Meanwhile Drew, weary of the battle and feeling sorry for himself, one day whilst under the influence of drink, decided to take his troubles to his laird. He would understand and know what to do. The Laird listened sympathetically and promised to act.

Andrew was duly summoned to the mansion house. Dressed in his Sabbath clothes and nervously twisting his bonnet in his hand, he was ushered into a sparsely furnished room at the back of the house. His heart sank as he entered. Seated at a table was not the Laird as he had been led to believe but the Factor, a much feared and hated man, who, it was well known, would stop at nothing to do his master's bidding. After explaining that his master was away on business and that he had been instructed to deputise, he pompously went on, *"Andrew Young, ye are summoned here tae answer a very serious crime. Ye have been caught having an illicit and sordid affair with a collier serf, the property of our laird and master."* Andrew opened his mouth to reply, but was rudely told, *"Nae interruptions Young! Jist confine ye'sel' tae aye or nae!"*

He continued, *"As ye hae pleaded guilty Young, there are three punishments I can gie ye. Ma decision is final, because whatever I decide will be endorsed by the Laird. First, I can hae the said serf flogged and chained in the iron collar tae a pillar on the pit bottom. Or I can hae ye dismissed frae the Laird's service. This of course means that the Laird will mak sure that ye never get employment again in Scotland. Last but not least, I can dismiss ye and yer family frae the Laird's service and evict the lot of you from your tied cottage. Now Young, which is it to be? I have three weeks afore the Laird comes back to make up ma mind."*

Suddenly the Factor's manner changed. His foxy face took on an even more sly and cunning look as he whispered, *"Noo Young, if within these three weeks, you come tae me asking for a job in oor Laird's pit, I will deal with your request sympathetically, knowing you are doing it for love... aye love!"* Rising to his feet he scowled as he hissed through his teeth, *"And if by any chance ye repeat this conversation I will call ye a liar. We hae nae witnesses. Noo get oot!"*

Andrew found himself on the steps of the mansion reeling at the reality of power. His parents had brought him up to believe that the Laird was a wise and caring master who treated all who served him as if they were part of his own family and that as head of that family he would always knew what was best for each member. So when he received the summons he had gone believing as a free man with rights, he would be given a fair hearing and just punishment which he could accept. He never doubted that he would be given an opportunity to ask for help and guidance in finding a legal way out of his dilemma. After many sleepless nights seeking a solution, he had made up his mind that if the Laird said it was legally impossible then, he would volunteer to barter his freedom, if that was the price he had to pay to marry one of his serfs.

Instead he found himself powerless, with no rights and with no access to appeal or redress. He was as clay in the hands of a ruthless schemer who, wielding absolute, albeit delegated power, was prepared to destroy a trusting and loyal family in order to get one more serf for his master's pit.

And so it was that the young Andrew emerged from his baptism of fire a man. A man fired with a fierce determination to dedicate his life to the cause of liberty and justice for all, be they so called freeman or serf.

The year was drawing to a close and excitement was mounting at Niddrey Pit as the Yule holiday drew nearer. It was a typical Monday morning with the pit resounding with the curses and oaths showered on those coal-bearers, unlucky enough to be carrying for colliers suffering from 'big heeds', the result of their sabbath drinking. Maggie Lugton was trying her best to hide a badly swollen black eye, the result of her weekly beating from her drunken husband Lugs.

Big Bell, whilst helping the children to strap their creels on their backs, was giving Maggie some sound advice. *"Gawd wumen, show some spunk! Stand up tae the bastard. I keep tellin' ye, if ye canna bash him back then dinna feed him. Starve him an' sleep wi' the bairns. That'll settle his hurlie!"*

Before Maggie was able to give her stock reply, *"But he's a guid man when he's sober,"* Bell, with a withering look of utter contempt, walked away muttering to herself, *"What's the use! I may as weel save ma breath. I sweer she enjoys it!"*

Only Andy McVie and his coal-bearers were on top of the morning. His cocks had won at the cockfight and, not being much of a drinking man, his wife and children would be in for a treat at the fayre, after he had another flutter of course.

In the adjoining room, Nettie and her sisters were busy loading coal into her slyde (a wooden tub). When it was full Nettie put her arms through a leather harness, did up the heavy buckle at her side, and then fastened the hook on her back to the tub chain. Straining every muscle she started to drag the heavy load along the muddy track, while little Lottie pushed with all her might behind. As they moved away her father stopped hewing. His anxious eyes followed them until they were swallowed up in the blackness. He shook his head. He was at a loss to understand what was happening to his once chirpy chatty daughter. These days she rarely spoke, far less questioned or argued, not even with her mother. In fact, when Janet had broached the subject of marriage to the smith, Nettie just shrugged her shoulders saying, *"Aye if that's what ye want. Wha does it matter onywey?"*

But James had insisted any talk of marriage be postponed until after the Feast of Fastern E'n. *"Bide awhile!"* he said, *"she still needs time to get o'er Jemmie's death."*

One Sabbath he had followed her and found her sitting on Jemmie's grave, staring at the wall, a picture of misery and dejection. *"Mind ye,"* he had said to Janet later, *"I canna understand her. Only at Easter I heard her tell Alice and Lottie that we should a' be happy fir Jemmie, 'cause he was noo in Heaven wi' the angels!"*

Meanwhile panting and groaning, her body bent double, Nettie was straining every muscle to dislodge her tub, which had become wedged behind a rock. Startled, she let out a scream as someone dropped down from a room above and landed in front of her. In the faint candle light she could just discern the outline of a tall collier. Before she knew what was happening, an arm seized the chain behind her back and effortlessly hauled the tub out of the hole while the other arm clasped her round the waist and a voice whispered in her ear, *"Nettie, ma Nettie, ma ain rose!"*

Hit by a thunderbolt of joy and happiness, then lashed by a storm of fear and foreboding Nettie cried out,

> *Oh Andrew, Andrew, what hae ye done?*
> *Forfeited yer freedom fir thirldom,*
> *Gave up yer light fir ma dark,*
> *Tae become yin o'us, a race apart.*

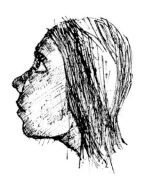

## CHAPTER 7 A MATCH AND A MATCHING

It was Shrove Tuesday, the feast of Fastern's E'en. In the shadow of Arthur's Seat a fayre was in full swing. Crowds of people were milling around stalls and booths where each vendor was trying to outcry his neighbour in an effort to persuade folk to part with their few hard earned bawbees. *"C-a-a-ll-e-r h-e-r-r-i-n'! C-a-a-ll-e-r h-e-r-r-i-n'! Wha'll buy ma caller herrin' new drawn frae the Forth?"* cried a buxom fishwife from Fisherow.

*"H-a-d-d-i-e-s! H-a-d-d-i-e-s-! Fresh loupin frae ma creel!"* yelled her handsome sister, while Jeanie the 'buckie wife' sitting at an improvised table surrounded by customers eating platters of shellfish, spiced with vinegar, kept up her gentle cry, *"C-a-l-l-e-r ou! C-a-l-l-e-r ou! Caller partans! Cockles! Buckies!"*

Nearby, Rantin' Nan, the mad salt sellar from Leith, was liberally showering curses on all who dared to look and not buy. But folk just smiled and shook their heads saying, *"Puir Nan, she's nae the full bawbee!"*

That day it would have taken more than Nan's rantings to upset the good natured crowd who were out to enjoy themselves and make the most of one of the four annual half holidays. The weather was perfect, a beautiful spring afternoon with an azure blue sky and a slight breeze blowing across Duddingston Loch. What more could they ask? Around the stalls the air was sweet with the aroma of freshly baked bread wafting from an oven on a horse-drawn cart. There the baker's wife was doing a roaring trade selling loaves and gingerbread men.

Standing on the edge of the crowd surrounded by a gaggle of giggling girls, Johnny, a handsome young Jew, flirted as he flaunted his gawdy beads, brightly-coloured ribbons and gay kerchiefs. Now Johnny had an eye for colour: he also had an eye for a pretty girl. *"Come ma bonny lassie,"* he was whispering in the ear of a blushing young servant girl. *"Buy zee bonny blue ribbon tae match zee bonny blue e'en!"* Then bending down, and without taking his leering eyes from her face, from the corner of his mouth he hissed at two ragged little boys touching his wares, *"If ye didna vant tae buy ma beads, tak your snottery nose oot o' ma tray!"* For good measure he landed a hefty kick up the backside of the smaller lad.

In their scramble to get away, the urchins bumped into two pretty girls, scattering turnips from the basket they were carrying between them. A staid, polite potter, who had been quietly calling, *"Pitchers, platters and porridge bowls here!"* ran to their aid and helped retrieve their produce. Rewarding him with a shy smile and a *"Thank ye, kind sir,"* the girls walked away to resume their cries, *"Neeps, wha'll buy ma neeps? Neeps like succar!"* Wistfully he stood watching them disappear from view behind the near-deserted weavers' booth. Here Duddingston Dodd and his fellow weavers were struggling to sell a length of cloth to two shrewd guidwives. Pulling and tugging as they examined every inch of the yarn the women haggled over the price. Dodd, desperate to clinch the sale, smirked as he whispered to the scrawny, tight-lipped wife, *"Noo Mistress, if ye were tae mak yersel' a goon frae this braw piece o' cloot, yer guidman micht tak a second fancy tae ye!"*

Flinging down the material she glared at him, as with a toss of her head she snapped, *"Nae thank ye sir! Nae wey will I pey fir his second fancies wi' yer fancy prices!"* Pulling her plaid tightly around her scraggy frame, she flounced off in a rage shouting over her shoulder to her friend, *"I'm awey tae buy some kail frae Jenny. At least she'll nae rook a body!"*

*"Gowdy, gowdy!"* cried a dairy maid, holding up a hunk of cheese to tempt the guid-wife as she strutted past. A lad tried to coax her with a smile as he cried, *"Soor dook Mistress! Soor dook! Try ma soor dook Mistress!"* She succumbed and drank the sour milk on the spot- the liquid seemed to have a miraculous calming effect.

Someone else was far from happy, Kate Oswald a thin jittery creature who hailed from over Craigmillar Castle Brae was in trouble. One of her hens had escaped and landed in a barrel of oatmeal belonging to a cantankerous bully, a farmer from Wanton Walls. Loudly giving her a piece of his mind he told her in no uncertain manner what he thought of her and womankind in general. In her haste to grab the hen, she then knocked over her basket of eggs, smashed most of them and burst into tears as he bawled at her customers, *"Trust a bloody weman tae mak a mess! She's as handy as a wee pot wantin' an erse, that yin!"* Further afield in the shadow of Arthur's Seat, away from the din, children were merrily dancing round the maypole. The many coloured plaited ribbons fluttered in the breeze as they wove in and out to the gentle music of a fiddle and a drum while an artist sat quietly in the background painting the scene.

Standing in the crowd of onlookers, the Macgraw family were almost unrecognisable in their best clothes. Wide eyed, Alice, Lottie, and the two boys Lachie and Robbie stood watching the dancers, as they relished with pure delight every slow lick of a stick of gundy held in their coal-ingrained hands. This was their first fayre and their first taste of the candyman's wares. They were mesmerised. Already that afternoon they had watched jugglers, stilt walkers and fire eaters, listened to strolling players singing songs of battles long since fought, and watched a strange mediaeval play they could not understand. But best of all they loved the puppets. Together with other children in the crowd, they booed the wicked stepmother, cried a little for the princess she turned into a frog, and cheered the prince who saved her with a kiss.

Lachie generously offered a lick of his sticky delicacy to Nettie who was standing behind clapping her hands and stamping her feet in time to the music. She smiled and shook her head saying, *"Naw, it is yer Fastern's E'en present!"* She was happy. Her normally gaunt sallow face was flushed and her brown eyes sparkled as she smiled up at Andrew by her side. As the music quickened she flung back her head and started to dance, twirling round and round. The ragged plaid slipped from her thin shoulders to reveal a skimpy pale green blouse and a dark green linen skirt. At that moment her girl friends arrived on the scene and gaped at the spectacle. Nettie birling again for effect said, *"Look lassies, ma weddin' goon! A present frae Faither and Mither!"* Then lovingly fingering an emerald green ribbon holding back her long auburn hair, she smiled with pride and looking up at Andrew said lovingly, *"Andrew bought this fir me frae Johnny the Jew."*

Excitedly and with a twinge of envy the girls gathered round, touching the skirt and crying, *"A new goon! Aw, but it's braw! And sic a bonny ribbon frae sic a braw lad. Aw, but ye're the lucky yin, Nettie Macgraw!"*

Nettie beamed with pride. Although her mother had bought the clothes from a travelling second-hand clothes hawker, they were new to her and her friends. None of them had ever handled, far less possessed, any new garments.

Just then the figure of Big Bell, bare-footed and resplendent in an ancient, tattered red cloak came striding across the field, her dirty tousled greying hair blowing in the breeze. On reaching Janet, she bent down and whispered in her ear. Janet then nodded to her husband James, who with the rest of the Macgraws started to move. This was the signal for their friends to follow. First to move was Big Bell's eldest daughter Kate, and her two brothers. Following closely behind came Andy, Jess, Maggie, Lugs and their families, and bringing up the rear were collier friends and relations from Easter Duddingston Village.

All fell in behind Big Bell, who, with cloak billowing in the breeze, marched over the field to where a stout balding monk stood patiently waiting with arms folded across what at first glance looked an outsize chest for so small a man. Without a word he signalled first to Nettie and Andrew to stand before him and then to the rest of the company to form a circle around them. When he was satisfied everyone was in position, he extracted from beneath his robes an enormous book, which he hugged firmly with two hands against his chest. Reverently lifting his eyes to Heaven, he proceeded to chant in Latin something inaudible to all but the couple standing before him. Nevertheless, the company instinctively seemed to know when to respond with *"Amen".*

Laying down the book he took the couple's hands, placed them together and said, *"Andrew repeat after me.... I, Andrew, tak thee, Nettie, fir ma wedded wife, tae have an' tae hold, till death us do pairt."* Then to Nettie, *"I, Nettie, tak thee, Andrew, fir ma wedded husband, tae love, honour, and obey until death us do pairt."* Pronouncing them man and wife he added, *"Those whom God has joined together, let no man put asunder!"* As the couple knelt before him, he made the sign of the cross and laying his hands on their bowed heads gave them his blessing.

The couple rose. The monk smiled, congratulated them and opened his book. Using a quill pen he mixed up ink and then proceeded to register the marriage by recording their particulars on the page. Closing the book with a bang, he replaced it under his robes, gripped it firmly against his chest, and sauntered off in search of others requiring his services.

'Book 'n Bosom' a well known figure at local fayres, lived in a friary on the banks of the River Esk. He joined together in holy matrimony couples wishing to be married, as well as others, who had made a *'Handfast Contract'*[2] the old Scottish custom of trial marriage and then, having lived together for the stipulated period of a year and a day, wished the Church to ratify their marriage. The Reformed Church frowned upon this old custom and so Book 'n Bosom was finding that more and more couples were opting for marriage straight away. Nevertheless business was still brisk and today was no exception.

As friends and relatives gathered round congratulating the couple, Nettie's happiness was momentarily marred when she saw a fleeting shadow of intense sadness cross her new husband's face as he scanned the faces of the crowd. He was searching in vain for his family. She knew that their absence put the final seal on their total rejection of him as their son. He had hoped that somehow they would find it in their hearts to forgive him and come to his wedding. But now he knew that their decision was final and he must live forever with that knowledge.

Bell, sensing Andrew's disappointment, stifled a sympathetic sigh. Grinning from ear to ear she quickly enveloped the couple in a bear-like hug, bellowing as she did, *"Weel Andrew lad ye've done it noo! Ye've pit a knot in wi' yer tongue ye canna tak oot wi' yer teeth!"*

When the laughter died down she took command yelling. *"Noo fir the weddin' dance!"* Taking off her cloak, she rolled it into a bundle and tossed it to Andrew saying, "*Tak this! It wull dae fir the bowster!*" To the others she yelled, "*Richt, laddies on this side and lassies on the ither!*"

Lining up, the dancers waited until Janet, followed by the rest of the company, started to sing. This was the signal for Andrew to start dancing up and down the row of girls.

> *Wha learned ye tae dance?*
>
> *Babbity Bowster, Babbity Bowster,*
>
> *Wha learned ye tae dance?*
>
> *Babbity Bowster, Babbity Bowster.*

Andrew still dancing up and down sang -

> *Ma Nettie learned me tae dance,*
>
> *Babbity Bowster, Babbity Bowster,*
>
> *Ma Nettie learned me tae dance,*
>
> *Babbity Bowster brawly.*

The company asked,

> *Wha gaed ye the keys tae keep?*
>
> *Babbity Bowster, Babbity Bowster,*
>
> *Wha gaed ye the keys tae keep?*
>
> *Babbity Bowster brawly?*

Andrew replied,

> *Ma Nettie gaed me the keys tae keep,*
>
> *Babbity Bowser, Babbity Bowser,*
>
> *Ma Nettie gaed me the keys tae keep*
>
> *Babbity Bowser brawly.*

Clapping their hands and singing at the top of their voices the girls collectively ordered Andrew to,

> *Kneel doun and kiss the grund,*
>
> *Kiss the grund, kiss the grund,*
>
> *Kneel doun and kiss the grund,*
>
> *Kiss yer bonny lassie oh!*

On the command 'kiss the grund' Andrew, who had danced up to Nettie, placed the improvised bolster at her feet, took her hand and invited her to kneel beside him. As they knelt together on the `bowster', he kissed her on the mouth to loud wolf whistles and cheers.

The dance then continued as another lad took the bowster and started to dance as the others sung. He in turn selected a girl and they paired off. This went on until every unmarried lad and lass had a sweetheart for the day. But when Bell's thirteen year old daughter Kate was chosen by Geordie Lugton, the self-styled answer to every village maiden's prayer, Bell was not amused. She was heard to mutter darkly to herself, *"She maun dae better than that. Muckle heed and nae wit that yin! I'll pit a hole in his slydie, see if I dinna!"* At that moment a shrill whistle pierced the air and a loud voice yelled, *"Clear the field for the main event o' the efternoon! Folks, this is what ye hae a' been waiting fir. The men's fitba' game!"*

A gang of apprentices fooling around, kicking an inflated pig's bladder deliberately ignored the request to leave the pitch. Losing patience the exasperated organiser bawled, *"Come on ye! That's nae fir it. Get aff!"* But it fell on deaf ears. The lads continued to ignore him and carried on cursing, swearing, and laughing loudly at each other. It was only when two hulking stewards confiscated the bladder and burst it with a knife that they slowly swaggered off, thumbing their noses at the organiser as they went. *"I dinna ken what the young yins are coming tae! In oor young days, we widna hae dared treat oor elders like that. O'er muckle time on their hands- that's their trouble! Nae half day holidays in oor time. They dinna ken they're born nooadays!"* muttered the man to himself. Finally the field was clear and in the crowd a self-appointed master-of-ceremonies, much the worst for drink, bawled, *"Come on folks, let's hae a big welcome fir the twa best village teams in the Lothians!"* As the crowd yelled and clapped, the drunk lubricated his throat by swigging from a near-empty bottle of whisky which he was clutching by the neck. As the noise died down, he managed to steady himself by standing on one leg and stretching both arms upwards. Holding this peculiar position, he warmed to the task in hand and yelled at the top of his voice, *"Hud on tae yer nebs 'cause first on are the boys frae FISH…ER …OW. Stinking o' fish as ever but the meanest kickers this side o' the Forth…. here they come but awe what a stench! Awe! for pity's sake lads, could ye no hae had a wash afore ye came?"*

The fishermen were a fierce-looking bunch: brute force and solid muscle rather than skill was clearly to be the order of the day. Only a drunk or a fool would have dared to talk to them like this. Not surprisingly, the opposition looked anxious and stood dithering at the side of the field. Were they about to change their minds and go home? The fishermen glowered at them, impatiently stamping their feet and kicking hummocks of grass in exasperation. Sensing that the game could be over before it started, the drunk shouted, *"I dinna blame ye lads o'er there. It's no as if ye're getting pied fir this. Come on everybody, let's hae a really big cheer fir the brave weaver-boys frae DUD…DING….STON. They're great wi their hands but are they any guid wi their feet? Aye, here they come! We a' ken they've nae chance really but gie them a big clap. If they're no kicked tae death, the stink will surely get them!"*

From the start it was evident that Fisherow was the better team and that the white-faced weavers did not stand a chance against the brawny weather-beaten fishermen.

Meanwhile the wedding party were enjoying the game, cheering and encouraging the weavers. When it was over some of the young colliers arrogantly boasted *"We can dae better then that!"* and against the advice of their elders decided to ask if they could field two teams; Niddry Village and Easter Duddingston. *"Changed days"* muttered Andy when he heard the Organiser readily agree without as much as a murmur. *"Maybe he's a bit deef and didna pick up we're colliers, ye better hurry up an' start afore he changes his mind!"* They borrowed a ball, but before they could start Andy shouted, *"Hud on a menute! Ye've forgotten something! Yin o' oor players wis married the day, was he no? Weel we maun mark the occasion in the time honoured wey!"*

*"Mistress Young!, aye Nettie that's ye! dinna look sae surprised, ye'll hae tae get used tae it- let's hae yer ribbon?"* Bemused, she took it off and handing it to the player, Andy tied it around the ball. *"Richt lads. the Niddry Nodders, followed by the Easter Duddingston Dodgers wull noo dae the traditional lap of honour around the field ahint the bride and groom!"*

Many of the crowd who had left after the previous game, drifted back when word got around that colliers were to play. Scratching their heads they were left wondering what was going on, when they saw two teams doing a lap of honour and the game not yet played. But once round the field, the game started immediately.

The gang of city apprentices, learning who the teams were, howled with laughter and shouted, *"Ye gawds! Broonies play fitba! What next!...Wha dae they think they are? Nae self respecting team wid play them! They ken that. That's hoo they hae tae play yin anither; But we'll see aboot that! That lot, they widna ken where tae start, farless hoo tae kick or heed a ba'. Come on lads, lets gie them some lessons- let's show them hoo tae kick a few heeds in- broon heeds eh!"* With that they tossed their bonnets in the air and crying *"Yippee! yippee!"* charged across the grass, stopping where the collier women and children were patiently waiting for the game to start. A handsome cocky lad sidled up to Jessie. Looking her up and down, he pinched her cheek and looking into her eyes whispered, *"Aye, but ye're a bonny Broonie!"* Waving to his friends to follow, he yelled over his shoulder, *"A bit o' a'richt this Broonie, come an' hae a keek lads!"* Quick as a flash, before Jessie has time to make up her mind whether to be flattered or frightened, he lifted her skirt exposing her bare leg and buttock. She screamed, instinctively looking towards her Mother who was standing with the other women.

But it was Bell who came to the rescue. Like a streak of greased lightning, she shot from the crowd. Planting her bare feet firmly on the ground, with arms akimbo, majestically she pulled herself up to her full height and glowered down at the lout, who, still holding the skirt in the air, froze with fright. Motionless he stood there, a petrified human statue, hypnotised by two wild dark eyes staring out of the head of a weird apparition in a tatty scarlet cloak.

An ugly silence descended on the crowd. With not so much as a flicker, Bell's eyes kept boring into his, while the gang stood stunned in the background. Women, with children clinging to their skirts, turned pale and trembled. But Big Bell stood resolute; firm as a rock; a sentinel defending her tribe.

The pregnant silence dragged on and on. Suddenly an old women belched, the tension snapped, the lad's head jerked resuscitating him. Dropping his gaze and the skirt, he screwed up his face, nonchalantly shrugged his shoulders and followed by the gang sheepishly slouched off, muttering darkly, *"Christ, a She-Deil in the flesh if e'er I saw yin! God alone kens what other manner o' supernatural beings live doon among that lot, in the Dungeons o' the Demons!"*

The gang were to say the least, a bit disgruntled, when they saw that the football game has started. But nothing daunted, they mingled with the onlookers intent on finding an excuse to start trouble. But no one paid any heed. The crowd was too busy cheering and yelling encouragement to a small slight player, who was tearing up the field, skillfully dribbling a ball before him. Twice he was tackled and twice he foiled his opponents, while onlookers yelled at the top of their voices, *"Pass it Jock- pass it!"* Neatly tapping the ball with the side of his foot, he passed it to a tall youth who, responding to the roar, *"Noo Lankie, heed it in- heed the ba'!"* effortlessly headed it into the goal. The crowd went wild with delight. The apprentices found themselves caught up in the excitement as they flung their bonnets in the air, jumping up and down and thumping each other.

Now these lads were football fanatics who took their football seriously. They could recognise and appreciate good football when they saw it. Judging by their commentary, this was by far the best game they have watched for many a day. So instead of jeering they found themselves cheering and yelling their heads off as they shouted, *"Come on Jock, get stuck into that wee runt!- Richt Lankie, noo heed the ba' Heed it in!"*

The game though rough, was played strictly according to the rules, with everyone agreeing that the best team won. It was Easter Duddingston, with two goals to their opponent's nil When the game finished, first to invade the field were the apprentices, vying with each other to shake hands with the winning team and slap the two star players on the back. The Organiser, who once again had the task of clearing the field for the next event, heaved a sigh of relief when he saw the gang leave; this time without persuasion. They were dragging their two new found heroes, Jock and Lankie, off to the Sheeps' Heed Inn for a celebration drink.

Already there were players lined up for the next game and raring to go. But this time they were players with a difference. They were female! It was 'the Married Women versus The Single Lassie's Fitba' Game. By tradition the married women must win, so Nettie, playing her first football match, was on the winning side, although there were some who said of the result, *"It's a fix!"*

By the end of the match most of the women were saying, *"I'm fair waubit"* and were only too happy to sit down and await the last event of the day. By this time there was hardly a man in sight, most of them were either in the Ale Booth or at the Cockfight.

*"Noo folks! Noo Folks!"* yelled the now familiar voice of the Organiser, *"The......G R A N D F I N A L E !....Auld Scotland's ain MORRIS DANCERS !- Oor weel kent and weel lo'ed Scottish*

Dancers hae travelled all the wey frae the fair city o' Perth tae be wi' us this day. Folks!... let's gie a Lowland welcome to Scotland's maist famous MORRIS DANCERS!" A roll of drums, followed by the jingle of bells, heralded the entrance of the dancers. A cheer went up as they danced in. What a spectacle! Thirteen dancers weaving in and out, dressed in bright red and green tunics, dark tights, white shoes and flowered hats, while hundreds of tiny bells, regulated by the skilled movement of their bodies, produced sweet musical chimes as glass concealed in the flowers,(put there to avert the Evil Eye) flashed and twinkled in the afternoon sunshine. The more they danced the more the crowd loved it. They clapped, whistled and yelled "More - more!" Then, when five of the dancers mounted their partners' shoulders and, held only by their feet, were carried round and round in an intricate and rumbustuous number, the audience held their breath. Noisily they demanded encore after encore. Eventually the dancers marched off to thunderous applause ringing in their ears.

"Time tae go hame! let's find yer Faither" cried the mothers, dragging reluctant, but happy children, many of whom, for the rest of their lives would remember that day. They heard the men before they came into view carrying Andy shoulder high and chanting, "Niddry.....N-i-d-d-r-y.......guid auld Niddry!"

"Gawd they're reamin' foo!" cried the women, anxiously scanning the beaming faces. Many heaved a sigh of relief when they spied their spouse reasonably sober, while others, not so lucky, consoled themselves with the thought, "Weel efter a' it's a half holiday, it only happens four times a year!"

Now the Niddry Nodders might have lost the football game, but the Niddry Cocks; Andy's to be precise, had well and truly beaten all contenders at the Cockfight. Gamblers among them had a field day. Judging by the state of the majority so had the Ale Booth Keeper. But as the women said "It is a half holiday".

By this time the crowds were streaming out of the fayre. As they passed the noisy but happy wedding party, many were seen to give them a wide berth as, with a "holier than thou" look, they furtively watched out of the corner of their eye, the antics of Lugs and a few of his loud mouthed cronies embroiled in a drunken brawl. But they showed no interest in the other colliers walking ahead, carrying exhausted toddlers on their shoulders or helping their wives carry kail while they patiently played and laughed with older children, many of whom were still full of energy and mischief.

Still keeping their distance though, many of the crowd deliberately walked as far away as possible. When it came to the point where they had to pass the colliers on the rough track Mothers gathered their children to them, hiding the little faces in the folds of their skirts and shouting, "Dinna look bairnies- that's the broon yins- they bring bad luck!" One guidwife cried over her shoulder to her inebriated husband staggering behind, "What mare can ye expect frae that Godless lot; Damned before they dee they are!" A deaf old crone, shuffling behind, pulled her plaid over her head and as she went by yelled to the others in front, "Aye! I hae it on guid authority, that doon where they come frae, they nae only get a keek at Hell Damnation but at Auld Hornie himsel'!"

Bell stopped; glowered; poised her head ready to charge. Changing her mind she frowned and shrugging her shoulders commented wryly to her neighbour, *"Callin' names brakes nae banes!"* Flinging back her tattered cloak, with a withering look she strode on majestically. It seemed the day was not yet over for the wedding party. On reaching the village Bell shouted, *"Noo folks, aff hame and hae a rest! Then as many o' ye as want tae, come tae ma hoose fir a Fastern's E'en wedding celebration, jist like the yin ma folks gave me when I was married at Wanton Wa's"*

Since coming to work in the pits, Andrew had lodged with Big Bell, his Father having turned him out with the parting shot, *"Get oot! Ye are nae bringing yer pit glaur nor yer pit whore here. Ye hiv made yer bed, noo lie on it! Get oot and stey oot. From this day on this Young family has nae son!"*

Janet and James, though welcoming Andrew as a future son-in-law and dismissing rumours circulating in the pit about him, erred on the side of caution and asked that they wait three months before getting married, saying, *"Jist gie yerselves time tae mak sure, ye are sure!"* Reluctantly the couple agreed. By the end of the twelve weeks they were more than ever determined to wed. Nettie confided in Bell that she would have dearly loved to have the blessing of the Kirk on their marriage, but as colliers were debarred from worship in the Kirk, sadly she knew it was an impossible dream.

Bell, a romantic at heart, recalled envying a cousin of hers who had run away with her lover and been married by a travelling friar at a fayre. Making enquiries she found out about Book 'n Bosom, then helped Janet plan a fayre wedding, while at the same time promising the couple *"Ye'll hae the best wedding Niddry village has seen fir mony a day!"* So here she was, true to her word, about to make it a day to remember. After an hour's rest, the guests, all intent on having a good time, started to arrive, squeezing into her one roomed cottage and bringing small gifts for the bride and contributions in kind for the evening festivities.

The young ones, when asked to huddle up close to each on the two straw pallets were more than willing to oblige. The older women, with the exception of Auld Leib, squeezed together on the box bed, while the men squatted on their hunkers and resting on their heels, placed their hands on their knees. Auld Leib, by virtue of her age and high standing in the community was given the only seat in the house, a three legged stool. As it was now the gloaming, Bell lit the room with two candles supplied by James. She stoked the fire with coal brought by the dour Dave Erskine no less, who had taken everyone by surprise by agreeing to come. This was the first time, many of them had ever seen Dave out of his pit clothes, as he lived the life of a recluse after his day's toil was done.

James formally welcomed everyone, thanking then for coming to his daughter's wedding and taking the opportunity to thank his wife's best friend Bell for all she has done for Nettie and Andrew.

Embarrassed, Bell brushed aside his compliments saying, *"Weel, since coming tae bide here, he's become like yin o' ma ain!"* With that she got down to business saying, *"Weel freends let's start* oor *Fastern's E'en celebrations. Ma Granny, wha wid be sitting at the fire knittin' wid start us aff by reciting the traditional rhyme. I'll try tae remember it!"* After a false start and a scratch at her tousled head she just managed to say.

> *First comes Candlemas.*
>
> *Syne the new mune,*
>
> *The neist Tyseday after that*
>
> *Is aye Fastern E'en*

After a pause and a reminiscent smile she went on, *"Then Mither wid say,"*

> *On Fastern's E'en we had a rockin'*
>
> *Tae ca' the crack and weave oor stockin'*
>
> *And there was muckle fun and jokin'*
>
> *Ya needna doubt.*

As she finished, James, grinning at the women, jokingly remarked. *"Weel ye collier wemen certainly find time tae crack, yaketty yak! yaketty yak! But the guid Lord, in his wisdom, did nae see fit tae gie ony o' ye time tae knit a stockin'! But wha kens! yin day he jist micht! and then us colliers chiels will strut like birkies tae the pit, wearing woollen stockings, jist like oor Laird!"*

This was met with roars of laughter from the men as in their mind's eye each fancied themselves decked up in woollen hose. All that was, except Lugs, who, still drunk, was sitting huddled in a corner furtively drinking the ale, which was supposed to be his contribution to the festivities. Only a few folk, among them Bell and his daughter Mary, heard him slur, *"Hud on! I ken a guid yin aboot a leg in a stockin'!"* Bell seeing Mary's face go scarlet when she heard her father about to tell one of his obscene jokes, cut him short by saying kindly, *"Aye Lugs, later! but first as is the custom, we maun hae oor fortunes telt. Lieb, wull ye kindly oblege?"*

Auld Leib, the much respected village spaewife and herbalist struggled up from the stool to acknowledge the applause which greeted the unanimous request. Having brought most of them into the world, treated their family ailments, and been involved in many a family brawl and vendetta, she knew all there was to know about most folk. So as she painstakingly foretold something special and personal to each one in turn, some beamed with pleasure and relief, while others looked fearful and visibly shook. One thing was certain. Auld Lieb was held in awe by one and all and her prophecies were taken as gospel. By the time she finished going round the room, her cranky old voice was almost inaudible. She looked tired and weary. Awkwardly lowering her rheumaticy old bones on to the stool, she asked Nettie and Andrew, whom she had deliberately left to the last, to sit on the floor, one on either side of her. By shuffling her feet she moved the stool nearer to the fire to warm her work worn calloused hands. Then fumbling in the pocket of her skirt she produced a bottle containing one of her concoctions, which she uncorked and shakily put to her lips, gurgling noisily as she gulped it down. Wiping her mouth with the back of her hand she carefully replaced the cork and hid her bottle away. Stretching out her arms she groped for the couple's wrists, found then, and gripped them tightly. As the flickering firelight played on her gnarled face she was seen to wearily close her eyes and to everyones' dismay, appear to doze off. An eerie silence filled the room. Folk shuddered. *"Is she deed?"* young ones whispered in alarm. But no! she was groaning! Her hands were seen to move as her nails dug deep into the couple's flesh and with eyes still veiled she started to chant in a strange alien voice.

> *Fir ye twa I see a thorn an' a rose.*
>
> *The thorn is the thorny path o' life ye'll tread thigither*
>
> *The rose is the bonny wild briar, that grows in yer heerts.*
>
> *Nurture it weel an' tend it wi' loving care*
>
> *An' it will blossom an' bloom into the Rose of Creation,*
>
> *An' when folk frae ilka land, taste its Heavenly nectar*
>
> *An' breath its Divine perfume*
>
> *The world could ince again*
>
> *Create a Garden o' Eden; this time fir a' mankind.*

As her voice trailed off she opened her eyes, stood upright and with a toothless grin, acknowledged the company's adulation.

By now Bell was quietly making preparations for the crowning event of Fastern's E'n…the baking of the Infra Cake…the Dreaming Bannock. Tonight this would double for the Wedding Cake. She had already built up the fire in the middle of the room and waiting until it was smokeless she invited the guidwives present to sit round it with their legs pointing inwards. Into a bowl she tossed a few handfuls of oatmeal, then passed it to Janet who broke in some of the cracked eggs she had bought cheaply from Kate Oswald that afternoon. *"Noo cloukit weel"* said Bell as she poured in liquid while Janet stirred vigorously. *"Mither used beef bree, but we hae rabbit bree, a gift frae the best poacher in Niddrey"* she said as she winked at Andy while adding the salt. Janet gave it the final stir, then passed the bowl ceremoniously around the circle. Each guidwife in turn, took the horn spoon, stirred the mixture and closing her eyes silently made a wish.

The bowl was then passed to Auld Leib, who sitting on the stool, held it up with two hands to Bell who said, *"Noo whees't folks!, ye maun a' keep michty quiet while Leib weaves the Magic Spell. Remember, if ony yin speaks the Spell wull be broken an bad luck wull follow ye fir a year an' a day!"* In a hushed silence Leib intoned an incantation, while one by one, Bell slowly dropped lucky charms into the mixture. The Infra Cake was now ready for cooking. With great pride and ceremony Bell produced her most cherished possession…her Mother's gridle. This she placed with care on the glowing embers. Nettie as the youngest guidwife present was given the honour of pouring the batter on to the gridle. As it began to cook: Jess turned it: Janet removed it when ready and placed it in a dish held by Maggie.

The Wedding Cake was now ready and carefully laid aside to await the evening's grand finale. Meanwhile other bannocks were being made, using the same recipe, but omitting the spell and the charms. When ready, they were broken into pieces, passed round, eaten and washed down with rabbit and nettle soup, which Bell had prepared earlier as the others rested. When everyone had eaten, the entertainment started up again with James asking his cousin Andy, *"Can ye mind the ballad Grandfaither used tae sing tae us bairns, aboot a Niddrey serf in feudal times, wha belonged tae the Lord o' Craigmillar Castle? It was ca'd, 'The Lass o' Niddrey Mill?"*

*"Aye"* replied Andy, *"Gawd! As if I could forget! If Grandfaither taught us bairns onything woe betide us, if we didna remember every word!"* Together they sang…

> *For long I lived in auld Scotland*
> *A serf for aye without reprieve*
> *Ma life was sold to suit the Laird,*
> *And mony times ma heert did grieve.*
> *O wi' ye love by Niddrie Burn,*
> *I long to stroll o'er vale and hill*
> *To hold yer hand to plan oor life*
> *My Kirsty fair o' Niddrey Mill,*
> *Craigmillar's Lord ma family owned*
> *Tae satisfy the gentry's life*
> *But I had ither plans in store,*
> *Far frae the bitter toil and strife.*
> *I lo'e a lass, a Niddry maid,*
> *Wi' a' the love a man can gie*
> *An' swear ma life and her's yin day*
> *We'll share the gither full and free.*
> *And so fra bondage I escaped*
> *Tae Albion's plain a minstrel bold*
> *I sang at Castle, Coort and Hall*
> *Yet never yince ma faith I sold.*
> *A Prince's dochter saught ma love*
> *But aye my Kirsty filled ma mind*
> *Ma servant lass, tho' puir in wealth,*

*Is richer than the ither kind.*

*Revolting peasants then I joined*

*Wat Tyler's men wi' courage strong*

*I learned the truth o' that great ficht*

*And still for Kirsty I did long.*

*An' noo, back in ma native land,*

*I'll marry Kirsty at the fayre.*

*Ma spirits high, ma wandering o'er*

*Nae mare fir gentry's whim's I care.*

*I am a freeman, serf nae mare*

*An' wi' ma bride freewoman too*

*Curse serfdom an' its cruel laws*

*Curse lairds an' castles an' their crew.*

*"But if he cam back tae Niddrey, hoo was he free then?"* asked Lottie. *"Cause he managed no tae get caught fir a year an' a day. That's the law lass... an still is tae this day!"* Auld Leib told her. Katie piped up, *"Mither can I sing the song Granny used tae sing tae me at Wanton Wa's?"* *"A'richt",* agreed Bell, *"But I doot ye'll find room tae dance."* Undeterred Kate rose and squeezing in between two of the men squatting on the floor she somehow managed to dance up and down on the spot as she sang,

*Katie Bairdy had a coo*

*Black an' white aboot the moo*

*Wisna that a denty coo,*

*Dance, Katie Bairdy*

*Katie Bairdy had a cat.*

*Wha could catch baith moose and rat,*

*Wisna that a denty cat*

*Dance, Katie Bairdy.*

*Katie Bairdy had a hen,*

*She could lay both but an' ben,*

*Wisna that a denty hen,*

*Dance, Katie Bairdy.*

As she sang, some of the young ones struggled up, found a spot and joined in the dance, singing the song over and over again. Beginning, to find the repetition a bit much, the women started to diddle a well known Scottish Reel. The men clapped and tapped their feet while the dancers moved fast and furious, up and down. Exhausted, they collapsed laughing in a heap on the straw pallet. Katie looking to see if Geordie was watching her, gave him a shy smile. He winked. Her Mother glowered.

And so the night wore on. Many were the yarns spun, songs sung and jokes told. It must be said that Lug's obscene *'Guid yin aboot a leg in a stockin'* brought the roof down, although it was tame compared with the others which followed as the ale loosened tongues.

But the surprise of the evening was when Dave Erskine volunteered to sing. He could have been affected by the barley bree, or maybe he just felt happy. He took everyone by surprise (himself included if the truth was known) when he found himself saying *"I'll sing an auld Edinburgh ballad I used ta sing when I wis a wandering minstrel in the days afore I wis arrested as a vagabond and enslaved tae the pit. It's ca'd 'My Fair Ladye'."*

In a deep baritone voice he sang,

> As I gaed by the Luckenbooth,
>
> I saw a ladye fair,
>
> She had long pendles on her lugs
>
> And jewels in her hair.
>
> And when she came to oor door,
>
> She spiered at wha was ben
>
> O, hae ye seen ma lost love,
>
> Wi' his braw Hielandmen,
>
> The smile aboot her bonny cheek,
>
> Was sweeter than the bee
>
> Her voice was like the birdie's tree
>
> But when the meenster cam' oot,
>
> Her mare began tae prance
>
> They rode into the sunset
>
> Aye on tae the coast o' France.

*"Alas folks"* said Bell, *"All guid things maun come tae an end! Its time tae go! Back tae auld claiths and parritch fir us tomorra! But first, as is the custom. we maun see the bridal couple safely to their new hame!...Just in case ye tak cauld feet Mistress Young and try tae run hame tae Mither!"*

Still laughing, the company left the cottage and as they stepped out into the dark they were met by four of the men carrying lighted torches made from kail runts. The torch-bearers fell in, two on either side of the bridal couple, directly followed by Janet holding high the Infra Cake, while the rest of the company, banging their bowls with horn spoons and singing at the top of their voices, brought up the rear. As the procession slowly wound its noisy way through Niddrey Village then up the muddy track to Cleekhim, where the couple will now live, people came to their doors shouting good luck slogans smattered with bawdy jokes, which brought a blush to the bride's cheek. Eventually the cavalcade reached Cleekhim Village and stopped outside a tumbledown hovel where the company encircled the couple as they sang with gusto:

> *Welcome tae yer ain fireside*
>
> *Health and wealth attend the bride,*
>
> *Wanters noo yer true weird*
>
> *Joes are spied, by the Infra Cake!*

On the words 'Infra Cake' James stepped forward, took the Wedding Cake from his wife's hand, laid it on the flat of his hand, lifted it and smashed it on top of his daughter's head.

As the pieces scattered to the ground, the young ones scrambled to find a piece containing a charm. In the thick of the melee was Geordie, roughly kicking and shoving everyone out of his way, determined to get the biggest piece. Great howls of laughter went up (the loudest coming from Bell it must be said) when he pulled out the button and everyone spontaneously chanted, *"Geordie Lugton's gonna be a bachelor, a bachelor!"* Jessie's face fell when she found a thimble in hers, while Mary triumphantly holding up the ring was the envy of all.

But all was not lost. Bell held out hope for the disappointed as she reminded them, *"Lads and lassies if ye sleep wi' yer Infra Cake under yir heed ye'll dream o' yer ain true love!"*

The newly weds thanked everyone, said their farewells and as they made their way towards the door, the crowd yelled *"Andrie! ye maun cairry yer bride o'er the threshold!"* Picking her up as if she were a feather, he smilingly obeyed. The ragged plaid slipped from her shoulders, her long auburn hair cascaded down her back and the green skirt fanned out as he carried her inside and kicked the rickety door shut behind them to start their life together.

The crowd started to disperse, but not before Bell had made a bee-line for Kate. Gripping her arm as if in a vice, she was heard to say, *"Richt lass, hame wi' Mither!"* Glowering at the grinning Geordie, who obviously had other plans for her daughter that night, she hissed, *"An' ye lad! on yer slydie, before I damp ye doon wi' a dook in Niddry Burn!"*

## CHAPTER 8  THE JOUGIS AND THE KIRK

Four hours later as Bell had predicted, it was 'back tae auld claithes and parritch' as shadowy figures emerged from Niddrey and Cleekimin Villages, dragging reluctant, sleepy headed children along the rough track to work, As they neared the pithead, Andrew's grip on his wife's hand tightened as they watched each group in front disappear one by one down the ladder, as if gobbled up by a silent beast, lying in wait in the early morning dark for its human prey.

After three months working in the coal-heugh, Andrew still found himself at this hour of the morning, having to screw up courage to force himself to descend the ladder to face yet another day in the hell-hole. Niaively he had thought he could cope with what lay ahead when he became a collier. After working from sunrise to sunset in the open with the sky above, he was unprepared for the emotional shock which shook his body rigid when he found himself with only a candle for comfort, toiling in the eerie black of a subterranean cavern, with a rock roof pressing down, shutting out sun and seasons. As the weeks went by he had to get accustomed to a sixteen hour daily stint of hard physical grind, stripped almost naked in the clammy heat, or shivering in soaking wet clothes as he worked in water up to his calves. Gradually he became immune to the agony of lying on his side in a narrow seam, with arms above his head, wielding a short handled pick in order to get at the coal. At other times, crawling like a snail in the mud, choked with coal dust and gasping for breath in the thin, foul air, he would feel as if his blood vessels would burst. He, who had always thought he was brave enough to face most situations, was many a time gripped by the throat in sheer terror.

After ten gruelling days, his body, as if to say, *"Enough is enough"*, capitulated to a raging fever; aching limbs; nausea and finally delirium. Hovering eerily outside his body helplessly he watched from above while he struggled to hold up a crumbling, creaking roof with outstretched bleeding hands. Like dried twigs his arms snapped and he screamed as the rock devoured his bones and slurry drained his blood.

He recovered from the fever to be told two days later by Eckford, *"Richt Young, yer twa weeks training is up! Its time tae howk and draw yer ain! Ye'll hae tae find yer ain fermit bearers!"* Then, with undisguised glee, the Overseer proceeded to allocate him a 'room' as far from the ladder as possible. But as Bell said on hearing the news, *"Lad, it's an ill wind that blaws naebody ony guid!"* as off she sped to find her friend Jess Millar. Will Miller, alas, now lay along side wee Jemmie in his pauper's grave, while his widow unable to find work to support her family was facing eviction and beggary.

*"I've worked since I wis five when Faither first took me doon"* Jess told Andrew eagerly, *"An' if ye'll hae us as yer bearers Andrie, ma bairns and me wull work hard fir ye! Bell can vouch fir me, I'm a hard worker- I stand nae nonsense frae Doddie here, wha's seven, an' ma fifteen year auld dochter Jessie. Oh! I ken twa bairns is no enough, but we'll work hard I promise ye!"* Andrew needed no persuading, he considered himself fortunate to get Jess and her children.

Andrew now had other worries on his mind. He had something more than the hazards of pit life to contend with; something he had not bargained for; hostility and suspicion of the colliers! How it came about he was never quite sure, although he often wondered if it stemmed from what happened the first morning he reported for work.

Eckford, the Pit Overseer, an ignorant brute of a man, much hated by his workers, was, that Monday in a towering rage. Obviously not much of a scholar, he had, with considerable difficulty just finished writing down Andrew's particulars for his contract, when a group of colliers and coalbearers arrived at the pithead. Flinging down the quill he made a sudden rush towards them yelling, *"Lugton! I want ye!"* Blustering, red faced, bleary eyed Lugs jumped to attention and roughly pushing his wife and four children aside scurried nervously towards Eckford, crying *"Aye Sir! coming Sir!"* With eyes flashing, arms flaying and panting for breath, the Overseer charged like a raging bull up to the frightened collier. Shouting and poking his finger in his face, within minutes he had succeeded in reducing the man to a simpering, fawning dog-like creature.

The others, anticipating trouble, quickly scuttled off leaving only Andrew within earshot. He could not help but overhear Eckford lambaste the poor collier unmercifully. It seemed that the row has something to do with stones in the coal. Loudly cursing him, the Overseer threatened the cowering creature, first with a flogging, then a fine- and finally to nail him to the pit bottom in the jougis. Lugton, cringing and almost on his knees, like a terrified parrot, kept screeching, *"Aye Sir, ye're right Sir! It winna happen again Sir. Ye ken me Sir, I widna dae sic a thing- it must hae been yin o' ma bearers. I'll skin her alive Sir, I swear I wull Sir, I'll swing fir her, I wull Sir!"*

Eckford, his face by this time a deep purple, seemed unable to stop himself, as he ranted and roared, accusing Lugton *"Y're naething bit a common thief, a swindler an' a liar intae the bargain, robbing oor Laird o' what is richtf'lly his. Jist ye wait until he hears o' this. He's ordered me tae ferret oot vermin like ye! an' tae report ye tae him personally. Ye ken wha' that means!"* Lugton did indeed! Passionately pleading, and almost on his knees he begged, *"Oh Sir jist gie me yin mare chance- yin mare chance Sir. I hae a wife an' bairns tae think o'! It'll no happen again I swear Sir!"* As the Overseer kept up the tirade, periodically he would glance over his shoulder to where Andrew was standing. After a time Andrew became aware of this, then slowly it dawned on him that the display of authority and power, for some obscure reason, seemed to be being enacted for his benefit. *"But why?"* he thought *"Oh maist likely, that's his wey o' showing new-comers wha's gaffer in the pit!"*

Now Eckford was in no doubt who was gaffer in his pit- Eckford. But the worry for him, right now, was for how long? And he had good reason to worry! Recently output at the pit has slumped. The Laird, blaming his Factor, told him politely, but in no uncertain terms, that he held him personally responsible. He also made it crystal clear that he considered Factors expendable and so if things did not improve, his would be the head to roll. The Factor seeking a scapegoat, turned on his Overseer and blamed him for the falling output and the smouldering unrest among the colliers, the root cause of the trouble, according to the Laird. So venting his venom on his minion the Factor vowed, *"Mark ma words Eckford, if things dinna improve, an' improve quick, I'll get anither Overseer! There's plenty mare where ye cam' frae!- an' when I dae... mak nae mistake its back howking coal ye'll go!"* Rubbing his hands together he sniggered as he lowered his voice and raising his eyebrows whispered *"Jist think Eckford what these howlin' wolves doon there wull dae when they get their filthy paws on their freendly Overseer!"*

Eckford. a crawling toady at the best of times, quickly got the message. In a panic he promised, *"I'll ferret oot these bastards maself Sir, wi' ma ain hands an' see they get their just desserts Sir! an' I'll find weys tae mak anither cut in the wages of these lazy buggers. They're far tae weel peyed fir the work they dey! It's their high wages that mak the price of coal sae dear fir oor Laird, is it no Sir?"* The Factor cut him short, *"Aye, it is that! So dae what ye must, an' dae it yer ain wey!, I'll nae spier hoo! I'm only interested in makin' guid profits fir the Laird. Yer job is tae maintain law and order in the pit, see that the serfs earn their wages and that the Laird gets his just rewards,...Richt noo ye hae four weeks tae improve output...if no.... tae the wolves ye go!"*

The Factor, a ruthless man, full of his own importance, saw his job as one of managing his Master's pits, extracting maximum coal yields and maximum profits, with minimum personal hassle for his Master the Laird. The Laird in turn, did not interfere, asked few questions and rarely went near the pit. Indeed few of the colliers have ever seen the Niddry Laird, the man who owned them body and soul and for whom, their labour made such handsome profit. They certainly had never seen him or any member of his family down the pit!

Two days after the ultimatum, unexpectedly the Factor sent again for Eckford and with a self-satisfied smirk condescendingly informed Eckford, *"I think I can be o' assistance to ye in yer hour o' need!"* The Oversee, sick with worry at the implications of their last encounter, was about to gratefully heave a sigh of relief, when, hearing the nature of the help he stopped short. The Factor was saying, *"I personally hae persuaded a man frae the Laird's estate tae cam an' work in the pit. He is young an' strong an' what's mare he can read an' write! The Laird is michty pleased wi me and wants ye Eckford, tae personally train him....He says he's a God-send an' could be a great asset tae us, jist at a time when the Laird needs intelligent an' loyal recruits fir his pits".*

Immediately Eckford smelt a rat, *"Asset ma a..."* he thinks *"God-send be damned!... Dae they think I'm bloody daft? I ken what that twa are up tae!"* Mimicking the Factor he mumbled under his breath, *"Train him Eckford!- Teach him a' ye ken Eckford- then he'll tak ower yer job Eckford! Gawd that's it! I see it a'! Naebody in their richt mind wid cross the Laird's dyke an' come tae work in his pit. I bet The Laird has made it worth his while!- No that we'll ever ken!- He'll keep his hands clean! That snivellin' Factor wull dae his dirty work fir him!...Asset ma erse!. I ken what that pair are up tae!...God-send!... Planting a bloody spy mare likely! But I'll cook their goose! That twa wull find oot I'm nae as green as I'm kail lookin'!"*

*"So this is their bloody spy"* thought Eckford as he raged at Lugton, while all the while watching Andrew out of the corner of his eye. *"I'll show ye Young wha's gaffer here an' hoo weel this gaffer runs his Laird's pit and protects his property and richts!"* When he was convinced that Andrew had the full measure of his authority and power he dismissed the luckless Lugton shouting, *"Richt Lugton, this time ye'll forfeit four days pey. Ye're gettin aff lichtly! Next time it's a correction hoose fir ye- Noo get oot o' ma sicht!"* With that he walked away. Abruptly he stopped and as if it was an after-thought, he casually yelled after Lugton, *"As ye're here, ye may as weel be the yin tae tak Young here doon and show him the ropes!"* Sarcastically adding, *"This clever gadgie wull need nae mare than twa weeks before he's able tae howk and draw his ain....Wid ye no agree collier Lugton?"* Taken aback at the turn of events Lugton could not find the words to respond. When he had first become aware of Andrew's presence he had been momentarily thrown. Until then he was unaware there was a witness to his row. On seeing that the onlooker was not only a newcomer to the pit, but a stranger to the village, he was first furious, then fearful.

Lugton, known as Lugs to friend and foe alike, panicked as his crafty mind conjured up a picture of what this would do to his image when cronies in the Ale House heard about it. He prided himself on being known as one of the pit's rough hewn, hard drinking, gambling he-men. As his fearful blood-shot eyes met those of the tall handsome young stranger, an instant, intense, all consuming hate flared up inside him….a hate on which he would feed for weeks to come.

Lording his skills over the raw recruit's lack of knowledge of pit workings, in the weeks that followed Lugs treated Andrew like a galley slave. He did everything in his power to make the new recruit's life a misery. He showed him as little as possible, put every conceivable obstacle in his way and when he found something to find fault with, made sure everyone in the pit, in particular the Overseer, heard about it.

It did not take the artful Lugs long to cotton on to the fact that Eckford hated Andrew and that nothing pleased him more than when he saw the new-comer in trouble and belittled in front of the men. The fact that Andrew did not appear to Lugs to have the guts to retaliate, only added fuel to his hate train; the train Eckford stoked daily with whispered innuendo.

So when Andrew became ill, Lugs gleefully gloated, telling everyone, "*See I telt ye! Ten days and he's oot fir the count! He micht hae the book learning, but he's nae man! He's a spineless weakling. He'll never mak a collier that yin!…..A' he's fit fir is humping coal wi' the wemenfolk!*" Whispering behind his hand with a nod here and a wink there, he would say "*Tak it frae me, I hae it on the highest authority that Young is nae recruit. He's a spy, aye a spy in the pey o' the Laird. He's here tae ferret oot what's going on… tae gie the names of the troublemakers and tae clype on them wha dinna gie their pound o flesh! Jist watch how Eckford treats him different frae the rest o' us… Jist watch how he sends fir him an' speaks tae him on his ain!*"

Lugs conveniently omitted to add that it was every time he would report him. Never once did Lugs miss a chance to drop hints, make snide remarks or wild accusations about Andrew. At other times he simply said "*Noo ask yersel' why should ony-yin leave the Laird's service and cross his dyke tae work wi' us? There must be a guid reason. He' got the book learning and a trade, he wis a gardener ye ken!?. Noo dinna tell me ony man in his right mind wid gie up a' that fir a lass… and a collier lass at that! Nae! tak it frae me, he is a spy, the Laird's tailpyet, that's what he is, Believe me, I hae it on guid authority, frae yin that kens!*"

No prizes for guessing who 'the yin that kens' was! The threatened Overseer, masterminded the sowing of the seed of hate as he lay in bed, tossing and turning, unable to sleep, working out how he could save his own miserable skin. Crafty Eckford, knew men and the nature of the beast! He knew where to find fertile soil to plant his seeds of hate. Lugton more than lived up to his expectations! With the exception of the Macgraws, Bell, Jess and Andy, the rest of the colliers believed Lugs and gave Andrew a wide berth. When he came within earshot, conversions would abruptly cease with a quick, "*Sh, sh, here comes the Laird's tailpyet!*" Cheeky children, encouraged by their parents sang as he passed,

> *Tell tell Tailpyet.*
>
> *Yer tongue shall be slit,*
>
> *An' a' the rats in Niddrey,*
>
> *Wull git a wee bit!*

Things came to a head when after two months, Eckford lampooned Andrew in front of the colliers, brutally telling him what lay in store for him if his output did not improve. By now Andrew was well aware there was a big push in the pit by the Overseer to increase output, and that there was a move afoot to cut wages and costs yet again, But he failed to understand why he should be singled out. He knew his wages were less that some of the others, yet he worked as hard. Something was amiss, But what? It was true that when he started to work on his own behalf, he found he could not bring himself to fill his bearer's creels to overflowing, as others did. Many a time he had felt a lump in his throat as he watched women and children with backs almost bent double cry in agony as they struggled up the ladders under the heavy load. If he had not seen it with his own eyes he would never have believed that such thin, emancipated and crippled frames could carry such burdens. He often thought to himself, *"Folk in the world above widna believe that such cruel slavery exists in their ain land, an' as long as we're oot o' sicht doon here, we're oot o' minds!"*

When Jess saw him only half fill the creels, she would have none of it, saying *"It's the System! It's nae yer fault Andrie!' It'll only cause trouble fir the bairns an' me if we are seen tae cairry less than the ithers... and besides, it'll mean less wages fir us a'... Nae Andrie....things maun aye be somewey!... This is oor lot in life; this is the cross the guid Lord gave us tae cairry, the cross that'll get us intae the Kingdom of Heaven, that Domain o' Love, oor Father in Heaven hae promised us!"*

Lately Jess seemed preoccupied and worried. She was having trouble with her daughter. The young Jessie had been very close to her Father and after his death had for a while been depressed and miserable. Suddenly she changed and now seemed to be playing her Mother up; something she would never have dared before. It seemed she had developed more than a passing fancy for cocky, conceited Geordie Lugton. At least once a day Jessie would go missing to be found by her Mother, cuddling Geordie in a dark corner. It seemed that nothing her Mother could say, nor do, could put a stop to it. Jess would have spoken to his Mother, Maggie Lugton, but for some unknown reason, Lugs, who normally overworked and bullied his family, was turning a blind eye to his son's skiving.

A couple of days after Eckford had confronted Andrew, Jess was seen to extinguish her candle and hide in a dark corner. There she watched as her daughter struggling to drag her slyde, disappeared into the darkness. Minutes later the mother darted off in the same direction to reappear dragging a howling Jessie by the hair and punching her unmercifully, as she screamed *" Go on, tell him ye limmer!...Tell Andrie what ye hiv been up tae!.... Oh God forgee ye! Yer Faither wull turn in his grave!.., what a wey tae pey back the man wha saved us frae being flung on the mercy o' the Parish."* So saying, she flung her daughter at Andrew's feet and giving her a resounding kick in the backside shouted *" The truth ye limmer, tell him the truth!"* Andrew appalled at Jess's brutality dragged her off and tried to quiet and question the howling Jessie. Eventually he dragged the story out of her.

It seemed that once a day Geordie would lie in wait for her as she pulled her slyde past a worked out room. Making sure no one saw then, he would rub Andrew's mark from the slyde and replace it with his Father's. Taking over the harness he would leave Jess hiding while he pulled the slyde to the foot of the ladder as if it were his own. There the coal would be loaded into his sisters' creels and became part of his Father's output.

As the sobbing girl finished, something in Andrew's brain exploded. He saw red! Roughly flinging her aside, he rushed to where Lugs, stripped naked to the waist was hewing the coal. Grabbing him by the back of his trousers, snatching his pickax he flung it to the ground with one hand and with the other landed a vicious punch to the unsuspecting collier's head. yelling *"Tak that ye bastard!"* Lugs, unaware of what had hit him, fell unconscious to the ground. Andrew spun round, grabbed the startled Geordie and landed him a punch between the eyes as he yelled *"I'll learn ye no tae steal frae me!"*

Colliers, hearing the commotion dropped their picks and ran towards them shouting, *"A ficht, A ficht. Geordie is hammering the Tailpyet"* As they crowded round, someone grabbed a candle and holding it up so that the light fell on the battling pair the colliers yelled with venom *"Go on Geordie, let the bastard hae it! - smash his face in - mark him fir life! Leave him so that he'll never spy on ony yin again as long as he lives."*

As the mob's roar for vengeance pounded his ears, and the vicious arrow of their collective hate pierced his very being, Andrew's brain screamed *"Show no mercy - you'll get none - It's him or you!"* The beast in him responded and like a crazy creature, he unmercifully rained blow after blow on his opponent. Geordie, though small and undernourished was no coward. He lashed out with all his might and landed two damaging blows, drawing blood. The hysterical mob yelled and cheered him on shouting *"Go on Geordie...Death tae the Tailpyet!"* The battling pair, punched, pummelled, rolling over and over on the muddy rock floor. By now the hysterical crowd were demanding nothing short of death to the Tailpyet. Andrew, taller, fitter and better nourished had the advantage and the stamina. Gradually Geordie tired. With a final devastating blow to the side of his head Andrew stepped back as his opponent crashed with a splatter, unconscious, face down into the mud. With blood streaming down his face, pulling himself to his full height Andrew faced the hostile mob and somehow managed to yell menacingly through his haze of pain, *"Richt! Any ye lot want a dose o' what he's got?"*

After a moment's uncomfortable silence a cheer reverberated through the pit as someone grabbed Andrew's aching arm and holding it high above his head shouted *"Three cheers fir the winner!"*

At that precise minute a voice thundered through the pit, *"What the hell's gang on doon there?"* It was Eckford. In a flash the men, like rats deserting a sinking ship, scurried back to their rooms and started to hew, leaving Andrew standing alone with the unconscious Geordie at his feet. Even the prostrate figure of Lugs instinctively responded to the dreaded voice of authority. As it pierced his brain his eyes popped open and staggering to his feet, holding his head between his hands, mumbled as he shuffled along *"Aye Sir, coming Sir!"*

*"Richt Young, caught ye red-handed!"* yelled the gleeful Eckford, as he ran towards him. Andrew said nothing. Giving the unconscious Geordie a vicious kick in the ribs, the Overseer yelled

"Hey you! get up!" But Geordie just lay there. He was out cold. "Richt Young! What's going on? What's he doing lying there?" Andrew still said nothing. "Richt, ye ken fichtin' in the pit is a serious offence, I demand to ken wha started it and why?" he roared. Still Andrew did not answer. Shouting so that the others could hear above the steady clink clonk of their pickaxes Eckford yelled " Richt! Wha is gonna tell me whit this is aboot!" No answer. The men went on steadily working.

"So that's it! Naebody saw ooything! I ken ye a' saw whit happened, an' ye were a' here. I heard ye a' cheering. I'm no deef nor daft! Ye dinna need me tae tell ye the punishment fir fighting in the pit. If naebody wull tell, an' I canna get tae the root o' it ye'll a' suffer~ an ye ken wha' that means! Turning to Andrew, in a low wheedling voice and trying not to be overheard he whispered "Come on Young! Ye've got mare sense than that ignorant lot! Ye're no like them... ye're different. I ken that!. Ye tell me whit's at the bottom o' this. It must be something serious when they are a' clamping up like this. Jist name the troublemakers stirring things up in this pit! Ye an' me ken fine that's what the Laird wants tae ken. Tell an we'll o'erlook yer pairt in it!"

Straining their ears a few colliers could hear snatches of the conversation. They feared the worst. Lugs came out in a cold sweat. But they need not have worried. Eckford got no answer, only a stony silence. "A'richt" he yelled, angry and surprised. "Can it be, that he is nae spy," he was thinking, "Jist anither bloody ignorant serf!"

"Weel Young" he yelled, loud enough this time for others to hear, "If ye, or ony o' that lot winna tell me what's going on, then ye'll be the yin I'll mak an example o'! I'll personally report ye tae the Laird: fine ye four days pey an' ye'll spend the next 24 hoors in the jougis." With that he yelled "Stoddart come here." Stoddart, dropping his pick as if it were a hot brick, without a murmur did as he was told and hauled Andrew along the pit bottom to where the jougis hung. There Eckford roughly clapped the iron collar around his neck, snapped it shut, fastened it with a key, and attached the short chain to a pillar of coal. There with head held erect, unable to move, Andrew would stand for the next twenty four hours.

When the Overseer was out of sight, Nettie, Bell and some of the men. who previously had shunned him, took it in turns to give him sips of water along with words of encouragement and gratitude. At first Lugs could not comprehend why Andrew had not jumped at the chance to report him and give Eckford the reason for the fight. Switching loads, everyone knew was considered a very serious crime in the pit! So relieved and grateful was he, that he dispatched his daughter Mary to Auld Lieb's to ask for a portion to relieve Andrew's pain. This he personally administered to the prisoner. It deadened the pain and probably accounted for the hallucinations that followed. Out of the dark haze of pain and anguish as in a dream Andrew saw Venus. Not the gentle, sylph-like naked Goddess who had risen from the waters of Niddrey Burn, but a wild demented creature....

It was Nettie! Like a deranged beast she was fighting to avenge her loved one and fighting the only way she knew how. She kicked, punched, thumped, bit, scratched and tore out the hair of poor, duped, love-sick Jessie.

Next night as Andrew lay exhausted in body and mind on a pallet next to Bell's two sons, he was appalled and frightened at how easily he, who professed to abhor violence, had, when threatened, instinctively succumbed to the primeval beast within and fought like an animal for survival. And worse, how as victor he had wallowed in the glory. Already he had come to see, how, the 'broon yins' after a century and a half of slavery, herded together in appalling conditions, poverty stricken, and forced to live apart from their fellow men, treated like animals, they responded like animals. They had became clannish, inward looking, bigoted and brutalised, with their lives a breeding ground for suspicion and ignorance.

By the time he fell into a troubled sleep he had convinced himself that his fight was but a skirmish - a primeval response by the herd to rid it o' the enemy they had been so easily made to believe had come to destroy them. *"Aye"* he thought, *"If only that loyalty and unity could be harnessed tae challenge authority and demand our rightful place in society!"*

It was James, his father-in-law who taught Andrew his mining skills. He showed him how to work rhythmically and rapidly; how not to waste his strength on clumsy movements and how to recognise and interpret warning noises heralding roof falls, flooding or black fire damp. Describing the day to day hazards in the pit James would say, *"Oor Maisters dae nithin' tae prevent accidents. Doon here we depend on yin anither fir oor safety. Yin false move can kill or maim us a!"* Auld Wullie McVie would ruefully add, *"Aye! a' coal owners care aboot, is gettin' as much coal oot as they can, never mind hoo or at what cost!"* With all the impatience of youth, Andrew would question why they bowed so meekly under their yolk! *"Wi' State, Kirk, Army and the Coorts controlled by oor Maisters hoo can we dae ither!"* was the retort *"But still we keep fichtin'. God alane kens how mony in Niddrey and the Lothians hae gied their lives, or hae been transported. Jist look around, and see hoo many o' us, hae scars that we'll cairry tae oor graves- fichtin' fir the right jist tae be treated as human beings, aye human beings!"* Many were the times James had to restrain his impetuous son-in-law saying, *"Andrie ye maun hae patience! First learn tae be a guid collier an' prove yer worth afore ye start tae agitate. Tak pride in yer craft! Aye its a craft, never mind what folk say! Then use yer book learning tae find weys tae ficht the cruel system that wrongs us an' huds us doon!"*

On the Sabbath Andrew would teach his wife and later his children, to read and write. With the exception of the radical pamphlets given them by a shoemaker friend, the only book the family possessed was the Bible he had given Nettie. Every spare minute she could find, she spent reading the Holy Book. The more she read, the more she turned to religion, learning whole passages by heart. When reading from the Book of Corinthians, she once said *"Oh I remember the minister reading this passage aboot faith, hope and charity. I did'na understand it, but it stuck in ma mind, as Mary McVie hud her wee sickly bairn baptised Faith that day, in the hope she wid be saved. But she deed the next!"*

Often when depressed and despondent she would ask her husband, *"Dae ye think the day wull e'er come, when colliers wull be allowed back tae worship in the Kirk again? - I remember when I wis a wee lassie, saying ma prayers in oor Loft in Newton Parish Kirk. Oh Andrew, saying them noo at ma bedside is nae the same... Neether wonder God disna hear us!"*

Andrew on the other hand, never came to terms with the Kirk's treatment of colliers. The more he read from the Good Book, the more alienated he became from the faith that once had been the centre of his life. He saw the Kirk using religion to uphold the Establishment, while making the poor believe that their suffering was the Will of God. Nevertheless, he was happy for his wife and her family when, one Sabbath, Nettie came from her parents' cottage in a state of great excitement crying, *"Oh Andrew, hae ye heard the guid news? ~ the Kirk Session is gang tae let us back intae the Kirk. Oh Andrew, God is guid!"*

It was a red letter day; a day for great celebrations indeed! The Macgraws joined families from Niddrey, Cleekimin and other mining communities in the Liberton Parish, to celebrate the long awaited answer from the Kirk Session to their petition. For five long years they had been begging the Session to reinstate their right to worship in Newton Parish Kirk. Now at last they had a reply. But James cautioned them saying, *"Afore we get too excited, let's hear the conditions. Dinna forget we've been here afore. This is the second time in oor lifetime we hae been shut oot the Kirk!"* Recalling the first time Wullie McVie said *"Aye James is richt! Can ony o' ye forget that day fifteen years ago, when the Elder read oot the conditions the Kirk Session laid doon afore they wid let us back tae worship?'*

*"Gawd!"* said James, *"When we heard them we were dumbfoonered! They were unbelievable! Tae this day I remember them by heert, the near nigh impossible conditions that pompous, pious Kirk Elder read oot tae us!"* *"Sae dae I!"* chorused Andy and many of the others, as one by one they rattled them off:

*'Build an outside stair on the blind side o' the Kirk!'*

*'Repair the roof, mak it wind and watertight!'*

*'Erect a loft of given dimensions and construct a slot, where we can hear and see the minister, but be unseen by the congregation!'*

*'Enter the loft by the staircase, after the service has commenced and leave on a given signal frae the minister before it finishes!'*

*'Maintain the loft, staircase and roof at oor ain expense!'*

*'Keep yer brats, at least 800 yards frae the precincts of the Kirk at all times!'*

*"Gawd! Remember hoo we jist stood there open moothed, thinking hoo could the likes o' us ever find siller tae dae a' that!"* sighed Wullie.

*"Aye! an' a' I could think was they widna ca the Lairds bairns, brats!"* said Wullie's wife. *"Aye Wullie"* mused James, *"Sae desperate were we tae belong tae God's Family again that we'd hae done onything, aye onything! "We starved oorselves! Aye and God forgie us, we took the food oot o' oor bairns' mooths telling them 'Better hungry bellies here on earth, than nae life in the Hereafter.' Hoo we did it, only the guid Lord Himsel' kens! But in the end we did everythin' that Session demanded o' us!" "An'"* went on James, *"We kent fine they laid doon these conditions, thinking there wis nae chance o' us meetin' them, But God wis guid an' we did! Sae the Session hud tae let us back!"*

"*Aye! the Lord God was mercifu'*" agreed auld Wullie between bouts of coughing and spitting. "*An' every Sabbath fir ten happy years, in a' kinds o' weather we colliers trudged fir miles tae worship in oor Loft in Newton Parish Kirk. An' it didna tak the bairns lang, tae learn tae stey oot o' sicht an' keep as quiet as the Kirk moose!*"

"*Aye*" said Andy with a laugh, "*mind how when auld Bauldy Bain wid fa' asleep an' snore like a pig, he'd be poked in the belly wi' the lang pole shoved through the door keekhole. He'd jump, sweer under his breath, then hiss 'Will some yin tell that gadgie, that a winkin' cat's nae always blind!' - Come tae think o' it Wullie, we ne'er did see wha the gadgie was, that sat ahint that door, spying and poking us thro' the keekhole. But he kent where tae poke where it hurt maist, I can tell 'e!*"

"*Whaever the 'Keekin'-Tam' wis, at least he set e'en on us, even if were only yin e'en!*" commented James dryly, "*No like the Laird an' his landed gentry freends, farmers, craftsman and labourers sittin' doon below, praying in their pews, kennin' fine that they hud made shuir, their e'en could'na be defiled by the sicht o' us outcasts o' the human race, praying above to the same God. Aye the same God!*"

"*Min' ye, little did we think, that as they sat piously praying, they were busy scheming hoo tae get rid o' us fir guid!*" ruefully said Andy "*Sae when we were telt frae the pulpit, that the Kirk wis tae close doon and a new yin built, we were sae happy we sang hymns a' the wey hame in the rain, but we soon learned there wis naethin' tae sing aboot. They had conveniently forgotten tae tell us that there was nae room in the new Hoose o' God for colliers! It wis left tae the Clerk tae tell us that the Session had ruled that oor Petition, ten years afore, only applied to the auld Kirk nae the new yin! We could'na believe oor ears. But there it wis, colliers oot in the wilderness ance again!*"

"*Aye*" muttered Wullie sadly, "*Wandering ance again, but ne'er losing sicht o' the Promised Land! Colliers alwayis hae been a deeply religious and God fearing lot. Withoot God's promise of a Life Hereafter, how else could we thole this Hell on earth! So ye see there wis' nithin' else fir it, but tae start a' o'er again and humbly petition the Session tae let us worship in the New Kirk. That was five years ago. And noo at lang last today we hae an answer!*"

"*Ah!*" said Andy beaming, "*But this time things are different! We're tae get a Gallery nae less- aye a gallery, nae a loft like we hud afore. And there are nae conditions, an' we're no expected tae build or maintain the building. Ee! But that's grand news man, is it no?*"

"*I, fir yin say- wait an' see. I'll believe it when I see wi ma ain e'en. Nae afore!*" said the ever cynical James. "*Nae James Macgraw, fir ance ye're wrang! Times hae changed! Ye wait an' see!*" retorted Janet, his normally silent wife. James waited and when the time came he refrained from saying "*I telt ye sae!*"

Colliers **had** to find the money to fit up the Gallery and conditions were enforced! These were...

There would be an outside stair by which colliers and their families must enter and leave unseen by the congregation.

A fellow Christian, from down below, would still sit watching through a keekhole, waiting to poke any who dare misbehave or not pay attention.

On the Sabbath the gallery was opened colliers were granted special permission to go down into the body of the Kirk.(After the congregation had left of course!) There they viewed the two commemorative plaques which they had been allowed to fix on the wall beneath their gallery.

As they crowded in admiring the two beautifully inscribed tablets, James was heard to whisper to his neighbour, *"Well maybe, fir ance, we've beaten oor Maisters at their ain game!"* Nettie, one of the few present able to read, had been asked to give a running commentary. Using her finger as a pointer, she was proudly explaining to a sea of admiring upturned faces, *"This is the colliers' petition plaque. It commemorates the fact, that in the year of oor Lord, 1742, colliers' o' this Parish were granted the richt tae worship in Newton Parish Kirk. The tablets show the colliers' motto; the tools o' oor craft and names of some of us colliers- Adam, Kinghorn and Archibald".* As she talked, her ever lively imagination started to run riot. Her brown eyes lit up and sparkled, as she enthusiastically asked her audience *"Aw! folks, isn't writin' a wonderfu' thing?"*

*"Aye! fir them that can read an' hae nithin' better tae dae!"* shouted a female voice from the back of the crowd. Ignoring the comment, Nettie excitedly rattled on, *"Writin' gies power! Oor betters hae ei kent hoo tae use it to further their interests!"*

*"Hoo lass?"* enquired an old man.

*"Weel jist tak a keek at the ither plaques roond the Kirk Wa's an' see fir yersel'es hoo them that hae the power around these pairts, hae used the writin', not only tae keep their memories alive, but tae mak sure the cruel system that huds us doon lives efter them!"*

Expecting the usual blank or hostile stares, she stopped, anxiously scanning the upturned faces to see if any understood, far less agreed. But she need'nt have worried, a heartfelt cry reverberated round the Kirk, as, with one accord many shouted, *"Aye oor Maisters hae ei done that alricht!"*

Greatly encouraged, she hurriedly went on, *"Weel folks! maybe the writin' on oor tablets canny gie us power to change the system, but it gies us an other power. Power we hae never had afore!"*

*"Power fir what?,"* cried an impatient voice.

*"Power tae talk frae the grave!"* she retorted

*"Talk frae the grave, Gawd! she's at it again- what next!"* cried a woman at the back as she noisily stalked out followed by her two friends shouting, *"Plaque! Waste o' guid siller we say- there's mare needy things tae spend oor hard earned bawbees on than the likes o'that!"*

Nettie, pretending not to have heard went on. *"Aye tae warn generations yet unborn, o' the length man's cruelty tae his brother and sister man wull gang tae keep their power an' wealth."*

Stopping for breath, she thought for a minute then went on, *"Andrew of'en says that yin day a' puir folk in Scotland wull be able tae read an' write!'*

*"That'll be the day! Oor maisters wull hae nane o' that!"* scoffed the sceptics."

"Weel," said Nettie, "Ye could be richt! But suppose, jist suppose, that yin day, the Laird an' his ilk find it in their interest tae educate their workers..... Let's shut oor e'en an' imagine hunners o' years frae noo, when we're a' deed an' gone an' this Kirk is still here. Maybe standin' on the very spot w're standing on noo wull be folk bearin' oor names. But these folk wull no be ragged like us, They'll be weel clad, hae shin on their feet, be better fed, better hoosed an' mare enlightened. An' as they read oor message on this plaque fir themselves they wull be hearin' oor ghostly voices coming frae the grave, tellin' them aboot a time lang syne, when powerfu' families in Scotland, used the State tae mak colliers an' salters legal slaves, and the Kirk tae mak them believe their poverty wis the Will o' God, not something thocht up by them, sae that they could hud on tae the riches an' power oor toil an' suffering gied them!"

## CHAPTER 9 **ARLED BAIRNS**

In time Andrew grew accustomed to pit life, accepting its hazards and taking each day as it came, while living for the Sabbath. In the first two years of their married life the couple worked every Sabbath making their tumble-down, vermin infested hovel into a home. Andrew's years of labouring in the Laird's gardens gave him skills beyond that of coal hewing. They started by repairing the thatched roof, making it wind and water tight and closing the smoke hole. Moving the hearth from the centre of the room to a wall, they built an ingle and then a chimney. Before they could tackle the cleaning of the reek stained walls they had first to remove decades of spider webs hanging in great clusters from the sooty rafters. When finished they lime washed the walls.

It was the custom at that time for the Laird to present every collier with a tree trunk on his wedding day. With his, Andrew made a box bed, a three legged stool and a meal kist, the top of which was used as a table. The cottage having no ceiling, dry stane walls and an earthen floor, was very damp in winter. Nevertheless compared with their neighbours, the Youngs lived in luxury. Many of the wives were lost in admiration, and nagged their husbands to improve their hovels. But none had the confidence or energy left after their week's toil to attempt such an unheard of undertaking. Other women, green with envy made bitchy remarks behind Nettie's back, saying, *"She wis aye a queer yin that, wi' her high falootin' ideas an' pernickity weys. She spends her life trying tae get rid o' the pit glaur.' 'De ye ken, they used tae say that on the Sabbath she stripped hersel' stark naked- aye stark naked, an washed a' ower, in the burn. Imagine that'! 'Aye, her heed's in the clouds that Nettie Young! Wait till she has a creel fu' o' bairns, she'll come doon tae earth wi' a wallop."*

At times Nettie tried reasoning with them, but she may as well have saved her breath. When bitchy to her face, she would agree with them saying. *"Al'richt! I ken that ance I hae bairns hinging round ma skirts as I toil in the pits, I'll hae nae time nor the energy tae improve ma hame!"* Getting angry she'd go on, *"But why should we onywey! The Laird should see that his workers hae decent hames tae bring up their bairns. Jist tak a keek o'er his dyke, an' see hoo he and his family live. Even his animals are better hoosed and fed than we are! An as fir the pit glaur! Why should we hae tae bring it hame wi us? Why can't the Laird gie us tubs o' water an' soap tae wash some o' it aff at the pit-heed?"*

An outburst like this would be met with looks of utter astonishment followed by contempt. Hurriedly the women would make an excuse to leave whispering to each other as they went, *"Gawd that Nettie Young, she's at it again! Wha dis she think we are?... Tubs o' water an' soap at the pit-heed.. what next! She forgets what side o' the dyke we were beget!... A' that book learning is filling her heed wi' queer notions!"* Others would say, *"It's puir Andrie we're sorry fir! That wife o' his is going saft in the heed!"*

Andrew, now a much respected and popular member of the community since the fight, had become one of its accepted leaders. The book learning that so many had once scoffed at and so lightly dismissed, was now seen as an asset to the community. Here was someone, who could not only read and write better than anyone they had ever known, but someone who had the words as well as the courage to speak up on their behalf. On one famous occasion he had somehow managed to go over the head of the Overseer to the Laird. Presenting the colliers' fears that the flood water would overtake them before the Overseer was prepared to act. The Laird, to everyone's amazement, agreed to abandon the pit earlier than planned.

Once the couple had made their house habitable Andrew turned his attention to the surrounding ground. Here he had to clear away a huge muck midden plus the growth of decades. Fencing off a strip of land with a hawthorn hedge, he set about planting onions, carrots and turnips as well as the colliers' staple diet, kail. On the Sabbath, when coming back from Kirk or the Ale House, men would stop and stand watching him. But none could be persuaded to dig a plot for themselves.

About this time a new vegetable was being cultivated in the gardens of the rich in Scotland. As a gardener in the Laird's estate Andrew had grown it and now saw its potential as a supplement to their meagre diet of porridge and kail. But how to get the seeds posed a problem. One evening at a Friends of the People Society meeting he met up with a childhood friend again. The son of the estate millar, he agreed to ask the estate gardener for some seeds. They thrived. When the second years' planting yielded a heavy crop, the Youngs decided to invite neighbours to their cottage one September Sabbath, for what Bell called, 'A Harvest Supper'. Her contribution was her speciality, bannocks made on her Mother's gridle. Under her guidance Janet and Jess made a pot of Hotpotch, with onions, carrots and turnips. Nettie, borrowing the largest cooking pot in the village, rubbed the earth from the strange new vegetables, covered them with water, liberally sprinkled in salt, then boiled them over the fire. Her Mother cooked the kail in her own cottage.

It was just as well it turned out to be a balmy Sabbath evening, as villagers not only from Cleekimin, but from Niddrey turned up. Word had got around and folk were curious to taste the new fangled food. Bringing their bowls and spoons, and in many cases liquid contributions to the evening merriment, they squatted on the ground around the cottage garden. Nettie's heart sank when she looked out and saw how many were there. But Auld Wullie McVie, ever the optimist, consoled her saying, *"Oh dinna fash yersel lass! The Lord will provide. Remember the parable o' the loaves an' fishes!"*

Maybe at this point the womenfolk added a bit more water to the soup, as every outstretched bowl was filled, with compliments afterwards for the cooks. *"Never hae we tasted sic grand soup!"* all agreed. Some hand must have hurriedly added a few more 'tatties' to Nettie's pot as there was one for each bowl, served with a spoonful of kail and a bannock. Never since the wedding had there been such a sumptuous meal. Everyone sang its praises, *"Man! but that wis grand- we've ne'er tasted onything like it- nor eaten sae muckle. It's a feast fir King Jamie himsel'!"* they cried, smacking their lips and licking their bowls clean.

*"Aye!"* said Andrew, *"Noo ye can boast ye hae eaten what's served up at the Laird's table -aye- an' at the King's! They ca' it the potato!"* Andrew was learning fast. At this point he knew better than to suggest that other colliers grow them for themselves. A few might, in their own good time, but not if wives nagged or neighbours nudged. Bell was the first to ask for some of his seed potatoes. Fiercely independant as ever, she insisted in return she would teach Nettie how to cook soups and stews using Andrew's other vegetables, *"Jist as Mither taught me doon at Wanton Wa's"* she promised. At the same time she tried to teach Nettie to knit, but without success it must be said. *"Better stick wi' the book learning lass"* sighed Bell, defeated for the first time in her life.

Gradually a few of the neighbours started to cultivate a strip of land and on the Sabbath as they worked in their plots they would shout to each other, good naturedly decrying each others' produce. On one such evening when they were comparing turnips, Andy turning to a new son-in-law, said, *"Weel, big or sma' this family wull hae something ither than kail this winter tae help keep the wolf frae the door. An' if we're aff work, sick or idle, wi' nae money coming in, at least we'll no starve, as we done mony times afore!"*

*"An' it' micht save some o' ye young yins frae gettin' caught in the spider's web o' debt,"* shouted auld Wullie McVey from next door. *"Nae chance o' that fir me an' ma wife- we didna believe in tick!"* confidently replied the newly wedded husband.

*"Dinna be sae sure lad! When I had ma accident years ago an' couldna work fir four months, an' there wis nae money comin' in, the Pit Shop offered me food on credit until I was back tae work. At the time it seemed a God-send. Back at work they claimed ma first week's wages- leavin' us wi' naethin'. This meant we hud tae ask credit that week and so it went on week after week, month after month like the horse gin. An' then we hud idle time and nae wages again. An' sae the debt grew. Tae this day I'm still in debt and doobt if I'll e'er git oot this side o the grave. Once in that web, the spider ne'er lets go! Gawd we jist canna win!"*

*"But the coal owners win a' the time!"* retorted Andrew. *"The Midlothian coal owners meet regularly tae fix prices in their truck shops an' ye a' ken the high prices they charge, Combination Laws dinna affect them! But if mare than three o' us meet the gither tae discuss oor livin', we're breakin' the law an it's a correction hoose fir us, or worse!"*

Nettie and Andrew were married three years, when, after a miscarriage and a still birth, Adam their son, was born. He was a frail tiny morsel of humanity, whom Bell, who delivered him, was fearful would not survive. Nettie, in a weak state after a difficult birth, prayed earnestly to God to spare him, and pleaded with Andrew to have him baptised. Ever anxious to please his wife, respecting her wishes and, at the same time sharing her unsaid fears, he reluctantly agreed, saying, *"Get the bairn baptised if ye feel ye must, an' I understand why, but as his faither I jist canna stand at the Font and, wi' the minister as witness, accept the Laird's arles for ma son's future labour. In law, he's pairt o' a family yoked tae the pit onyhow. This custom only maks the faither a party tae his serfdom. That I'll never be!"*

She found little understanding or sympathy from the minister, who refused to baptise the baby without the father being present. But two years later, his successor, a more enlightened man, baptised Adam and his little sister Janet.

Nettie with Andrew's help managed to conquer her claustrophobia, but all her married life she was haunted by a secret dread she never could share with him. She lived in terror that one day the Wrath of God would descend on her husband and some terrible catastrophe would befall him, because of his refusal to go to Kirk. Many a night she lay awake trying not to let her mind dwell on the fact that according to the teaching of her Kirk her husband was already condemned to Eternal Damnation, and therefore, they could never be together in the Life To Come. When she tried to voice her fears, Andrew just shrugged them off saying *"I'm maybe nae fir the Kirk, but I'm still fir Christ! I still try tae live according to his teachings. A' the Kirk can dae is ex-communicate me! The Law of Scotland no longer punishes folk for religious offences as it did a hundred years ago. I'll jist hae tae tak ma chance wi' Eternal Damnation!"*

Andrew may not have succeeded in influencing his wife's religious views; indeed he did not try, as he always encouraged her to think for herself; something unheard of among colliers and most men in these times.

But they were as one politically. Sharing his conviction that colliers in Scotland were being deeply wronged, they committed their lives to the fight for liberty and justice for all.

As the years went on more and more of their fellow colliers joined in the discussions sparked off by the illegal pamphlets the couple read aloud to any who would listen. From these they learned not only of the unrest and disturbances in the Lothian Coal Pits, but of the battles that were being fought by other Scottish workers; agricultural labourers, weavers, spinners, and factory workers, who lived in squalor and worked in appalling conditions for near starvation wages. Although severe and vicious punishments were meted out to those who dared challenge the system many were the brave men and aye, women, who suffered and gave their lives in the fight for liberty and justice in Scotland at that time.

## CHAPTER 10 **A UNION OF BROTHERS**

It was now 1745, Scotland was embroiled in the Jacobite Rising. Not many miles from Niddrey, Prince Charles Edward Stuart, the young Pretender, routed Johnnie Cope at the Battle of Prestonpans. In some quarters, including the House of Wauchope, there was great rejoicing.

When the news of the battle reached Niddrey and Cleekhimin villages, many there saw no reason to rejoice when they heard what an indignant Jock o' the Mill had to tell them. *"They say its nae secret,"* he said *"that the Laird's six year old son and his tutor were seen crossing the enemy lines cairrying a basket o' strawberries, a present fir the Prince as he camped at Duddingston the nicht afore the Battle. An' dae ye ken what was in the bottom o' oor young Maister's basket? Siller! Lots an' lots o' siller fir the Prince's Cause."*

*"Oh aye!"* angrily cried colliers, *"He has siller tae spare fir the Jacobite Cause, has oor Laird, but nane tae pey his folk a livin' wage- us wha mak that siller fir him."*

As the shallower and more accessible seams of coal in Niddrey became exhausted, so the depth of the pits increased. Families working the Peacock Tail seam in No. 3, the Laird's deepest pit at that time, found themselves having to face yet another hazard. This was the highly inflammable and explosive gas, known as fire-damp. On reaching the pithead one morning, for the second time that week they were informed that there was a build up of fire-damp and they must wait until Tam the fireman had it cleared. After thoroughly soaking his clothes in water, Tam went down alone into the working place, and there, with a naked candle, burned off the gas. The courage that this act called for, was now accepted as part of the day's work. Given the all-clear, the colliers and bearers descended and worked steadily all day to within an hour of 'Lowsing Time'.

Suddenly, without warning, it happened. An almighty explosion ripped the pit apart and the roof caved in. What followed was a nightmare. Working non-stop through the night, colliers from neighbouring collieries, without a thought for their own safety, frantically dug till they reached their entombed comrades. There they found many suffering horrendous injuries and barely alive. Seven were dead. Among the dead was ten year old Lachie Young. Nettie his Mother, suffered injuries to her leg, but the rest of the family escaped unscathed but for the horror and trauma that haunted them for the rest of their lives. From that day on, Andrew became obsessed with pit safety. In the immediate aftermath of the disaster, the coal-owner promised safety measures, but the token gestures they finally implemented, did not even begin to tackle the problem.

So colliers were thrown back on their own resources. Having heard of pit-men who took birds down the pit, Andrew and others, from that day on, took their tame linties with them to work. Colliers were unable to detect the oderless gas but a bird would succumb quickly, thus giving warning to the humans. In common with the other mothers in the pit, all Nettie asked of life was to see her children freed from its shackles. Many a time, when trudging down the track beside the Laird's dyke she would hoist her little daughter up until she could see over it and say *"If ever ye're free, try tae get a job as a servant in that big hoose, jist like Grace, the aunt yer faither has telt ye aboot."*

Perhaps it was as well that James did not live to see the day he had so often foretold would surely come: the day colliers and other workers in the Lothians rioted in the streets of Edinburgh. He would have seen his daughter Nettie there, together with her husband and others from Niddrey and Cleekhim. Many were arrested and sentenced to punishment in a house of correction.

The Lothian coal owners, worried by the riots, held a meeting and within the confines of the law, legally punished the rioters. At the same time they tightened the screws of serfdom. Colliers, who before the riots had been woefully saying *"Things canna get ony worse!"* were wrong. So wrong! Wages, already pruned to the bone were slashed even further, with the collier now having to pay for the sharpening of his tools in addition to providing his and his bearers' candles. Competition from the North of England pits, where the quality of coal was higher and easier to get at, was the excuse coal owners gave.

In spite of the fact that it was unlawful for groups of more than two to meet together, many met in secret to discuss wages or working conditions. One such group, made up from colliers from Easter Duddingston, Niddrey, Cleekhimin and other pits in Liberton Parish, met clandestinely at Niddrey. Some of the colliers, including the Youngs, had only the day before, been released from the house of correction.

The day was long past when Nettie was tolerated by the men only because she could read and write. They now recognised her as one of their best versed speakers, and a political activist willing to make any sacrifice asked of her.

Today Andrew had brought a stranger to the meeting. It was someone he had met while serving his sentence. The man gave no name, only that he came from the Kingdom of Fife. He showed the audience a document which had come into his possession, recording, how a few years before, when coal was 2/2d a cartload, the Wauchope family had made a profit of £11,384.4.8d. *"An'"* said Andrew *"they tell us oor Scottish pits dinna pey- weel here is written proof that they dae! An' as oor Maisters ne'er tire o' tellin' us- facts are chiels that winna ding!"*

*"An' what'll oor Laird's profits be noo?"*, shouted the Niddrey colliers. *"Muckle mair than that!"* answered Andrew *"In spite o' what they tell us, we a' ken that since the Union of the Parliaments, coal-owners hae greatly increased their wealth. Jist look at oor ain Laird! Look at the muckle sums o' siller he hae spent makin' improvement on his mansion hoose. Aye!, he an' the rest o' the Scottish coal-owners maun be gettin' a guid price fir the coal we howk fir them! They say that the growing hame and foreign markets canna get enough coal and that Scotland is the highest exporter o' coal in the world today! So ye'd think, wi' sic a high demand fir their coal, an' when it's nae secret that the owners canny get workers tae gie up their freedom tae dig it oot, that they wid improve the lot o' their colliers. But naw!"*

*"Wha should they?"* cried a voice from the crowd, *"They dinna need tae! Fir nearly 150 years we hae been their property, wi' nae human rights at a'!"*

*"Aye!"* said the stranger rising to his feet and flinging wide his arms as he thundered *"Their's is the power and the glory in this land; theirs tae dae with us what they please! They mak the laws; laws that dictate wages and conditions an' mak maximum profits for themselves as weel as perpetuating the system that huds us doon!"*

*"Where is the justice?. How much longer must colliers thole this cruel bondage. Fir o'er three hundred years we've been forced tae endure social injustices as if they were theWill o' God, no a human invention thocht up by oor Maisters solely fir their profits. Hoo much longer must we suffer their barbarous punishments, transportation and aye, even death, afore we are freed and get oor rightfu' place in this, oor ain country. Why is it, that only colliers and salters are excluded frae the Habeas Corpus Act of 1701- The Act that gi'es protection against wrongful arrest and imprisonment to the Scottish people, but not to us. Why?....Are we not also Scots?"*

*"Are we no also human beings?"* shouted a voice from the crowd. *"Aye! By these Acts o' Parliament colliers and their families hae been ostracised, stigmatised and forced to live as a race apart!"* went on the stranger. *"But noo, from the stubborn struggle that has glowed for centuries in the heerts*

and minds o' the brave men and women o' this section of the Scottish nation who were, and continue to be, gravely wronged, a new spirit has arisen and is spreading like wildfire thro' the Scottish pits proclaiming,

*Rise like lions after slumber.*

*In unvanquishable number-*

*'cause we are many, they are few.*

*Brithers and Sister colliers, today I bring this message to the Niddrey Pits- Colliers of Scotland Unite. Let Unity be oor watchword and oor rallying point. Together we will create a collective voice to challenge oor Masters and ficht for freedom and justice for all. Join our Brotherhood. Swear the secret oath o brothering, pledging oorselves tae unite and stand by yin anither!"*

Next day as Nettie hauled her slyde passed a deserted room three women lay in wait for her. Jumping out they knocked the candle from her mouth, pushed her to the ground and held her there. Yelling hysterically they reigned punches on her. *"Tak that- that'll teach ye nae tae hae secret meetings wi' oor men! Ye shouldna be meddlin in men's affairs! That's something us wemen ken nothin' aboot!"*

*"Ye're place is at hame looking after yer bairns, no oot galavantin wi oor men! Did that mither o' yours ne'er tell ye, that the guid Lord put us wemen on earth tae look after men, bear their bairns an' cairry their coal!"*

In the pitch black Nettie could only recognise the loudest of the screaming voices. It belonged to Jessie, who after bearing two of Geordie's children was now married to him and having more than her share of trouble. *"For Christ's sake, what's this?"* thundered the voice of Big Bell, appearing from nowhere. Recognising her daughter's voice she yelled, *"Jessie, dinna vent yer spleen on Nettie Young if yer Geordie is up tae his auld tricks, ye hud better look elsewhere. He certainly wisna wi' her last nicht. We a' ken where she wis, at the meetin' wi' her man. Her mither had her bairns!"* Holding high her candle, Bell angrily scanned the faces of the women in the flickering light, as she roared menacingly *"weel, if ye'll nae tak heed o' what Nettie Young says I'll mak the lot o' ye listen tae me! I'll bash in the brains o' the first yin tae move! Instead o' hammering her, ye should be glad that at last there is a woman in this pit wha can talk up fir us. An' yin that kens as much as ony man,...aye an' mare than maist 'cause o' her book learning. Why winna ye listen when she tells ye what she hears at the meetings or reads in the pamphlets?" God forgee me, but mony a time I wish that the first woman wha tried tae cairry coal had broken her back! But she dinna! An' the result it that this livin' hell is oor lot in life. But must it be the lot o' oor bairns? We're their mithers- it is us wha should be daeing something aboot it! If ye listened to Nettie Young, ye'd ken that it's only here in the Lothians and in the Fife pits that wemen and children hae tae work underground cairrying coal."*

*"Aye, horses and ponies dae it in ither places, an' they're better fed an' treated than us humans are!"* chirped up Nettie, dragging herself up from the mud and wiping the blood from her face. *"An' because the men are better paid, they can afford tae keep their wives at hame tae look efter the wee*

*bairns, no tak them in their creels tae the pit like we hae tae dae! And what's mare, o'er the border in the English pits, women work only on the pitheed- no underground! Mind ye, they work fir starvation wages like us and are exploited jist like we are, but at least they are free, no legal serfs like us!"*

As Nettie stopped for breath, Bell holding high the candle, glared at the women as she cried impatiently *"Wemen I've telt ye afore an' I'll tell ye again! It's time the voice o' us mithers was heard coming up the pits tellin' the world what gangs on doon here."* She quickly added, *"Aye an' tellin' hoo weman an' bairns are used as human beasts o' burden, forced tae cairry burdens far beyond oor strength, an' o' the terrible injuries an' deaths we suffer tae get oot their coal. Aye! an' mak them understand what it's like tae hae tae drag wee, feered, hungry bairns tae work in this hell hole fir 16 hoors a day. Ne'er kenning, if this'll be the day yin o' them, or their faither or mither, wull be maimed, killed or drooned in the flood water. ....An' fir what- sae that a few rich families can get even richer!"*

*"Aye"* shouted Bell, *"Wemen, when are ye gonna get it intae yer thick heeds that we're oor ain worst enemy. We shouldna be fichtin' yin anither, that's what oor maisters wants.....keep us at yin anithers' throats an' it taks oor minds of what they're daeing tae us. As mithers we should a' be sticking thegither an' fighting along wi' oor men for freedom from this cruel poverty and bondage."* Shaking her fist at them angrily she blew out the candle and shouted as she stalked away *"Women! Mithers o' Niddrey, fir Gawd sake listen tae her, an' dae somethin', ...naebody else is gonna dae it fir ye- naebody else cares- git that intae yir thick heeds!"* As they walked back to the ladder Bell sighed and shaking her head said sadly to herself, *"Sheep herd thegither.... Eagles flee alane!...Nettie Young, she's a wuman afore her time!"*

Each spring when the wild primroses were in bloom, Nettie and Andrew would take their children on a pilgrimage to a hallowed spot beyond the dyke encircling Newton Parish Church Kirkyard. There a carpet of pale yellow primrose now covered the unsanctified ground where wee Jemmie, Wull Millar and countless other colliers, young and old lay at rest. The family would kneel and offer up the prayer Nettie had first said for wee Jemmie, some twenty years before.

> **Father in Heaven, cam doon frae above**
>
> **An' tak wee Jemmie, wi care an' love,**
>
> **Keep him safe, till morning is nigh,**
>
> **And we meet in the sweet bye 'n bye.**

Reverently picking three posies of primroses the family would carry them into the Kirkyard. There, repeating the prayer, they would lay one on the grave of each of their two children; Andrew, who died from diphtheria when he was six and ten year old Lachie who lost his life in the pit.

The other posy they carried along the banks of Niddrey Burn until they reached a disbanded pit on Niddrey Edge- the unsanctified grave of Big Bell. There she lies, entombed for all eternity. Killed in an explosion, trying to save the children. She died as she had lived, defending and protecting the child coalbearers in their daily dice with death, while urging their Mothers to raise their voices with their men and fight for freedom from their cruel bondage.

The family stood in silence as Nettie, struggling to kneel, reverently laid God's first roses of Spring on the ground which now covered the disused shaft. Only her husband heard her whispered plea.

> *Deep doon in dungeons grim confine,*
>
> *Where wemen greet an' bairns pine*
>
> *Bell, cradled in rock, yer vigil ower us keep,*
>
> *Frae the land o' the leal where ye sleep.*

As she struggled to rise he took her calloused, work worn hand in his. Where once there was a mantle of gold, scraggy greying locks now swept back from a bald patch on the front of her head. Her once lovely body was now twisted and crippled. But as he gazed deep into the soft brown eyes, he saw, reflected in the window of her soul, untouched by time and suffering, the same blithe and loving spirit of long ago.

*"Oh Nettie, ma ain Nettie- ma Venus o' Niddrey Burn!"* he whispered as he squeezed her hand and gently helped her up.

## CHAPTER 11 **FREEDOM DAY**

*"Rab wake up! Fir Gawd's sake listen! What's that?"* cried the distraught croaky voice of an old beggar, sleeping in a ditch on the outskirts of Easter Duddingston Village. His youthful companion, none too pleased at being rudely wakened from his dreams on such a glorious morning, snarled, *"What dae ye think it is? The last trumpet!"* *"Mare like an army on the move!"* groaned the old man as the now unmistakable tramp, tramp, tramp of marching feet grew louder and louder. *"Christ! Maybe it's the law. Quick! Oot o' here!"* yelled Rab, jumping up and grabbing his bundle. Scrambling through hawthorn and thistles, they stopped and stared. Over the brow of the hill, under a sea of banners, came a great wave of human jetsam- a motley assortment of grinning black-faced men, ragged lads, lassies, mothers with babes in arms and children at their skirts. All were singing lustily as they danced to the raucous accompaniment of blaring trumpets, beating drums, and bewitched fiddles.

*"Ye Gawds! The children o' Israel!"* muttered the old man, hastily crossing himself. Rab's response was to roughly push the old man into the procession as it passed, crying *"Go*

on, *auld yin, join the multitude. Wha kens, we micht land up at the promised land!"* As the crowd pressed relentlessly on, the frail old man had to hobble hard to keep up with the others. Rab, press-ganged by two dancing girls, quickly found himself caught up in the infectious hilarity.

At the gates of Duddingston Mansion the procession ground to a halt. Cap in hand, two of the leaders approached the gate keeper, who, while having great difficulty in retaining his vicious dog, listened attentively to what they had to say. Shouting *"A'richt! Wait there a meenite!"* he disappeared up the driveway, to return a few minutes later followed by a group of estate workers. Slowly the massive gates swung back to reveal the men stationing themselves at intervals along the tree-lined drive, their narrowed eyes full of suspicion. The procession, now subdued and orderly wound its way up the avenue to halt before an elegant mansion house, built on the lines of a Greek Temple. A murmur of awe and admiration ran through the crowd as they gazed in wonder at the beautiful building, the like of which, they had never seen before. Waiting to greet them on the terrace was the Earl of Abercorn and his family. Although many in the crowd were his serfs, until that day, few had ever set eyes on him.

Removing his bonnet, the leader stepped forward and bowing low, the hushed crowd heard him say, *"Yer Grace, we, yer humble servants, colliers o' Easter Duddingston, Niddrey, Inveresk, and salters of these parishes, hae come this day tae respectfully thank yer Grace fir pushin' thro' Parliament the Act that' frees us colliers and salters frae the shackles o' serfdom."* Turning to the crowd he yelled, *"Brither an' sister colliers, and salters let's show oor everlastin' gratitude. Three cheers fir oor saviour, the noble Earl o' Abercorn, the member o' Parliament, wha cared enough aboot us, tae get us delivered frae bondage! Hip ..hip...horray!"* For miles around the countryside resounded with the roar. And what a roar! Two hundred voices charged with emotion, elation and joy. Such joy!

In the crowd Adam Young stood with his youngest son perched on his shoulder. Smiling up at the boy they joined in the cheering, they yelled till they were hoarse. Tugging his son's leg, Adam shouted *"James always remember this day! Yin day ye'll proodly tell yer grandchildren- I wis there! Aye, I wis there the day Scottish colliers paid homage tae the Earl o' Abercorn, the saviour wha freed us frae bondage!"*

When at long last the cries died down, with a magnanimous smile, the Earl stepped forward saying, *"Colliers, coal-bearers, and salters, this is an historic occasion! Today, the first of July in the year 1775, will long be remembered as a milestone in the history of Scottish Coal Mining. From this day henceforth, Parliament has decreed that colliers and salters shall be freemen!"* The rest of the sentence was lost in thunderous applause. Lapping up the adulation and gratitude with a smug self-satisfied smile the Earl waited patiently until the noise died down then continued. *"I'm sure you will all agree, that this is not an occasion for long speeches. It is a time for joy and celebration. Is it not? So I will detain you only long enough, to bring further good tidings. To mark this auspicious occasion, Parliament in its wisdom, has decreed that the first day of July will, from henceforth be known as 'Freedom Day' and be an annual holiday for colliers and salters!"* The crowd went wild! Women, with tears streaming down their coal-ingrained faces, jumped for joy as they hugged their husbands and bewildered children. Rough-hewn hard men, visably moved, cried *"God bless yer Grace!"* And why not! Colliers had fought for 170 years for this day to dawn! Many silently offered up a prayer of thanksgiving to God for their deliverance, while others, among them the Macgraws, the Youngs and McVies, remembering the struggle and sacrifices of their forbears- wished God could have spared them to see this day!

With a regal wave of the hand, the Earl and his family withdrew, the applause still ringing in their ears. Once the great door of the Mansion clanked behind them, the procession reassembled and made for the gates in an orderly manner. But once outside, the crowd went wild. dispersing to celebrate in time honoured fashion- each according to his or her need or inclination!

As for Rab the beggar, he spent an unforgettable day with the two dancing pit girls. So taken was he with red headed Nell Young, that when he left her at midnight, (three sheets to the wind it is true), he slurred, *"Oh but ye're ma bonny Nell! I lo'd ye the meenite I set e'en on ye. Tae prove it the morra I'll git a job beside ye in the pit, a place wild horses couldnae hae dragged me yesterday!"*

Next day, down the three Niddrey pits, many were the castles built in the stinking air. The young, foot-loose and fancy free, dreamed of crossing the ocean to seek fame and fortune in the Americas. Others would be off to the west of Scotland, where it was said pay and conditions in the pits were better. Some fancied work on the land, while many of the girls saw themselves as servants, dairymaids or workers in one of the fine new factories springing up in the new towns. *"Aye"* thought Adam wistfully in the cold light of day, *"Fir the maist o' us, wi a tied cottage and up tae oor necks in debt tae the Pit Shop, we're still trapped!"* Others facing reality could only agree, but consoled themselves thinking *"But sharily things maun git better noo!"*

There was at least one among who saw no reason to cheer; the oldest man in the village; Geordie Lugton no less! He was by now, well into his 'fifties, having out-lived two wives, two sons and most of his contemporaries. Geordie hadn't changed. Like his old ferret, he'd lost his teeth, but not his nature. How right his cronies had been when they said, *" Oh him! He'll see us a' oot!- Looks efter number yin, dis Geordie Lugton. An'somehoo alwayis finds a wumen tae mither him!"* Others would sneer saying, *"Nae chance o' that yin gettin' himsel' mixed up in pit politics- alwayis tae busy oot chasing the wemen. Nae jougis or correction hoose fir him! ~ Ale hoose or whore hoose maybe!- but nae correction hoose!- Mind ye, he's alwayis yin o' the first to tak the benefits ithers ficht fir, is oor Geordie!"*

Right now Geordie, sitting in state in front of a dying fire, couldn't see why colliers needed to be free. His long suffering daughter-in-law, was greeted with a tirade on the subject as she returned home from the pit soaked to the skin after being caught in a thunderstorm. Paying scant heed she thought to herself, *"Weel it's maks a change from the usual greetin' and girnin' aboot his aches an' pains!"*

Then she saw the fire! Only by fiercely biting her lip did she manage to hold back tears of rage and frustration. Before going to work she had left it set, ready to light to cook the evening meal. In spite of it being a scorching hot day, the malicious old man had deliberately lit it, then let it die out just in time for her home-coming. Too tired to argue or get angry, ignoring his incessant rantings she wearily rekindled the fire and started to make the porridge and kail. Suddenly her hackles rose when it dawned on her what he was saying. *"Tae be honest wi ye, fir the life o' me I dinna see why colliers want tae be free. That lot! they dinna ken when they're weel aff! I say oor Laird kens what's best fir us. He understands things the guid Lord ne'er gied the likes o' us the brains tae ken aboot. Jist see hoo guid he is tae us, hoo he taks care o' us in oor auld age, lettin' us bide on in his village!"*

*"Auld age!"* she hissed under her breath glaring at his back. *"If the Laird's sae guid tae ye, hoo come that me, a wedow wumen- wha's naw even yer ain dochter is lumbered wi ye? An' hoo is it, that noo yer choked wi' the spit an canna work fir yer guid an' kind Laird ony mare, its left tae me an' ma faitherless bairns tae provide fir ye?"* But as usual, she would not dare say it to his face. Instead she meekly went about laying the dripping wet clothes around the fire, whilst vowing to herself that one day she'd explode and do something drastic- like empty the contents of the porridge pot over his head. But not today! *"The bairns wid hae tae gang tae bed wi' empty bellies. Efter a' he is their grandfaither!"*

On the third morning of that July, Adam was met at the pithead by a group milling round a notice pinned up on a shed door. They were impatiently calling, *"Come on Adam, read this! What dis it say?"* Hastily scanning the page before reading it aloud, Adam's face fell.

*"What's wrong?"* they cried in dismay.

*"Noo we ken why the bonny Earl wis sae keen naw tae detain us! He micht hae let slip the truth!"*

*"What truth man?*

*"Weel fir a start,"* replied Adam dryly, *"nae Americas fir ye young yins- Weel, no fir at least anither ten years or mare!"*

*"Ten years, what dae ye mean?"* they shouted,

*"Jist that! Anither ten lang years!"* Turning to Rab, who true to his word, had started work the day before, Adam went on *"The truth is, that freedom is fir folk like Rab here. Folk wha are coming intae the pits fir the first time, but fir us colliers, it's a case o' live horse an' ye'll git corn!"* Reading slowly from the notice he said, *"All bound colliers under 21 hae anither seven years tae serve: above 21 and under 35 hae ten years; above 35 and under 45 anither seven and over 45 three mare! An' that's if ye live that long! An' what's mare! this ye'll ne'er believe. We've no tae be given oor freedom. Oh naw! We've ta go cap in hand tae the coorts and claim it!"*

*"Claim it!... what dae ye mean?"* they cried in alarm. *"Ye dinna believe me! Then listen to what it says: `Colliers claiming their liberty shall obtain a decree in the Sheriff Coort."*

*"A decree!....What the hell's that?"*

"When ye canna read or understand big words, it wid be a brave man among us wha'd face the coorts. Jist think hoo a Sheriff would bamboozle us!" shouted an old collier.

"An' what aboot us wemen?" cried Geordie's daughter-in-law.

"If ye're under 45, then its anither ten years for ye as weel Mistress!"

"May the Lord hae mercy on us!" cried the other fermit bearers in despair.

"And" went on Adam, " listen tae this! Jist in case ony among us wid dare tae think that ye can ficht fir yer richts, Parliament- what wis it the bonny Earl said? Oh aye! Parliament in its wisdom hae passed anither act, called 'The Combination Law'. This maks it an offence, for twa or more tae combine thegither tae discuss wages or improving working condition. It also outlaws strikes!"

"Then, efter a' that- fir them that mak it- ye'll be given yer richts under the Habeus…"

But by this time few were taking in what Adam was saying. Standing there, stunned, speechless and forlorn, they made a sorry spectacle. So when the hated voice of the Overseer barked from behind the door where he had been listening, "Richt ye lot get doon below! an' start howkin! Ye've wasted enough o' yer Maister's time!" without as much as a squeak they blindly obeyed- like the well trained human animals they were.

Adam at 31 had ten more years of serfdom to serve. In the years that followed he was twice indited and twice sentenced to serve in a correction house for inciting colliers to form a Combination[3]. For these offences the date on which he was due to gain his freedom was put forward a further four years. But on his 43rd birthday, as the result of a pit accident he died… his dream of a life as a freeman thwarted.

Beneath the bridge, hidden by a great oak growing on the bank of Niddry Burn, an old collier squatted on his hunkers watching the comings and goings on the Wauchope Estate. James Young, crippled in an accident that had paralysed his right arm and left his other hand minus two fingers, was no longer able to work. During the day, while his family toiled in the pits he would hobble down to the mill and trespassing under the bridge which ran beneath the Wauchope dyke, he would furtively follow the amazing transformation taking place on the estate. Day by day over the past year he had watched the constant stream of carts loaded down with timber, stone, iron, plaster and cement wending their way through the great iron gates. In the grounds the air resounded with the relentless noise of hammering, sawing and cursing as the outside of the great building took shape under the hands of stonemasons. On the ground men mixed great tubs of concrete and plaster while others sawed and stacked up timber ready to be fashioned it into joists, floorboards, windows, frames and doors.

On the Sabbath evening, when James and his wife Alice sat round the fire with their family, he would entertain them with tales of what had gone on in the estate while they were down below.

None would dare venture into the estate, but most of them had at one time climbed the dyke and gazed with awe at the magnificent mansion house and vast parkland.

When James first told of the lavish renovations, some of the elders were seen to wink at one another, shake their heads and mutter *"Aye, that's oor James geing his imagination a treat again!"* But when at the Inn, they overhead Auld Dunky recount an accident he had witnessed at the entrance to the Laird's estate, they began to wonder if there might be some truth in his stories. It seemed that a cart-horse had fallen on the ice and from under the tarpaulin had toppled a huge marble mantelpiece, the like of which Dunky had never seen.

Years before the Wauchope Mansion had been damaged by fire. Now in 1823 it was being restored to its former glory, with no expense spared. On the north east, a magnificent new wing, designed by the fashionable architect Robert Adam was nearing completion.

According to James this now included many handsome apartments. Spacious rooms with high, ornate plaster ceilings, large glazed windows and beautiful fireplaces. Many of the rooms were now in the process of being furnished. Beautiful carpets from the East, fine inlaid furniture by famous craftsmen and paintings by renowned artists all wound their way to Niddrie. In the grounds James watched new approaches being made, lodge houses being built and the parkland and gardens being extended and redesigned to include waterfalls, orchards, greenhouses and vinaries. Already Niddrey Marischal, nestling like a jewel in the lush green countryside of the Lothians, was considered one of the most beautiful country seats in Scotland.

From his hide-out beneath the bridge one man in particular fascinated James. He was a young stonemason working on the chimneys. For hours the old collier would sit enthralled, his eyes following every move as the craftsman skillfully carved with care and precision, on what by now were distinctive and much admired features of the Mansion- the ornate chimneys. Most times as he sat there the thin coal ingrained face expressed admiration and appreciation, but there were times when he would glance sadly down at his useless hand hanging limply by his side and sigh. As far back as he could remember James had liked nothing better than to whittle away at wood with a knife. Indeed the pride of his mother's cottage in Niddrey Village had been a dove carved by him. Later in life when he worked in No. 3 pit he took to sculpting the hard shiny Parrot coal and even succeeded in making a flute, which he taught himself to play.

James, the youngest of Adam's children, was quiet, solitary, and self contained- very different from the rest of the family. Alice, his mother, had been Adam Young's second wife. She was not only much younger than her husband, she was also his half cousin. By the time James was twelve years old and working in the pit, all his half brothers and sisters had left home. Like them he had attended the Parish School his family had often gone without to pay for the penny classes. An avid reader, Adam encouraged his sons to read anything they could lay hands on. So when the Dominie[4] offered to loan James a book on Scottish history, he took it home thinking it would also interest his father. To his surprise he found it contained stories of Craigmillar Castle, the awesome fortress he could see standing stark and bleak on the skyline as he made his way to work in No. 2 pit in the early mornings. All he knew about the castle was what his father had told him about its owner, Sir Alexander

Gilmour, who had been the Member of Parliament for Midlothian when the slavery act was abolished. James' vivid imagination ran riot as he read the book and learned of the part the castle had played in Scotland's history. So intrigued did he become, that every Sabbath that summer he would make his way up the brae and sitting beside the castle dovecote would watch the dooes.

While whittling away at a piece of wood James would conjure scenes from the Castle's gory past. He fancied he could hear the howls of battle as the Earl of Hereford's Army, sent by Henry VIII to Scotland on his 'Rough Wooing' mission, plundered, pillaged and burned all in it's path. Capturing the castle he set it alight and taking Sir Simon Preston prisoner made him walk barefoot to London. As the castle burst into a raging inferno James imagined he could hear again the terrified screams of women and children as they fled, pursued by Butcher Hereford's murderous hordes. At other times James would conjure up the sickening stench of blood as in his day dreams he witnessed it gush forth from the veins of the Earl of Mar, as his brother, James III had him brutally bled to death in a warm bath in the castle.

Balmy summer days would remind the young lad of happy times at the Castle. Times when the ill-fated Mary Queen of Scots (the royal babe who had been the unwitting cause of the 'Rough Wooing') spent some of the happiest days of her short life in what she herself described as 'the clear sweet air of Craigmillar'. On such days James would hear again, resounding through the Deer Forest, the clatter of hooves as the young Queen, accompanied by her ladies, galloped up the brae on their way from Holyrood Palace to the Castle. There in Craigmillar, not only did she wine, dine and dance but also, it was whispered, planned the death of her husband Darnley.

As the day would draw to a close the young James would reluctantly make for home. On reaching the top of the Wisp Brae he would climb into a high tree and looking back watch the sun sink leaving the Castle starkly silhouetted against a darkening blood red sky. Then he would see it as it was in days of old- a grim, forbidding, mediaeval fortress standing sentinel over the lands of Niddrey and Craigmillar. A fortress whose impregnable walls stifled the cries of anguish and despair of the myriads of prisoners who had languished and died in its dungeons.

Walking home in the glooming, the young pit-lad would fancy he could hear all around, floating on the breeze, the spectral sighs of serfs, as they toiled from sunrise to sunset on their feudal Lord's land, while their brother and sister serfs burrowed like moles in the bowels of the earth deep down beneath their feet.

Now in the summer of 1823 James was no longer able to roam the countryside he loved. No longer able to work, the highlight of his week was the Sabbath evening when he and his wife sat round the fire, while the family brought them up to date with pit news, gossip and scandal. He in turn would give a detailed report on the work going on the Wauchope mansion. Once that was exhausted, the children, who, up until then knew they must sit patiently waiting, would ask for a story. All his life James Young had the reputation of being the best storyteller in the village and as such was always in demand at village weddings, dances, feast day celebrations and fayres. His repertoire included stories and ballads handed down from his forbears as well as stories he had read and remembered. Favourites with the young males in the family were battles; the bloodier the better. Sometimes it was Prestonpans, Culloden or Bannockburn and nearer to home Butcher Hereford's pillage of Craigmillar or Bothwell and Francis Wauchope's skirmish at Niddrey Edge. The girls much preferred learning their Grandmother's ballads- prime favourite was 'The Lass o' Niddry Mill!'

When the children were in bed and the cottage was quiet, the remaining elders would settle down to listen to readings from pamphlets acquired by James' sons from political activists working in the pits or in the factories. Sometimes heated arguments flared up, often sparked off when discussing Tom Payne's 'The Rights of Man', or one of the 'Friends of the People' pamphlets on the French Revolution. But more often than not, it was the political action being planned in the Scottish Coalfields that roused the most passion. It was hardly surprising that James's children and now his grandchildren were the envy of the village. Although by now the old collier was frail, his body crippled and racked with the black spit, his mind was still as active and inquisitive as when he had been a lad. Indeed he was always telling Alice "As lang as the heert poonds, the mind maun spier!"

And now as if to prove it in the twlight of his life he had added a new dimension to his repertoire- a weekly report on the comings and goings at the Laird's Estate. A report he gleaned by clandestinely getting into the grounds and spying on what was going on. Alice lived in terror of him being caught. Blithely he ignored her warning, indeed seemed to thrive on the danger.

Summer had come late that year. Not only did this favour the work-force, but judging by the screams of delight and shrieks of laughter wafting across the parkland, the Wauchope children were also making the most of the Indian Summer. Watched over by a governess and a tutor the children learned their letters or sang nursery rhymes as they danced on the lawn. When in boisterous mood they would be encouraged to run off their energy by playing on a see-saw or on a swing, while the older ones would climb up into a tree house built in a great oak. At other times he would hear them squabble and hit out at one another, reminding him of his grandchildren. The older boys spent hours fishing in the burn, climbing trees, snaring rabbits, or noisily fighting imaginary battles around an ancient obelisk which lay to the north of the house.

James once heard the tutor tell them that a Stone Age Chieftain lay buried there, killed in a battle fought on that very spot. At other times he would hear blood curling screams as the 16th Century Battle of Niddrey Edge was re-enacted around the Ice House. Reporting on a battle his open-mouthed grandsons sat enthralled throughout, then bombarded James with even more questions than usual.

Not to be outdone, during the ensuing week, unknown to their elders, his enterprising off-spring decided they could go one better. Mustering an 'army' of pit lads and lassies, they rudely disturbed the peace of the Sabbath morning. Screaming and yelling they shocked and terrorised the village with their version of the blood curling battle, which they made even more realistic by a yelling accompaniment of ribald pit oaths- oaths no army of pit owner's children could ever emulate.

At least twice a day from his vantage behind the tree James would watch the servants bring the children cool, refreshing drinks and tiny cakes and serve them either on the lawn or on the banks of the stream. Afterwards the younger ones, exhausted by the heat, would be coaxed indoors to rest. *"Aye! fine feathers mak fine birds!"* said James to Nell his sixteen year old granddaughter, who for the umpteenth time had asked him to spell out every detail of the older girl's outfit. This was the pretty girl, who, shaded by a parasol that matched her beautiful pink dress trimmed with white lace, spent hours parading aimlessly up and down. James told Nell how the workmen whistled under their breath when they saw her rise from her easel, toss back her curls and walk sedately round the gardens. At other times they would stop and listen as her voice wafted up from the drawing room where she sat strumming a harp and singing love songs. *"Aye Nell"* he would say picking up his flute, *"Maybe the guid Lord didna see fit tae gie ye a harp, but he gied ye the voice of a linty. Come on lass, let's hae yer Great-Granmither's sang, '**The Lament O'The Arled Bairn'!"***

Crossing to where Rab, her father sat, Nell looking up at him would sing,

> *Oh Faither dear it grieves me sair*
>
> *The tear fa's frae ma ee'*
>
> *That I should slave an be sae puir*
>
> *I feel I want tae dee.*
>
> *I'm arled tae ma maisters's pit*
>
> *Why gie ye this tae me?*
>
> *Sixteen long hoors each day at it*
>
> *Deep doon below the sea.*
>
> *Cauld dark an dank the work I dae*
>
> *Wi' little pay tae show*
>
> *I never see the Sun's bricht ray*
>
> *Why dae I have tae go?*

Stroking her hair, which was already thinning in the front, her father answered...

> *Ma lass I've lo'ed you wi ma heert*
>
> *Since yir baptismal day*

*When first I signed that woeful chart*
*That arled ye fir aye.*
*A collier's lot has little tae it*
*But poverty an' death*
*Mysel' I'm choked wi' the spit*
*An' struggle hard fir breath*
*Your Mither an' me hae ither five*
*Wee hungry bairns tae feed*
*Yir pey tae keep us a' alive*
*Is aye in dreadfu' need.*
*Dont fault yir Faither fir the crime*
*That slaves ye tae the pit*
*It's just the system o' oor time*
*An' we've tae struggle wi' it.*

Nell unconvinced, looked her father in the face as she sang on:

*But faither ither bairns are free*
*An' dae nae work at a'*
*Why should this be the fate fir me*
*An' no the fate for a'*
*Ma face is white, ma ee'n are grey*
*Ma body's rackit sair*
*I'm auld afore ma weddin' day*
*An' scant o' claes tae wear.*
*There's lots o' lassies such as me*
*Who struggle at the coals*
*An' haul them tae the surface scree*
*Thro' laigh and watery holes.*
*When crawling in the darkened mine*
*I pray tae God above*
*Tae tak me frae this cruel grind*
*To his domain o' love.*

To which her father replied:

> *Such is the lot for us ma lass*
> *In bondage 'till we dee*
> *But someday it will come tae pass*
> *When colliers shall be free.*

"*Weel Nell*" said her granny, who, on hearing them sing that song never failed to wipe away a tear with the back of her twisted, black hand, "*There's yin thing ye can be prood oh lass- When ye gang tae the Domain o' Love, ye'll nae see yer family hae tae answer tae oor Maker fir using His Meenster tae sell wee babbies intae bondage at His Font!*"

One day while squatting behind the tree, James dozed off. When he awoke it was early evening, the estate was silent and deserted. He had never stayed that late before. Fearful that he might be seen, furtively he looked around before starting cautiously to pick his way over the stepping stones under the bridge. There he stopped, listened and hastily beat a retreat. Someone was approaching. He came out in a sweat thinking what would happen to him if he was caught trespassing on the Lairds land.

From his hide he watched as a young bearded man come into view. Dressed in dusty breeches, his white tunic sleeves rolled up to his elbows, a huge wide brimmed hat perched on the back of his head and carrying a mallet over his shoulder, the youth was leisurely strolling across the parkland whistling as he went. He was the stonemason on his way home to the tumbledown cottage where he lodged with an old farm labourer who, the year before, had been discharged because of his declining health and vigour. He had been allowed to stay in his dwelling on condition that he did the repairs, but he lacked both know-how and money to buy materials. Hence the reason he had been allowed to take in a lodger.

Suddenly James saw the mason stop in his tracks, turn his head and listen. Had he heard him wheezing? Desperately the old man tried to hold his breath! The effort almost choked him. Holding his hand over mouth he listened, but all he could hear breaking the evening calm, was the splash of the mill wheel as it rymthicly chopped the water. With a sigh of relief he watched the man turn about and making for the stream followed it under the bridge to come out on the other side of the dyke beside the Mill.

Ancient the Mill might be, but a buzzing hive of industry it was that September evening. As the giant wheel kept steadily turning, relentlessly driving the clanking machinery, men and boys ran hither and thither. Some were unloading carts of oats and carrying the bags into the mill to feed the giant circular grinding stones, others were shovelling the newly-ground, sweet-smelling, oatmeal into sacks.

After two disastrous harvests in a row there had been great rejoicing on Niddrey Estate as the Laird, his farmers, labourers, millers and colliers gave thanks in the Kirk for that year's bumper harvest. With the oats well ripened on the stalk the miller was happy- ripened oats meant less drying time in the kiln! The Laird, who owned the mill and the fields of oats, was happy. His mansion house girnals would be filled to overflowing, giving him plenty to pay in lieu of wages to his colliers and labourers.

By the time James managed to hobble under the bridge the mason was leaning on a fence chewing a piece of grass, obviously enjoying the bustling rural scene. After a while his eye caught the cluster of dilapidated hovels lying beyond the mill stream. It was Niddrey Village! Curiosity got the better of him. Gingerly using the stepping stones he crossed the burn and made his way to the village. The place was deserted except for a filthy old man dressed in tatters, who, crouching on his haunches outside a tumbledown cottage was dozing and wheezing in the sinking evening sun. Bidding him a courteous good evening, politely the mason enquired as to the name of the hamlet. This civil request was met with a blank stare. Thinking the man might be deaf, he repeated the question loud and clear. This time there was no mistaking the response. Although James was too far away to catch the exact words of the obscene reply, when he saw two filthy fingers being rudely poked in the mason's face he was left in no doubt as to where the mason was being dispatched.

James laughed out loud, "*Aye, ye've picked the wrang yin there- Nae chance o' Auld Dunky gieing anythin' awa fir nithin'!*" He chuckled as he watched the old man aim with deadly accuracy, a thick black spit which landed smack on the back of the neck of the receding stonemason. Agitated and upset, instead of retracing his steps under the bridge the young man stumbled towards the haven of the dyke. Flinging the mallet over the eight foot wall, he nimbly climbed on to the top. Safely astride, he hesitated, then gasped as a glorious sight met his eyes. It was a golden sun setting behind Craigmillar Castle.

Long after the sun had gone down, the mason was still there. Perched on the dyke, enjoying the peace and quiet, he was engrossed in watching the darkness gradually blanket out the surrounding, silent countryside. James had by this time left the mill, found a vantage point opposite the dyke, where he squatted contentedly chewing a blade of grass as he too watched the sunset. On a night such as this he was in no hurry to go home either. Suddenly he saw the mason start and listen as an alien sound broke the evening still. The eerie noise grew louder and louder as out of the glooming came a silent band of ghoul-like creatures, shuffling wearily along and dragging their scrawny young. Mesmerised, James watched the youth's face grow pale as he gripped the dyke and cried out in terror as the procession drew nearer. "*In God's name what's this- the March of the Damned on the road to Hell?*" Then holding his nostrils he yelled, "*Holy Mother of God, what's that stench?*"

The females in the pack, hearing the cry and sensing danger quickly and silently drew the young into the shelter of their skirts. Looking up, they drew back in fear and gasped as they espied, perched on the wall, a shadowy, white faced apparition with great hairy side whiskers, gawping at them from beneath a weird wide brimmed bonnet. Just for a second they seemed to falter then defiantly staring the stranger in the face, mutely they filed past dragging the frightened children. As they passed they could see him cringe as his face registered horror. Losing his balance he toppled backwards and with legs in the air vanished over the wall. *"Mither what ails that gowk?"* shouted Nell. Silently shrugging her shoulders her mother trudged wearily on.

Next day down the pit, to the accompaniment of great shrieks of laughter, the story of the Gowk on the Dyke was told, retold and added too. In the ale-house Dunky was plied with drinks and kept drunk for a week as he recounted how he, single handed, had defended the village from the inquisitive stranger. By the Sabbath Dunky was the village hero. True, his version of how he routed the stranger whom he now called that 'Beaky Gowk' no longer bore any relation to what James had witnessed. But no matter. Although there had never been any love lost between the two men, James did not grudge his long time critic his hour of glory and its bonus!

So, when two weeks later the Beaky Gowk had the temerity to venture back to the village everyone was ready for him. No way would he intimidate them! But even as he was saying "Good Day to you. I'm Hugh Miller, a stonemason working on the Laird's Mansion!" resolves were quickly evaporating as beady eyes perceived he came bearing gifts. The bottles of ale opened doors and loosened tongues. First to taste and talk was the Hero himself. Not that Hugh could understand a word Dunky, or any of the others villagers were saying.

It was to be several months before he would come to understand properly the local dialect. To him it was as if the 400 inhabitants of three adjoining villages, Niddrey, Cleekim and Hunters' Hall had developed a language of their own. He was amazed how strange and difficult their speech was, considering they only lived four miles from Edinburgh. Also how curious and outlandish many of their customs were. Perhaps that was understandable, as only a few had ever been to the city. The villages existed in isolation. It was as if they were buried in the bleakest and most isolated part of the Highlands of Scotland, rather than situated on the outskirts of its capital city.

When eventually Hugh was accepted and invited into their homes, he was appalled at the conditions under which they lived. Their houses were dilapidated hovels with uneven, earthen floors, damp walls, leaking roofs, smoke blackened rotting rafters, and unglazed windows, many with broken shutters, others just stuffed with rags or turfs.

Asking Dunky how long he had lived in Niddrey, he was told, *" Forty years. I've worked on Niddrey Edge Coals since the days the Niddry Laird bought ma faither an' oor family frae the Laird o' Inveresk!"*

*"Are you telling me you were a slave?."*

*"Aye Sir, I wis until 1799, when Parliament freed a' colliers!"*

*"But colliers were freed in '75!"*

*"Aye! sae they were, sae they were!"*

After a pause, puffing himself up with pride, he gave a knowing look and went on *"Aye! weel I ken that Sir! I wis there! Aye Sir, I weel remember as a bairn sittin' on ma Faithers shooders cheering* the bonny Earl o' Abercorn fir freeing us colliers frae bondage. But somehoo maist o' us there never got oor freedom. Only Young there an' his ilk e'er managed it!" The look of utter contempt he shot at James as he finished was meant to leave Hugh in no doubt of what he thought of his fellow collier.

Nodding his head he continued earnestly, "Aye, Faither always telt us tae trust oor Laird tae ken what's best fir us. No ony o' these loud-moothed pit trouble-makers, wha think, that 'cause they can read and write, think they ken it a! An' Faither wis richt in the end! 'Cause oor betters passed anither Act o' Parliament in '99, an' noo we're a' free colliers!"

"So Young, you got your freedom before the others!" said Hugh turning to James.

"Aye I did that!" replied James. "Oor family still bound when oor Faither Adam Young deid. His ten years had been extended when he was twice jailed fir inciting colliers tae form a Combination. On his death-bed he made me promise I wid go tae the Coorts and claim oor families's freedom. But it wasna easy. It took twa years. But we did it! I tried tae persuade ither families tae claim theirs but only a few ever did. Some were feered!" Glaring at Dunky "Ithers..they were jist ignorant!"

"But you never left Niddrey?"

"Naw I never did! Its true I ended ma working days a free collier howking in the Peacock Tail Seam in No. 3 pit. But like a lot o' us, having claimed oor legal freedom, we found oorsel'es tied anither wey. The debt ma family run up at the Pit Shop when Faither was ill and when he wis jailed in the correction hoose took years tae clear. Then when the time cam an' we were free, times were bad. Work wis scarce. Short-time an' pey-affs were the collier's lot. Often it wis the free-men the Maisters got rid o' first. Mony of these families finished up eatin' grass an' dying o' starvation. A cousin of mine's whole family finished up deeing o' hunger in a disease ridden, stinking hovel in the Lawnmarket in Edinburgh. Sae I kept ma heed doon, worked hard and steyed in Niddrey. It wis a case o' 'Better the Deil ye ken, than the Deil ye dinna!'"But ma sons are leaving Niddry. Ned an' his young wife Jess hae moved oot and are working o'er at the new Newcraighall Pit".

## CHAPTER 12 **THE MUCKLE ADVENTURE**

*"Mither, Mither, is it time to get up?"*

*"Naw Wull! go back tae sleep yet a while! An' whisht!- ye'll waken the bairn!"* whispered his mother.

In the straw bed where he slept with his eight year old brother, Jed, Wull Young lay wide awake, too excited to sleep. When saying his prayers he had earnestly asked God to make the sun shine next day. Before that he had persuaded his Mother to give the porridge an extra stir for luck, and now, so as to make doubly sure, he lay with his fingers tightly crossed. Today was the 1st of July, Freedom Day, the annual holiday. For pit children living in Whitehill Street, in the new village of Newcraighall, it was to be something even more special. It was the day of the 'Muckle Adventure'. Not that any of them had a clue what that meant- only that two Sunday school teachers had asked their parents' permission to take them away for the day.

Wull lay thinking, *"Faither is richt when he says we're lucky tae bide in this new village an' no doon the road in auld Niddry where we used tae stey wi' Granny, as its only bairns frae here that's gang on the Muckle Adventure."* Time to rise came at last. The heat haze blotting out the sun did nothing to dampen the excitement in the Young household. Dressed in their Sabbath clothes the children cried, *"Ta ta"* to their father, Ned Young as they left the cottage and walked beside their mother, who was carrying baby Mary, snugly sleeping in her plaid. Twelve year old Wull, looking like a cut-down adult, in a shiny threadbare black coat he'd never grow into, held his little sister's hand firmly, mindful of his father's warning to take good care of her. On her other side walked Jed, proudly sporting a bonnet held up by his ears. Bess, tiny for her six years, clad in a skimpy green dress and a wisp of a plaid, looked like a little elf a puff of wind would waft away.

When Jed saw that their next door neighbours, the Stonehouse family, were missing, he cried, *"Mither, Jockie's no here, can we knock him up?"* In answer to his tap, Jockie the eldest boy, peering out of two swollen black tear-stained eyes, peeped round the door at the same time as a man's voice from inside bellowed *"Shut that bloody door! I've telt ye nane of ye lot are bloody weel going' onywhere"!* Upset, the Young children looked towards their mother, who hesitated as if about to say something, then changing her mind told the children to catch up with the others. Jess Young knew better than to interfere. It was no secret that when at home or in the pit, the Stonehouse family, were daily subjected to cruel beatings with a leather strap. The granny, mother and five children lived in mortal fear of Joe, the violent drunken father.

Meeting up with other families they headed towards Old Niddry Station, where two years earlier, a branch railway line had been built by the Edinburgh and Dalkeith Railway Company to transport goods. This had revolutionised coal transportation. No longer would it be carried in carts over rough and dangerous tracks to seaports and cities. As the families made their way up the familiar rough track, there was no need for mothers to drag reluctant children. Bubbling with excitement, the youngsters, running hither and thither had to be restrained as a stage coach rattled past on the rocky, dusty track on its way to the Toll House at Wanton Wa's farm. Bess's lively brown eyes sparkled as Wull, pointing back at the pit, squeezed her hand as he whispered, *"Look Bess, the engine hoose monster is asleep the day!"*

Although she had been working in No 4 pit with her family now for six months, Bess still feared and hated that giant steam engine. It haunted her dreams. One night, waking up, sobbing and screaming, she had climbed in beside Wull pleading, *"Oh Wull let me sleep a'teen ye an' Jed- I'm feered! I keep dreaming aboot that horrible monster at the pit. Is it true that he clanks and clanks an' sooks up wee bairns, then spewes their bones intae the pond wi' a muckle splash?"*

*"A' richt, coorie doon"* said Wull making room and giving her a re-assuring cuddle. *"Gang back tae sleep. He winna hurt ye- he's nae monster, jist the pit engine. Ye'll get used tae him and tae the pit too in time Bess!"*

*"Bess I'll tell ye a secret!"* he whispered so as not to wake Jed, *"When I started as a pump lad in*

No 3, I wis feered tae! I used tae dream that the Deil jumped frae a room intae the flood waters an' turned them intae a roarin' river o' red blood. An' as he ran at it's heed he'd grab me as he passed and scream he was takin' me tae the Burning Fire!"

But today nightmares and cares were forgotten, as the children skipped, laughed and capered on their way to the Railway Station where they were to meet the teachers. And sure enough, true to their word there they were, having just alighted from the stage. Mr Woods and his daughter Jane, who as well as being teachers at the Kirk on the Sabbath, farmed over at Liberton Village. With a welcoming smile and a cheery *"Guid mornin' bairns"* Mr Woods asked *"All ready for the Muckle Adventure?"*

*"Aye Sir"* yelled a chorus of excited voices. *"Well,"* said Mr Woods, holding up a canvas bag *"Guess what I have in here? I'll give you a clue! Its something no Adventurer worth his salt should be without!"* The children looked blank. Mesmerised, they watched as he plunged his hand into the bag and produced a tin drinking mug and holding it high said, *"Ah a tinnie. But's what's inside it? See... a stock of gundy and.. paper streamers!"* He handed one out to each child and as they struggled to slip the string attached to the mug around their necks, a train came briskly into the station.

*"Guid day tae ye a'!"* shouted the driver, stopping the horses with a flourish.

*"Bairns"* said Mr Woods *"this is Mr Fox, the coal merchant many of you know already. But what you don't know is, that he is also a very kind man who gets weird an' wonderful ideas!"*

*"Children what does Mr Fox usually carry in his wagons?"* asked Miss Wood. *"Coal Miss!"* came the quick reply. *"But as you are not working today, there will be no coal! Do you think Mr Fox has forgotten it is a holiday?"* she asked. *"Aw Miss!"* gasped the children in sympathy, amazed that anyone could have such a lapse of memory. *"Never mind bairns!"* shouted the jovial Mr Fox from his seat upfront, *"As nane o' ye seem tae hae ony coal fir me, and as the horses, Pete and Auld Tam here, are raring tae go, we've hud an idea- Why dinna we pretend ye bairns are the coal an' we'll tak ye doon the 'Coal Run' Wid ye like that?"*

*"Aye"* they choursed.

*"Richt!"* shouted Mr Fox, *"Ship ahoy! All aboard fir the Coal Run!...... Let's gang where nae bairn has e'er gone afore!"* The children needed no second biding. With a mad rush they clambered aboard, unaware of the trouble Mr. Fox had taken to clean the wagons. Bess, dragged along by Wull, was terrified when she looked up and saw the side stretching almost up to heaven. But the teacher seeing her hesitate, gently lifted her up, telling her to hold tight to the side.

Once settled in. the children were asked to say thank you to Mr. Fox. *"And"* said Mr Woods *"Before setting off let's offer up a prayer of thanksgiving to our Father in Heaven for the day ahead"* When the final *"Amen"* was said, Mr Fox with a broad grin, cracked the reigns with a flick of wrists and yelled *"Gee up, ma beauties!"* With a loud *"Hooray"* from his passengers, they were off!

Clutching their brightly coloured streamers as they fluttered in the breeze and sucking for the first time in their lives a stick of gundy, the children waved a noisy *"Ta ta"* to their mothers. Little Bess, tightly gripping the side of the wagon, wistfully watched her mother and baby sister Mary fade from view. Picking their way gingerly between the rails, at first the horses moved slowly, unsure of the strange, noisy, shifting load behind. But gradually they gathered speed, until they reached a steady trot. The children quickly became accustomed to the weird sensation of the swaying wagons, which Jed said was *"like ha'eing wings an' fleein' like a muckle bird!."* But Bess smiled a secret smile. She knew she was being carried on the wings of angels.

When the train ran along the track behind the red tiled cottages in Whitehill Street, alarmed by the din, people flew to their back doors. Accustomed only to coal wagons passing, they could not believe their eyes. It was the train alright, but it was carrying two wagon loads of happy children, sucking gundy, flying paper streamers and yelling at the top of their voices, *"Hooray we're aff doon the coal-run!"*

Past Wanton Wa' farm with its fields of green waving corn, oats and barley they sped, through woods, where overhanging branches brushed their faces, to run beside a gurgling burn which suddenly disappeared underground. In answer to a question Mr Woods told some of the older boys that the train had started its 'Coal Run' at St. Leonard's Station in Edinburgh before arriving at Old Niddrey. They were now passing Newhailes, the magnificent mansion belonging to the Dalrymples. Some of the children had looked through the gates of the estate from the track, but never dreamed that such a large and grand house lay hidden in the trees. From time to time Miss Woods, who took her duties as a teacher very seriously, would volunteer information for any who cared to listen. This time it was, *"Do you know that last century, the famous Scottish Judge, Lord Hailes, lived in Newhailes and wrote 'The Annals of Scotland!' - a very famous book."*

Leaving Newhailes Estate behind, they came to open fields where a shepherd was calling to his dog as he rounded up his sheep. Beside a farmhouse a dairy maid, carrying two churns of milk walked through a field of cows contentedly chewing the cud. While tongues vigorously demolished the gundy, wide eyed and wonder struck, their heads in a whirl, most of the children looked if they were in a dream.

*"Noo!"* shouted Mr. Fox *"look yonder! What can ye see through the trees?"*

There was a pause, then a wild yell went up, *"A ship! - Aw' it's the sea!"*

*"Aye its Fisherow!"* said Mr. Fox *"The end o' The Coal Run. This is where ma train taks the coal ye bairns cairry up tae the pitheed, Once here it is loaded on yonder ships an' carried way across the sea tae strange foreign lands".* As Fisherow came into view they could see that not only ships, but small fishing boats were lying in the harbour. Yelling *"Whoa!"* Mr Fox stopped the horses. *"Richt bairns, everybody oot! The Coal Run ends here! This is where we abandon ship an' become 'Adventurers' exploring the lands beyond!"*

*"Tak a big sniff. Can ye smell the fish an' the sea ?"* asked Mr Woods.

Holding hands and walking in pairs, like the animals leaving the Ark, they wove their way in and out the busy folk bustling along the harbour. They watched brawny, weather beaten fishermen unloading their catch, mending their nets, or working on their boats as they prepared to sail on the next tide. Tall women, dressed in stripped flannel dresses with shawls over their heads and shoulders, strode past, carrying heavy creels of fish on their backs. *"Fishwives on their way to Edinburgh to sell the fish!"* said Miss Woods. For a while they stood watching a ship discharge its cargo of linen and calico, *"From Holland!"* said Miss Woods, who seemed to know everything. Leaving the harbour they made for the beach, jumping from the pier on to the sand with wild shrieks of delight.

By now the haze had lifted and the scorching midday sun was at its height. As Bess's bare feet touched the warm sand she jumped up and down laughing as the strange white earth tickled its way up between her coal blackened toes.

Flinging themselves down, the children rolled and played on the silver sands. Miss Woods showed them how to build a sand-castle surrounded by a moat. Using their tin mugs some of the older boys were allowed down to the sea to fetch water for the moat. But as fast as they filled it up, the water would disappear. *"An' now Adventurers, let's see if the tide has washed up any treasure trove!"* shouted Mr Woods as he made off along the beach followed by his motley band. As they walked they picked up seashells and holding the big ones to their ear, swore they heard the roar of the sea. Wading in the water they found crabs, eels, jellyfish and seaweed, as well as pieces of rotting timber, which Miss Woods said could well have come from a galleon, lost at sea one dark stormy night. They shuddered at the thought.

Bess, happy and content, sat with Wull on a rock dangling their feet over a deep pool. Dreamily she sighed *"Will Heaven be like this Wull?"*

*"Aye!"* he replied lazily smiling to himself, *"There the sun wull always shine, pit water wull be silver an' warm, an' pit glaur wull be saft an' golden like sand. Aye, an' pit bairns, washed clean in the blue sea, wull flee wi' the angels"* The minutes ticked by. Wull, daydreaming, was miles away as he watched a tall ship disappear over the horizon. He saw himself perched high in its rigging, eagerly scanning the horizon for pirate ships. He did not notice his little sister quietly slide down the rock.

Thinking of angels, she had sat staring into the crystal water. Unaware that she was slowly slipping, she smiled as she felt the gentle touch of water stroking her feet and quietly beckoning her down into the warm bosom of the pool. With eyes glazed and a radiant smile on her face, slowly she discarded first her plaid, then her dress. Timidly she edged first her little coal blackened toes, then her feet, legs and body into the warm pool. Spellbound she watched as the warm salt water trickled through her sticky fingers, washing away the blackness and leaving them whiter than she had ever remembered. Innocently she surrendered inch by inch to the tempting, silent call of the pool until she was lying down and letting the soft inviting water engulf her up to her neck. Facing the sun, with her long auburn hair floating out behind she lay there, content and happy, at peace with the world.

Purring like a kitten, she let the warm rays of the sun caress her face, while the gentle ripples of the pool, embracing her body, held her secure and warm in its comforting bosom.

After a while, an impish smile crossed the elfin face. Pulling off the ribbon holding back her hair, she plunged her head, face first, into the water.

The splash brought Wull back to earth with a jolt. He screamed, grabbed her by the hair, pulled her out, shook her, punched her hard, grabbed the dress and dragged it over the soaking wet hair. He was shaking. She was still smiling. Lucky for Wull, and Bess for that matter, no one seemed to have witnessed the incident.

Miss Woods, by this time tired and exhausted had flopped down and was lying surrounded by the younger children. The two men, having gone back to the train had just arrived back carrying two boxes and a churn between them. *"Gather round bairns!"* shouted the jovial Mr Fox. *"Farmer Wood and his bonnie dochter here, hae kindly provided vitals for us weary Adventurers!"* Flinging out his arm, bowing low to Miss Wood, with more than a twinkle in his eye, he said, *"Bairns, ye are aboot to partake o' a feast, the likes ye've ne'er seen afore! Liberton Cheese renowned throughout Scotland, bannocks, an' gingerbread men, a' to be washed doon wi' a mug o' Miss Wood's best soor dook!"* With a flourish he took her hand and gallantly kissing it said, *"An' all made by this fair lassie!"*

Miss Woods blushed. The children duly thanked her as instructed, while Mr Fox embarrassing her further, went on, *" Bairns she's an angel sent frae Heaven, is she no? See she's even brocht carrots fir Pete an' Auld Tam!"* Mr Woods said 'Grace', then the children tucked in. Never had they seen such a feast, far less tasted the renowned Liberton Cheese. True, some had to be coaxed to taste, but after the first nibble even the tardiest among them gobbled up every morsel.

*"It is sad Jockie Stonehouse is not here!"* said Miss Woods, *"A dip in the sea water would have done wonders for his arm. But never mind- the Stonehouse bairns may have missed the Adventure, but so that'll they'll know we missed them and have'nt forgotten them, Jed will you kindly ask yer mother to give Mistress Stonehouse the childrens' Adventurer's Packs an' their share of the food?"* Walking back over the mussel beds Mary McVie suddenly had an idea. *"Sir! Can we fill oor tinnies wi' muscles and tak them hame as a present fir oor mithers?"* Sir said it was a wonderful and thoughtful idea.

But all good things must end and so it was time to go home. The horses were given the carrots while the passengers, carefully clutching their tinnies stuffed with mussels, piled back into the wagons. This time the journey seemed to take hardly any time at all. As the horse-train trotted along the wagonway behind the cottages, the children could be heard singing with gusto a new hymn:

> **Jesus loves me! this I know**
> **For the Bible tells me so.**

Tired, but so happy, they knew He did…They loved Him too!

Racing home, the Young children burst into the cottage all excitedly yelling at once. There was so much to tell! Only their mother was in. She gave each a cuddle as they put the mugs of mussels on the table saying *"This present is fir ye Mither. There's yin fir Faither and anither tae tak tae Granny!"* Bess loved going to visit her Granny at Niddrey Village. Often on a cold winter Sabbath night, she would sit on the floor in front of the fire, snug and warm between her Granny's knees. While her work-worn gnarled old hands would gently stroke her grand-daughter's brow Granny would sing or tell stories of long ago. Tales of what village bairns got up to at Halloween, when boggles, ghosties and ghoulies came out. Happy times when Grandfaither came a coorting and sad times when there were strikes and the whole village starved. Sometimes she'd tell of a women called Big Bell, a wee deaf and dumb lass called Mary McVie or Lachie McGraw, the lad from Ayrshire who was press-ganged and made a serf in a Niddry Pit.

As darkness fell that July night the Youngs' cottage went quiet. Prayers had been said and the children tucked up in bed. Mother was quietly humming to the baby as she lay with her in the box bed. Wull lay wide awake. He knew his mother was feigning sleep. Father was out! They both knew where he was- at the Niddry and Craighall Friendly Society. His father had told him why it had been necessary for colliers to start such Societies. At the same time as fighting for a living wage, improvements in safety conditions and the abolition of child labour, they were trying to protect themselves from poverty in the event of death, accidents, sickness and unemployment- of which there was plenty! Already Wull knew the risk his father ran. He also knew he had been in a house of correction for his part in a riot during the 1824 strike and that he was now involved in talks, planning the first ever national strike.

Wull worried. Every time he heard a step outside, he would pray, *"Please God mak this Faither!"* Then when the footsteps went by he would sigh and bite his nails (already bitten to the quick) an' pray again, *"Please Father in Heaven- jist let faither come hame safely, Oh Lord I ken I'm a wicked sinner but I promise I'll be guid an' ne'er sin ony mare, if only ye'll please bring oor faither safely hame!"* He came out in a sweat just remembering the misery of the six months in 1824- when Edinburgh and District were on strike. Although just turned six at the time, he remembered the pangs of hunger, how there was no food for anyone, how the whole village starved. He knew what a black-leg was and how some of them had their ears cut off. *"Strangers from Ireland"* Father had called them.

At long last footsteps stopped at the door and Wull's waiting ear picked up the faint click of the sneck being gently lifted. Even before it had time to click back, he was asleep; a smile on his face. This had been the happiest day of his life. And God had brought their father safely home!

## CHAPTER 13 **THE COMMISSION**

Seated at a table in the thatched cottage in Whitehill Street, a thin, round-shouldered girl sat writing as if there was no tomorrow.

The black-blue tattoo on the hand grasping the quill was not the only legacy Bess Young had to show for eight years work in the pits. Although only sixteen, the hair on the front of her head was already showing signs of thinning. Lately she had developed a racking cough, which would not go away. Because of this, her father had allowed her to stay at home while the rest of the family went to Kirk. After they left, quickly completing her allotted chores, she had pulled a canvas bag from under her straw mattress, extracted paper and a quill, mixed up ink, sat down then between bouts of coughing started to write.

Only the jerky, nervous movements of her fingers as they ran through the long tangled auburn hair lying loose on her shoulders gave any indication of the frustration she occasionally felt at trying to express her thoughts in writing. The urge to put things on paper had been with Bess since she had learned to read at the village school, where her father, Ned Young paid for her penny classes. His wife Jess, for whom life had been one long weary struggle against poverty and hardship, could hardly be blamed for feeling that there were better uses for the family's hard earned pennies than spending them on a girl's schooling.

*"Laddies...weel that's different!"* she would concede.

Unable to read herself, she was nevertheless a good and caring mother, but she made it quite clear to her daughter that reading and writing came after all womanly chores and duties were accomplished.

So Bess became a secret writer. Utilising every spare minute, she'd go to great lengths to find ingenious and sometimes devious ways to make time in order to put her ideas on paper- even to the extent of going without much needed sleep. Inevitably the day came, when she could no longer go to school and her supply of paper dried up. Forced to turn to her father for help, she tried to explain her compulsion to keep writing saying, *" Faither, when I sat in front o' Granny's fire cuddled atween her knees as she telt her stories, it wis as if she was pressing them intae ma heed sae that I wid ne'er forget them! An' noo when she's deed, mony a time when I'm alane and feart in the pit dark, yin o' her lang syne forgotten tales comes intae ma heed an' its sae real Faither, that when I get hame, I jist hae tae write it doon! Ither times whan I'm rigglin' like a snail, haulin' ma slydie, I deeden the pain o' the harness by' singing her sangs. Oh Faither, in the shadow o' ma lamp I see her face watching o'er me, jist like she telt us Big Bell did with these ither lads and lassies lang syne!"*

Eagerly pulling her old canvas bag from beneath her straw mattress she opened it and extracting sheets of closely written paper, thrust them into her father's hand saying, *" Go on Faither, read them! Only the Dominie has set e'en on them. He telt me that I maun keep on writin', e'en if folk tell me I'm saft in the heed!"* As Ned opened them the first thing to catch has eye was the words of the Coalbearers Lament.

> *When I was engaged a coalbearer to be*
>
> *Through all the coal pits,*
>
> *I maun wear the dron brat*
>
> *If ma heart it should break*
>
> *I can never won free.*

Childhood memories came flooding back. He heard once more floating down the ladder the comforting wheezy voice of his Mother as she sang encouraging her frightened children to follow her up the perilous journey. *"I doobt if any o' us bairns e'er kent the words"* he thought as he read them, *"It wis enough jist tae hear her voice and ken she wis there!"* Flicking through the pages he could not believe his eyes. Page after page of closely written words telling stories. Stories he had learned at his mother's knee, and long since forgotten, they were all there. *"Oh Bess"* he murmured, *"If only yer Granny had lived tae see this, she wid be prood o' ye!"*

A lump came in his throat as he recalled the 1837 strike, when, in common with the rest of the village his family was almost destitute. Yet his mother, insisted he accept what he knew to be her last, so that Bess could keep on her penny classes. *"Ned,"* she had said, *"Ye colliers who can read an' write, hae used the learning tae find oot hoo the government works, an noo ye tell us that instead o' rioting in the streets to git better conditions, there's mare clout in withholding oor labour! Noo, if collier-lassies were tae git the learning and at the same time as using the brain, they wid listen to their wumen's heert...They'd tell us that if every bairn born were tae get the chance tae use tae the fu' the gifts the guid Lord gies us all.... an if the gifts were used tae practise oor brothering principles then folk wid share and care fir each ither and there wid be need tae ficht or strike to bring aboot a fairer world!"*

Standing there with his daughter's writings in his hand and remembering his mothers words, Ned knew the role he must play. There and then he rashly promised Bess that she would never be without writing materials. True to his word, he never failed her. Where or how he acquired it Bess never knew. She never asked. But that Sabbath morning it was not stories of the dim and distant past the racing pen was recording. It was of a fateful day just gone, when past and present forged and Bess found herself a vibrant, living part of her collier heritage.

The previous Monday had started off much the same as any other day, until the Overseer, looking agitated yet trying hard to be unusually civil, stopped the coal-bearers as they emptied their creels saying, *"Twa gentlemen frae the Government wants tae speak wi' ye!"* Herding the bemused women and children into a large shed on the pit-head, he had difficulty finding space to squeeze them all in beside colliers who were already there. Nervously twisting his bonnet between his hands, the Overseer took up a stance at a table, where two gentlemen were earnestly talking to the Manager. Behind sat two clerks, apparently engaged in recording their conversation. *"I understand Newcraighall is the biggest pit, not only in Inveresk Parish, but in East Lothian!"* one of the gentlemen was saying.

*"Aye Sir!"* replied the Manager proudly, *"We have 273 male colliers an' 127 female coalbearers!"*

*"And..."* went on the gentleman, reading from a document, *"I see that 71 of these males are under 18.... and 26 are under 13.....While 33 female bearers, seem to be under 18, and 11 of these under 13...Do they all work underground?"*

*"Aye Sir"* was the reply.

Standing up, the taller of the gentlemen, speaking slowly and clearly, introduced himself to the assembled colliers and coal-bearers saying, *"Good Day to you!... I am Sub Commissioner Franks and this is Dr. Scott. We have been sent by the Government to enquire into employment conditions of women and young children working in the Mines and in Manufacturing in Scotland. Do you understand what I am saying?"*

*"Aye"* murmured a few. He went on, *"Dr. Scott and I have been asked to report on what is happening in the East of Scotland Collieries, and that of course includes Newcraighall Pit."*

Smiling at the sea of blank, blackened faces he said kindly, "*There is nothing to fear! We are here to help. Just answer as truthfully as you can! Let us start by asking the children. Who among you can write your name? If so, please raise your hand!*" Counting the numbers, he turned to the clerk and said "*One in three*"

"*How many of you attend school?*" Only Bess and two other raised their hands. Others seemed unsure. As he kept asking questions, most seemed willing to nod their head or raise an arm, but when individually asked for a reply, they would furtively look to where the Overseer and Manager stood, then clam up, standing silent and sullen. When he saw this the Commissioner asked the Overseer to leave the room. Rising and leaving the table he and Dr Scott stationed themselves in the furthest corner of the room, well out of earshot of the Manager.

"*Let's start with the oldest girl- where is Agnes Johnston?*" A bent, slight girl nervously hobbled forward, "*That's me Sir! I'm 17 and am a road redder in the Tunnel Pit an' work on ma maister's behalf. I can earn fourteen pence a day. Afore that I worked since I was eight cairrying the creel 14 hoors a day fir ma faither!*" Dr Scott seeing her painful limp asked, "*What ailes your foot lass, let me see it!*" As he examined her she whinged as she whispered, "*Last year I broke my ankle Sir, an' wis aff work 12 months. Sir, cairrying coal knocks lots o' lassie's joints oot, it bends oor ankles an' crushes oor haunches....*" Abruptly she stopped and looked towards the Manager, as if realising she had said too much, her hand flew to her mouth. Flushing under her grime, but making sure he could hear, in a loud voice she cried "*Aw, but Sir, it's gettin' better, honest it is!... I can now work ma 16 hours luggin' the coal... I can Sir. An' if I dinna dae Faither's biddin' he gies me the strap!*"

The Doctor and the Commissioner exchanged glances. The clerks kept writing, intent on recording every word.

"*What do you do Alexander?*" asked the Sub Commissioner to an eleven year old boy. "*I'm a pump boy Sir!*" was the proud reply as he flung out his scrawny chest. "*I pump oot water at the bottom o' the pit tae keep the mens' rooms dry. I'm obliged tae pump fast Sir or the water could cover us*"

"*Do you ever work standing in water?*"

"*Oh aye sir, aften, the water nearly always covers ma legs and the men's as they sit an' pick!*"

"*Yours is a very important job Alexander, you must be a very brave lad!*" said Mr Franks. Alexander paused, then hung his head as he admitted, "*Naw Sir I'm no! Sometimes I'm get feered. Not long ago I ran away when the water came so fast I could not pump quick enough*".

"*Tell me, when do you eat during the day Alexander?*" asked the Doctor. "*Oh we didnae get anything during the day sir!*" came the quick reply, "*But Mither maks us grand porritch an' kail when we git hame at night!*"

"*When do you start work Alexander?*"

"*Three or five in the mornin' an' git back up at six or seeven at nicht!*"

---

120

"How many holidays do you get during the year Alexander?" Alexander thought for a moment then said, "Aw jist Freedom Day and every Sabbath!"

"Well" said Mr. Franks addressing the others as he patted the boy's dirty tousled head, "This eleven year boy helps to keep the pit dry, and he must at times keep the flood waters at bay. Now let's find a lass of the same age and see what she does?"

"Here Sir" cried a mother, pushing forward an undersized, sad looking girl. "This is ma dochter Agnes Moffat. She's worked wi' hir Faither since she wis eight Sir!" Roughly prodding the tongue-tied girl between her bent shoulders she yelled, "Go on ye limmer, dinna stand there, tell the gentleman what ye dae!" Nervously screwing her canvas apron in her hands, Agnes finally blurted out "I go doon wi' Faither at twa in the mornin' Sir and came back up at six at nicht!"

"And what do you during these hours Agnes?"

"Cairry ma creel up the nine ladders Sir!"

"Aye" shouted the Mother, "Tell him aboot the time yer Faither ruptured himsel' lifting yer creel on yer back- and hoo he's no the only collier that's happened tae Sir!

"I'm not surprised Mistress," replied the Commissioner, "As I understand a creel can hold three quarters to one and a half hundredweights".

"Aye Sir" shouted her Mother "An' ask the lassies hoo aften the straps brek an' the coal fa's oot and bairns coming up ahint are maimed....Aye an' ask hoo many hae been killed Sir!"

"Aye, that happens aften Sir!" chorused other mothers.

"Manager, how many times has this happened during the last year?" enquired the Commissioner. "I dont know Sir. I hae nae instructions tae keep records o' accidents!" was the instant defiant reply. The Commissioner looked aghast, then whispered to the clerk. Waiting till he finished writing he again turned to Agnes. "How many journeys do you make each day with that heavy load on your back Agnes?" She thought for a minute then said, "Aboot twenty Sir, as I hae tae fill 4 or 5 tubs!

"Twenty? You must be tired indeed when six o'clock comes!"

"Am very glad when my task is wrought. It is sore fatigue Sir, but like a lot o'ither lads an' lassies, we git the strap if we dinna do oor faither's biddin'. Last year I broke ma shoulder and had tae lay aff work idle!" Looking towards the table, Mr Franks shouted, "Manager, can you tell me how much coal each tub holds?

"Four hundredweight Sir!"

To Agnes he said, "Yes lass, you are right! Carrying one hundredweight of coal in your creel you would have to do 20 journeys to fill five tubs!" Calling again to the Manager he enquired, "What distance would Agnes cover on one journey along the road and up the ladders?" The Manager, counting on his fingers, finally called back, "365 feet Sir!" Making a quick calculation Mr Franks was heard to exclaim, " My God, Doctor Scott! That's equivalent to climbing St. Pauls Cathedral".

*"And if she does that 20 times that is twice up Ben Lomond in one day. Sounds incredible!"* said Dr. Scott. Turning to the clerk, in a whisper the Commissioner dictated a long statement.

Unable to hear what was being said, Agnes looked increasingly worried when she saw the Commissioner check what the Clerk had written. Frantically groping around in her mind to find something good to say about herself, she finally blurted out, *"But Sir, I can read an' was learning the two penny book!"* Then with a resigned shrug her voice dropped, *"But I canna dae it noo, as I have nae been to school for twa years!"* Thinking of something else she brightened *"Aw but sometimes I go tae Kirk Sir on the Sabbath, o'er at Lasswade".*

*"How many miles away is that?"*

*"Nye on four Sir"* someone shouted. *"Tell me what you know about the Bible Agnes?"* Her face fell. She thought then muttered, *"Naething Sir?"*

*"Those among you who go to school, when do you go?*

*"Efter work Sir!"*

*"After a 14 hour shift?*

*"Aye, Sir!"*

*"Is it free?"*

*"Naw.... oor Faithers pey the penny fir it Sir."*

*"Now!"* said Mr. Franks studying his list, *"I'd like to learn what a putter does?*

Bess standing with the rest of the putters helped push her friend Janet Moffat forward, whispering, *"Go on Janet, ye tell him what we dae!"* Eleven year old Janet, whose large, dark lifeless eyes stared out of a gaunt blackened face, reeled from the unexpected push. Unsuccessfully trying to straighten her already permanently curved spine, she stammered, *"W..we pu' w..wagons Sir!...We draw in harness!"* Ill at ease and having difficulty finding words she resorted to going through the motions as she attempted to explain, *"The harness goes o'er ma shoulder and ma back like this Sir... then it's fastened tae the tub chain... but because the seams are awfu' narra from the mens' room tae the horse road, we hae tae bend doon like this tae get through!"* She finished bent double, her back arched, her head almost in line with her knees and her hand in the small of her back pulling an imaginary chain.

*"How high are these roads Janet pulls her tub along?"* Mr Franks enquired of the Manager. *"24 to 30 inches Sir."*

*"Those wagons the children pull, how much coal do they hold?"*

*"Four to five hundredweight Sir!"*

*"Does your wagon run on rails Janet?"*

*"Oh naw Sir! We haul them o'er flat wet slippy floors....Oft'n the water covers oor shin!"*

*"Janet"* said the Commissioner, *"You have given us a very vivid picture of the work of a putter. We*

can see you, bent double, painfully dragging your tub holding four to five hundredweight of coal along wet and narrow seams until you reach the horse road, where I understand a horse drawn wagon will be waiting!"

"Do you like your job Janet?". The answer was almost inaudible, "Naw Sir, but Faither maks me like it!"

Who drives the horses?" asked the Commissioner

"Me Sir, I'm Robert Thomson, a horse driver!"

"And your age Robert?"

"Eleven Sir…. But next year I'll be a man and wull start tae howk the coal!" he said with pride. "Until then I'll drive the cuddies!"

"Do you like your job Robert"

"Naw Sir! But I lo'e the cuddies- we a' dae."

"Is the track dry Robert?"

"Naw Sir, the water of'en comes up tae ma knees"!

Bess and other putters interjected crying out "But Sir, horses pu' on iron rails, us putters hae tae pu' along muddy rocky tracks…It's naw fair is it Sir?"

Darkness descended early that November afternoon. Bess, her body racked by constant coughing was now feverish and light-headed. Feeling faint she edged against a wall, slid to the floor and sat with her arms hugging her knees. Unable now to see the faces, all she could do was listen as the stream of men, women and children, repeat and reiterate the horrendous conditions under which they laboured. Listening to an old collier tell how he and his father were born slaves, the property of the Inveresk Laird, Bess found her mind wandering as her gaze idly followed the shadows being cast by the candles now lighting the room.

Vaguely she was aware of the man's voice dramatically changing and the air becoming charged with emotion as he went on to describe appalling accidents, caused by roof falls, gas explosions, flooding, inefficiency and neglect. Carried away by his passion, others jumped up and as they angrily recounted their ordeals, Bess watched the shadows on the wall multiply, merge and dance in frenzied sympathy with the voices of despair.

Wilder and wilder grew the dance. Suddenly the shed door crashed open and a howling wind whirled in strange yet vaguely familiar images to swell the howling mass. Merging with the shadows, they obliterated the figures in the room, as swirling up from the dungeons of Mother Earth came ghostly voices, voices Bess knew of old… Lachie McGraw, Big Bell, Wee Jemmie, Nettie, Andrew and Adam Young, Wullie McVey, The Stranger from Fife and countless others. Harmonising with the voices of the living they burst forth in crescendo, pleading a place in the sun.

The findings of the Commission rocked the nation. There was a public outcry. Throughout Victorian Britain, wherever people congregated, one topic of conversation dominated all others. It was the Findings, or what was now called **'The Physical and Moral Conditions of the Children and Young persons employed in Mines and Manufacturers'**.

In Kirk and Cloister it was said, *"It is deadly physical oppression and systematic slavery of which we consciously believe no one unacquainted with the facts would credit the existence of in the British Dominion".* To one another... *"History will ask of us Men of the Cloth, how in God's name, in this civilised and Christian country, was it condoned and upheld by us!"* How indeed!

Scholars closeted in Seats of Learning assessing facts, read *"We find that one in every four is under 13 and that this degrading labour is barbarous and cruel, the remnant of the slavery of a degraded age. Six days a week, often going on through the night they are forced to carry creels holding a cwt of coal on these pitifully undernourished frames!"* A student asked, *"Professor, as coal is the pump primer of the Industrial Revolution, could it be concluded from these findings that its foundation was built on the backs of these women and little children?"*

Elizabeth Barrett Browning, in an emotive poem, *'The Cry of the Children'* voiced the nation's conscience. In Drawing Room and Soiree tears flowed freely as they listened,

> *For oh! say the children, We are weary*
>
> *And we cannot run or leap:*
>
> *If we cared for any meadows, it were merely*
>
> *To drop down in them and sleep.*
>
> *Our knees tremble sorely in the stooping,*
>
> *We fall upon our faces, trying to go,*
>
> *And underneath our heavy eyelids drooping.*
>
> *The reddest flower would look as pale as snow.*
>
> *For all day, we drag our burden tiring,*
>
> *Through the coal-dark underground.*
>
> *Or all days we drive the wheels of iron.*
>
> *In the factories, round and round.*

In streets, market place and inns, where few could read, folks knew the facts already; they lived with them! With a shrug of their shoulders, they cried, *"Facts are chiels that winna ding... Noo they are oot in the licht o' day what wull Parliament dae? Until all people win the richt tae vote, we can dae nithin'!"*

In the Mother of Parliaments, Honourable Members debated such facts as, *'..the degree of fatigue produced by the collier labour in this district is extreme. The tender and feeble powers of girls and boys of this age (eight and upwards) must be taxed beyond their strength by the uninterrupted labour of twelve hour average daily, labour called for at irregular periods, sometimes by day and sometimes extending all through the night. It is incredible that children of such tender years, toiling in such wretched conditions, working irregular hours, on meagre and unsubstantial food......The medical evidence shows that this labour is injurious to the bodily frame; from the exhaustion of their labour, they are in most instances too fatigued even to attend their evening school, should one be found in their neighbourhood and after taking a meagre supper of kail and porridge they are too glad to seek the ill afforded rest which is to prepare them for the toil of the succeeding day......A great number suffer from heart condition and asthma and are prematurely old by thirty years of age, when their bodily vigour declines and they become spare and find great difficulty in breathing.'*

Taken aback at the public outcry, Honourable Members legislated to forbid the employment of women and children underground. Then they paused; bowed low to the powerful Coal-Owners' lobby and agreed to allow boys of 10 and over, to continue to toil underground. None seemed to have concern at what would become of these women and children on whose earnings families depended. A small number were found jobs on the pit head, but many found themselves destitute. Single women and widows with children were made destitute and thrown at the mercy of the Parish, which often refused to help them. Many were driven to prostitution and crime.

Over at Liberton some women, desperate to find work disguised themselves as men. They were summoned to the law courts in Edinburgh where it is said, they displayed such ignorance in the most trifling things and made such ridiculous answers that the grave and reverend court was convulsed with laughter.

Six years later Bess Young was dead. Suffering from consumption, she and her baby died in childbirth. Against her parents' advice she had married Jocky Stonehouse, *"Lass, pity is akin to love!"* they told her, but she would not listen. *"But Faither, ye dinna ken him as I dae- he's no like his Faither."* But her mother had her doubts- would it be *"Like father like son!"*

Living next door to the Stonehouse family, over the years they could not help but hear some of the terrible rows and beatings that went on. Afterwards, hearing the door bang behind the father as he charged out in a temper making for the Ale Hoose, Jess would steal round the back door and offer help and comfort. Rarely was there ever any food in the house. Most rows seemed to be about money. He drank and gambled the family wages. Many a time the Young family shared what little they had with the starving Stonehouse children. Lil Stonehouse a proud and lonely women, would never accept anything for herself. She suffered in silence. All she ever would say was, *"It's God's Will!"* She never spoke about herself. All Jess knew was that when she was very young she had been a farm servant. How she came to marry Joe Stonehouse she never said.

But the years took their toll. At twenty five, worn out and defeated Lil died. Jess swore it was starvation and a broken heart. After her Mother's death the oldest girl had to take her place and bring up the younger ones.

But Joe's lifestyle changed little. The rows and the beatings continued with Jocky more often than not the scapegoat. When he was 12, to everyone's surprise, he left home. As the other sons grew up, to survive they learned to meet their Father's violence with violence. It became a way of life. Neighbours grew accustomed to hearing them fight then watch them drink with their Father at the Inn afterwards, as if nothing had happened. Jocky rarely joined them.

On the night of the 'Muckle Adventure' Bess had gone with her mother to deliver the childrens' tinnies and gundy. As Bess handed over the tinnie of muscles saying " *Here's a present fir ye Mistress Stonehouse!*" Lil had burst into tears, her first present ever! Bess had grown to know the family well. From that day on, she would tag behind Jed and Jocky as they worked in the pit or played in the fields behind the cottages. When other children taunted him, making fun of his withered arm or blackened eyes, she would hotly rise to his defence. In time she came to know where to find him when he escaped to be alone. He would be lying beneath Kittle Macevie Bridge or in the field with the farm horses. He loved horses.

In spite of his disability, Jocky managed to survive as a pit lad, driving horses until he was twelve. Then for the first time in his life it seemed that Providence smiled on him. Saying it was because he was impressed with the way he handled horses, the farmer at Wanton Wa's offered him a job as an agricultural labourer. Jocky left home and went to live in the farm bothy. What he didn't know was this was the farm where his mother had been a servant.

At twenty, Jocky married Bess and took her to live in a tied cottage on the farm where, for a year she laboured beside him in the fields. At first he was very proud of his clever wife and although Bess would have liked to teach him to read, she well understood why it was that the man in him could not accept his wife teaching him. But when she put his humorous and earthy stories into her writings and read them back, it gave him a sense of pride and he asked her to teach him his letters.

One Saturday night as they sat writing before the fire, Joe and a drunken cronie burst into their cottage demanding that Jocky go with them to the Inn. He refused. His Father went beserk, shouting, "*Christ it's easy tae see wha wears the breeks in this hoose! Neether wonder yer the talk o' the village, ye muckle Teenie! Lettin' a wuman lead ye by the nose, especially when everybuddy but ye kens she only married ye tae get awa' frae the pithead!*"

As Jocky rose and made to show them the door Joe suddenly lashed out at him with his fist. Momentarily knocked off balance by the unexpected blow, he heard his father yell to his cronie, "*Christ look at him- nae guts! ...Its easy tae see I didna faither this bastard!*" Turning on Jocky, he shouted, "*Christ, that sneevlin' whore o' a Mither o' yers shair made a mess o' ye ... couldna e'en mak a pitman o' ye!*" The colour drained from Jocky's face. The seed was sown. Never would he know the truth. His Mother was dead. All he knew was, that never once had she even hinted he was other than his fathers's oldest son, although there had been times in his life when he had wished he wasn't.

Then it was Bess's turn to reel. She could not believe her eyes. White faced and shaking, like a lost soul, Jocky rose and meekly followed the two men, muttering *"I'd better go wi' them- its the only wey they'll leave us alane!"* Lying awake in the early hours of the morning she heard her husband fumble with the sneck. He was drunk. She lay pretending to sleep, thankful he was back, but frightened of what might happen. Tiptoeing unsteadily into the room he lurched forward in the dark, banged into the table, scattering the papers they had been writing on. Angrily picking them up, cursing, he flung them on the dying embers. As they burst into flames lighting the room, he lunged towards the bed, grabbed his wife by the hair and punched her yelling *"Bastard or nae bastard, I'll show this village wha's Maister in this hoose, Aye! I aften wondered wha the likes o' ye wid marry me- an' noo I ken; tae get awa frae the pithead!"*

She loved him and always did in spite of his violent temper and the beatings. Next day he'd be sorry and would cry like a baby. She would forgive him, and go on loving him, knowing she always would. And she did.

When she died, heart broken and full of remorse Jocky showed Ned not only the bag containing his wife's writings, but a package he found under their mattress. Jocky knew what was in the canvas bag. Many a night, when first married they had sat reading her stories by candlelight or singing the songs together. He had a fine voice. Then, when he started to learn to read, they would write stories together. He had a scathing wit, a vivid imagination and a great sense of earthy humour.

But he had never seen this other package. When he found it, he had tried to read it, but as he had almost forgotten all he had ever learned before that fateful night, he could not understand a word. Ned opened the package. In it was a letter, a secret letter Bess had been writing to herself since she was sixteen. In it she poured out her heart. Her love for Jocky, their courting days under the Kittle Makevie Bridge where he would sing to her, or make her laugh by mimicking the Minister and scandalising pious Kirk Elders. Scared, she would warn him what Granny said happened to those, who brought down the Wrath of God by such irreverence. She wrote of the day they went to Newton Parish Kirk and stood in the Kirk reading the names on the tablet. How afterwards they found primroses still growing outside the old Kirkyard Wall. Many a time they had searched for, but never found, the old shaft at Niddry Edge where Granny said as long as there were Niddrie Coalbearers, Big Bell's spirit would keep vigil.

The letter told of the happiest day of her life, their Wedding Day. How Jocky had secretly planned a surprise, a train ride down the Innocent Railway. But it was also to be something more; a re-run of the 'Muckle Adventure' he had heard so much about. At Old Niddry Station they boarded the train, which was no longer two wagons pulled by horses, but described by Bess as *"stage coaches joined thegither and pu'ed by a puffing steam engine!"* As they sped down what was still the 'coal run', she was surprised, nothing much had changed in ten years. Giving Jocky a non-stop commentary, she omitted nothing even remembering some of Miss Wood's educational snippets.

Leaving the train they retraced the route the 'Adventurers' had taken; watched the ships and boats in Fisherow harbour; looked for the 'giant' Fishwives and then run barefoot along the beach, were they had, what her new husband laughingly called *'oor weddin feast'*. *"And"* she told Jocky proudly *"It was oor 'Muckle Adventure' that gave Mr Fox the idea that he could carry passengers and charge them"*. But because folk were awkward and could never make up their minds where to get off, he charged them all the same fare. That is how it became known as the 'Innocent Railway'. The letter went on to tell of their hopes and aspirations for their life together when they moved into their cottage. In also told of the fateful night her father-in-law had almost succeeded in smashing these hopes. How, as she lay in bed in pain she knew that somehow she must convince her husband that she loved him for himself and that he was worth loving.

As Ned finished reading the letter saying *"Take it- it is yours"* he handed it back to Jocky who broke down and cried bitterly. Picking up the canvas bag Ned found himself unable to open it.

Weeks later, still grieving for his daughter, alone in the cottage, in the room where Bess had been brought home to die, he became aware of a strange presence. It was not frightening, just warm, comforting and gently willing him to open the bag. Dawn broke as he finished reading. Rising, he snuffed out the candle and as he opened the shutters and watched night fading into day he fancied he could hear his daughter's voice whispering in the wind:

> **Deep doon in dungeons dark confine**
>
> **Where wemen gret and bairns pined**
>
> **Craidled in rock, their spirit bides on**
>
> **Tae guard oor richts sae sairly won.**

Clutching her sheaf of stories Ned cried through his tears *"Oh Bess, ma bonny Bess! Is it that yer spirit is destined tae find nae rest until someone comes along tae finish telling the story you began, the story o' the Niddrey coal-bearers"*.

## CHAPTER 14 **ELECTIONS**

*"Gentlemen, stop I beg ye"* yelled the Toll Keeper as he ran towards a band of young horsemen galloping up the Niddrie Toll Road. They seem scarily intent on jumping his Toll-gate. Sharply pulling up his horse, an arrogant young nobleman, screamed at him, *"Man, don't tell me you fail to recognise your Sovereign's son- His Royal Highness the Prince Alfred!"*

Taken aback, the frightened Keeper touched his forelock and bowing low to the Prince stammered. *"Y..Y....Yer Royal Highness, y. .yer humble servant! p..p. please accept m... ma humblest apologies!"* Meekly opening the gate and too afraid to ask for the toll he let the royal entourage through. New to the job, the Keeper was still visibly shaking as he watched the horsemen thunder up the road towards Niddrie Marischal Mansion, where the massive iron gates were open in anticipation of their arrival.

Meanwhile in the mansion house kitchen, nerves were jangling and tempers fraying. Servants and footmen, who had been on duty since five o'clock that Saturday morning, were running hither and thither preparing for the week-end shooting party.

Luncheon was ready awaiting the arrival of the guests. The meal, typical of the famous Wauchope hospitality, consisted of game soup, smoked salmon, pheasant, baron of beef, supplemented with fresh vegetables from the garden, fruit from the orchards and cheese and cream from the Mains Farm.

Housekeeper Sarah Turner, accompanied by the butler John Falside had just finished a final inspection of the preparations. Tight lipped Mistress Turner, displeased with some aspects of the presentation, was, in her usual autocratic manner taking Cook to task. Knowing that the cooking and preparation of the meal could not be faulted, Cook was outraged at what she thought was unjust criticism and a matter of opinion anyway. It was common knowledge that she resented and resisted many modern ideas the Housekeeper was trying to foist on the running of the Household. Returning to the kitchen muttering to herself *"It's been yin o' yon days!"* she looked around and saw the twelve year old kitchen maid, struggling to scour a stubborn stain from a large pot. *"Ye limmer!"* she yelled, *"Hae ye nae finished that yet? It's nae mare scouring pouther ye need, jist guid auld fashioned elbo'- grease!... Gawd! ye young yins nooadays, ye want things made easy- ye dinna ken when ye're weel aff!.."* She broke off as the door opened and the Butler burst in, holding high a silver goblet. Pointing to a dent, while his eyes went slowly round the room he demanded, *"Wha made this dunt in the Laird's siller?"*

A deadly hush descended. Pushing aside the little maid Cook marched over to where Mr Falside stood, joined forces with him, and together slowly they scrutinised every face in the room. It did not take much effort to detect the culprit. An agitated red faced footman, stammered, *"Sir, it wis me! I'm sorry. It slipped frae ma hand when I wis cleaning it!"* With a withering glance the Butler was about to open his mouth, when a jangling ring resounded through the Servants' Hall, heralding the arrival of the guests and summoning the staff to action stations. But before taking over his command as head of operations, the Butler took time to hiss in the unfortunate young man's ear, *"An' dinna think ye're saved by the bell!- I'll deal with ye later!"*

Now Royal visits were not uncommon at Niddrey Marischal. In 1860 Queen Victoria's son, Prince Alfred and Andrew Wauchope had became friends while serving as young midshipmen on board HMS St George. Now with the Prince studying at Edinburgh University, he and his young noblemen friends were often seen leaving Holyrood Palace, riding through the Queen's Park, thundering past Duddingston Mansion and up the Toll Road on their way to Niddrey Marischal Estate.

On this day, luncheon went well, with the Prince's compliments, conveyed via the Butler, restoring Cook's injured pride. So peace reigned once more in her domain as the staff started preparations for dinner. Without taking time to eat, the young footman hurried to the terrace to join the gillies and dogs waiting the arrival of the shooting party. Having recently acquired a tied cottage and become a father for the first time, he was distraught at the thought of the coming encounter with the Butler. He had seen evictions happen for less!

When the young gentlemen finally appeared they were accompanied by the Laird, whom Andrew was trying to persuade to join the shoot. *"Look Father,"* he was saying, *"the weather is perfect! An afternoon out in this crisp air will do you good!"* Mr Wauchope, who was not a well man, was at first reluctant, but eventually agreed. The shoot went well, with many pigeons and a few pheasants falling to the guns. The Laird, having bagged a few himself looked happy and relaxed. As predicted the air had brought colour to his usually pale face.

After a short rest, refreshed and relaxed, he was handed his gun. Lifting it to his shoulder he took aim and as the shot rang out someone screamed. Horrified, his son, who was standing nearby, turned to see the young footman slump to the ground, hit in the arm by the charge from his father's gun. Yelling out for a doctor he sprang to his aid! Dashing to the stables, a groom grabbed a horse, mounted and rode off. The injured footman was gently carried into the house to be treated for shock by Cook and Mary. The Laird was distraught and swore never again to take a gun in his hand. He never did.

In times of emergency it was to Mary, Cook would turn to for assistance. She knew she could use the housemaid's considerable nursing experience. When she was twelve Mary Young had helped her mother nurse Bess in the last weeks of her illness and had been there when she died in her arms. When she was eighteen she married Tom, a collier in Niddrie Pit. Last year he had been badly burned in a serious fire at the coal-face and although there had been no loss of life, many of the injuries sustained were to cause life-long suffering. Tom was one of those who would never work again. So now Mary, assisted by her aging mother was struggling to nurse her invalid husband, bring up their three surviving children and be the family bread-winner. She would always be grateful to her father, who after the death of Bess, swore none of his daughters would ever work anywhere near a pit-head if he had his way.

When she was twelve he had managed to get her an interview for a job as a kitchen-maid in the Mansion. The fact she could read and write might have been the deciding factor in tipping the scales in her favour with the Housekeeper who engaged her. But that cut no ice with her fellow servants, indeed, it only exasperated the situation. At first Mary hated the job. She missed her family and her friends. She was also fair game to a few members of the staff, who did not attempt to hide the fact that they resented having to work alongside someone, whom they considered beneath them. Someone whose father they referred to as *'Yin o' the moles!'*

Sent one day on an errand to the stables, Mary was accosted by a young stable lad. Whatever response he expected, it certainly was not the heavy kick she landed where it hurt most. No lad working there, ever again, laid a hand on Mary Young. Knowing what store her father and mother set on her working in the 'Big Hoose', she quickly learned the best way to survive was to bite her lip and get on with the job. Although it was hard work, long hours and little pay nevertheless she considered herself lucky to be there and in time came to derive self satisfaction from the job. She also learned many things, not only about the landed gentry and those who served them, but about herself.

One evening while serving drinks in the drawing room where the Laird and his family were gathered round the piano entertaining friends, an elderly Wauchope Aunt was persuaded to sing her party piece. Unaccompanied and smiling sweetly she sang...,

> When I was engaged a coal-bearer to be
>
> When I was engaged a coal-bearer to be
>
> Thro' all the coal-pits
>
> I maun wear the dron brat
>
> If ma heert it should breek,
>
> I can never be free.

As she sung, Mary's mining blood erupted. An intense uncontrollable anger welled up inside her. Only by stuffing her free hand into her mouth and reminding herself she was a servant there, did she succeed in refraining from screaming, "M'am hoo can ye! Dae ye ken what ye are singing? - It is the Coalbearers Lament- he dirge o' the wemen and bairns shackled tae yer family's pits fir life!" Mary was still working there in 1846 when Andrew Gilbert, the second son of the Wauchopes' was born. She watched him grow up against a background of wealth and access to the noblest in the land. Most of his childhood was spent between Niddrey and Yetholm in Roxburghshire- the family's other estate.

As a child the red-headed Andrew was a high spirited lad, who enjoyed nothing better than to escape from his tutor into the wooded parkland of the estate. There he would spend his days fishing, bird nesting or catching rabbits, where, rumour had it, his skill outshone the best of the local poachers. Despite being born into a household that boasted a library containing 2,351 volumes, Andrew was never much of a book reader. He never went to University and his scholastic education was of the smallest. He spent two years away at a school, where the emphasis was on character building and learning by doing. Later he was sent to a school for those intent in pursuing a career in the army, navy or other profession. He ran away! His favourite pastime was playing soldiers. This was probably influenced by the fact that, as a second son, he knew from an early age that a career in the Armed Forces was a strong possibility. And of course he came from a long line of military men. One distinguished Wauchope fell at Killcrankie. The young Andrew was often seen with his tutor in the Queen's Park, or on the sands at nearby Portobello, intently watching military manoeuvres, much of which was drilling of regulars and yeomanry cavalry. On returning home he would press-gang his sisters, Fanny and Hersey, his cousins Elizabeth and Nina Elliot, as well as children of the estate workers. These he formed into what he called 'My Household Troops'. Drilling them for hours he would reward each in turn with the honour of carrying the banner or beating the drum.

Often miners' children attending the village school would be distracted from their lessons, as through the window they would watch red headed Andrew, perched perilously on the stane dyke, the nine foot high estate boundary wall. There he would stand for hours, his hand shading his eyes, solemnly scanning the horizon for the approach of 'the enemy.' At other times he would station himself strategically on the wall, then, proudly take the salute as his troops marched past in the parkland below.

One day while his family were entertaining the local nobility, keen as always to show off his 'troops', seated on Donald his black pony, with drum beating and banner flying Andrew proudly led them up to the front of the house. There watched by his dotting parents and admiring guests he put them through their paces. When the applause died down, the children stood to attention, waiting the command to dismiss. But that day, the freckled faced young general had other ideas in mind. Not content with drilling his troops on the green, he decided the time had come to storm the Mansion.

*"Forward march!"* he commanded. Trained to obey without question, to the consternation of the adults, his troops found themselves marching smartly behind the pony, as it trotted up the steps of the mansion, though the front door, into the hall, through the dining room into the corridor and out the back door to the terrace beyond. Now Donald, never having come that way before, decided it fitting to mark his territory by leaving a generous deposit on the carpet. It was left to Mary to clean up the mess.

The day came when young Andrew decided to spread his wings. Escaping from his tutor he clambered over the dyke, where, unknown to his parents, he made friends with some of the village lads. One night they raided the joiner's workshop, carrying away a number of old cart wheels lying strewn around the yard. These they fastened to the doors of some of the cottages. Next morning villagers hurrying to work found themselves barricaded in. *"Aye,"* said Mary, *"We a' ken wha did it! but nane darnae say. It wid be laughed aff as jist anither o' young Andrie's pranks."*

When his gang played a trick on an old women by letting her hens loose in the night, the terrified victim screwed up courage and went to the Laird, asking for compensation. Mary never knew the outcome of the request, but in no uncertain terms she warned her sons, *"Laird's son or no, if ever I catch ye twa near that lot, ye'll no sit doon fir a week. Crabbit and an auld besom Aggie micht be, but in this village we dinna treat oor elders like that. Ne'er forget that!"*

Her husband Tom, a fiercely independant man, who had worked in the pits since he was ten, did not find it easy to come to terms with his disability. Not only was he now unable to support his wife and children, he could no longer play an active role in the political life of the pit.

In 1841 a milestone had been reached in the history of coal- mining when, at Wakefield, colliers finally succeeded in establishing the Miners Association of Great Britain and Ireland. Two years later Tom was elected Niddry delegate and together with Newcraighall delegate Wull Young (who was later to become his brother-in-law) they attended the Association's Conference in Glasgow's Trongate.

It was a memorable occasion. Carried along on a wave of euphoria, the air was electric as speaker after speaker, many fine orators, spurred the audience on to carry on the struggle.

A sense of great historical momentum filled the Hall as miners rejoiced. Many speakers paid tribute to the debt the Association owed to their forbears. Those courageous collier families, who, through centuries of poverty and struggle had survived by swearing the Oath of Brothering and living up to its principles. Those fearless men who, in spite of Combination Laws, threats of torture, imprisonment, transportation and death had kept urging their fellow colliers to unite and form a union to challenge the absolute power of the coal-owner and seek to have righted the grievous wrongs inflicted on the mining community.

Now that day had come! Delegates, representing seventy thousand miners in the UK and Ireland would carry back the torch of hope; blazing the message that miners throughout the land were now united and as brothers would henceforth speak with one voice. Like others in the hall that day, Tom and Wull left walking tall, fired with a fierce determination to hold in trust their precious heritage and carry on the fight for justice.

Less than a decade later, here was Tom, a casualty of the Coal Industry, one of it's many workers flung on the scrap-heap and forced to end their days poverty stricken and a hopeless cripple. In spite of suffering constant pain Tom's resolve never faltered. *"As lang as I hae breath in ma body I'll use what time I hae left on earth tae urge colliers tae join the Miners' Association tae cairry on the ficht!"*

Lizzie, Tom and Mary's only daughter, started work in the Mansion House the year Andrew Wauchope, now a Captain in the 42nd Highlanders (Black Watch) came home on leave from his Regiment in Egypt to marry Elyss, daughter of Sir Thomas Erskine in Fife. His leave over, he rejoined his Regiment, taking his young bride with him. In the Army since the age of nineteen, Andrew had spent very few of the intervening years at Niddrie or Yetholm. But his commitments had to change dramatically when his brother William died without issue and he found himself Laird of Niddrie. After two years of marriage, returning from Egypt with her husband, Mrs Wauchope gave birth to twins in London. A week later sadly she died. Her husband was distraught. Three years later the twins, who were being reared by their grandparents in Fife caught scarlet fever. Little William died. Andrew survived, brain damaged and unable ever to become Laird.

*"Ta ta!"* men cried to their wives as they joined the exodus of colliers noisily making their way along the dusty track through Newcraighall Village. Barefoot children, scraggy dogs and a handful of chickens ran wild and free. Newcraighall had no roads or pavements but it did have new two storied houses and a Miners Institute .

*"Richt bairns, time for bed!"* fathers yelled to howls of protest from boys playing football with a pig's bladder. Two of the younger colliers could not resist booting the ball as they passed. The herding call was repeated to less energetic lads playing marbles and a couple of older girls, pushing babies in ramshackle prambulaters, while others were tossing chucky stanes and champing red sandstone to sell in their play shops. Having filled their pails at the communal street taps, women had dallied for a gossip with neighbours sitting on front steps or on outside stairs relaxing in the balmy evening sun. Stopping their chat only long

enough to reply "*Ta ta*" to the men, without coaxing they responded to the childrens' plea for an extension, "*Aye alricht!- ye can play a bit longer!*" Why not! With the man of the house out for a couple of hours, wives could not see why they too should not enjoy a break before resuming the nightly chores of getting children to bed and men ready for the night shift.

Earlier a group of young miners and two girls had been fooling around outside Whitehill Street Post Office. By now they had stopped and were talking among themselves, well aware, that sitting on the adjoining cottage step, two village gossips were watching their every move. "*See that Kate Adams*" one gossip was whispering "*A shameless limmer that yins turning oot to be! Any excuse to mak eyes at Dave Young an' she's there! Canna leave him alane fir yin nicht. She kens fu' weel where he's going the nicht...Men's business, nae place fir wemon!*"

The group started making their way towards the school and as they passed the two women stopped talking and cocked their ears, hoping to hear what Kate and Dave were saying as they walked hand in hand behind the others. "*Dinna loose yer nerve! Gie him it straight*", was all they could hear Kate say. But it took no effort to hear Kate's parting shot as she left Dave at the school door. Tossing her dark curls, her bright eyes flashed as she laughed and shouted to the other girls. "*Fiddlers, dugs and fleas get intae feasts uninvited! But there is nae way us lassies wull get in thro' this door this nicht. But never mind- yin day women wull get the vote and then the hand that rocks the cradle wull change the world!*"

"*Not a chance hen!*" retorted a grinning miner as he limped in behind the lads. "*God made bonny lassies like ye tae look efter us men an' keep the cradle fu!*"

Removing their caps the group entered the hall to find only a few seats vacant. Noisily greeting the older miners they split up and scattered themselves throughout the room. Those unable to find seats squatted on their hunkers in the passages, while others huddled together at the back. Before he squatted down Dave had a good look around. Sitting at an angle on the end seat of the front row, his right arm along the back of his chair, was the Minister making a mental note of all who came though the door. "*Trust him tae commandeer a seat where he can see baith platform and audience!*" thought Dave At the opposite end of the row, also with his eyes fixed on the door, was the Colliery Manager. His beady eyes making sure he could be seen by his betters to be keeping their workers under surveillance.

Seated between these two were two Kirk Elders, the Estate Factor, the Dominie, tenant farmers and two pit overseers. Scattered throughout the body of the hall, out-numbered by miners, were farm labourers, artisans, estate servants and workers. When everyone was finally settled and after ascertaining he was being seen by all, with a flourish, the Manager slowly extracted the gold watch attached to an ornate chain which lay stretched across his pot belly. Just as he was about to consult it, the platform party arrived and the audience was obliged to stand until the entourage were seated on the small raised platform.

First came Sir Charles Dalrymple from Newhailes, followed by Colonel Andrew Wauchope. Bringing up the rear was the Midlothian Unionist Party Chairman and two officials. Sir Charles, quickly taking command, opened the meeting.

"Good evening, Minister, Kirk Elders, Dominie, and friends from Niddrie and Newcraighall. There is no need for me to introduce your Unionist Candidate for the forthcoming Election. Well known to us all, he is our well-respected and much loved Laird- Colonel Andrew Gilbert Wauchope, Laird of Niddrie! As we all know, not only is he Niddrie's Laird, he has given over 20 years of his life to the service of his Queen and Country. Twice wounded in action he is now a Colonel in the Black Watch Regiment, renowned throughout Scotland as a brave and committed soldier dedicated to Britain's Imperial Cause!"

He paused. Unionist supporters duly took the cue and applauded loudly. He went on, "But now, Colonel Wauchope, no longer content with being a successful soldier, is a man fired with political ambition. His one desire is to follow in the footsteps of his illustrious forbears, become your Member of Parliament and look after your interests in the Mother of Parliaments. Friends please welcome your Laird, Colonel Wauchope!"

As the applause died down and the Candidate rose to speak, a drunk, squatting in the aisle, spluttered between bouts of coughing, "G...G.. God bless yer G..G ...Grace!" From his vantage point the Minister graciously bestowed a benevolent smile on the culprit. Wauchope smiled and turning first to his Agent said, "Thank you Sir Charles for these kind words". Clasping his hands and looking round the Hall he went on, "Good evening friends! It is good to see so many well-kent faces here tonight and heartening indeed to see so many prepared to sacrifice such a beautiful evening in order to be with me tonight!

First, let me give you my word that my prime reason for aspiring to enter Parliament is to look after your welfare and your interests. After all, has not my family looked after the mining and farming communities here in Niddrie and Newcraighall for nigh on seven hundred years? And are we not all part of the Niddrie Marischal Family? All dear to my heart!"

Thunderous applause answered the last question. He went on, "Now let me make a prophesy.... Now that adult males have the vote- this year, you, the miners, farm and estate workers of Newcraighall and Niddrie will make history! Together you and I will topple Britain's Prime Minister. No longer will Gladstone look on Midlothian as his Seat and use it to perpetuate some of his radical and dangerous political crusades!"

This was met with loud clapping, stamping feet, cheers and catcalls.

Wauchope then outlined some of the Unionist policies. First among them was support for the Church of Scotland in their fight against disestablishment. This won him a wild round of applause from the Clergy, Kirk Elders and the many Kirk Members present.

Now Dave, Willie and others knew what was coming next. For the last two years they had followed Wauchope around the Constituency hustings listening carefully to his speeches. They varied little from meeting to meeting. Added to that, they carefully studied the reports in the newspapers and so, by now, they could recite his policies and stock answers by heart. When he had finished Sir Charles asked for questions, stressing that each questioner must give his name.

First to raise his hand was a Kirk Elder, a tenant farmer on the estate. His question obviously pleased the Laird and gave him an opening to speak further on Disestablishment. Judging by the applause this went down well with many- reinforcing the promise of many votes.

Then an Irish boothy worker from Wanton Wa's farm stood up, *"The name's O'Reilly Sir, And where would you be standing on the question of Irish Home Rule!"*

This brought a loud and firm reply *"I am opposed to Home Rule. I am opposed on the grounds that it would lead to the dismantling of the Empire. Ireland is not a nation in the sense Scotland is a nation- so why can't Ireland be content with 'local government' of the description enjoyed here in Mid-Lothian?"*

Paddy jumped to his feet- he knew 'why', but Sir Charles simply ignored him and pointed to one of two hands behind him, one of whom belonged to a worker on his estate. Both men made to speak- but while the mix-up was being sorted out, Willie Adams, squatting in the aisle, took advantage of the confusion and jumped in saying.

*"The name's Adams! Colonel Wauchope, I ken you nae longer own Niddrie Pits, altho' I understand ye're a shareholder in the Company. So on behalf of a' Niddrie Miners I say how pleased we are to hear ye say ye wull safeguard our interests. Can we therefore tak it that you will be in favour of abolishing mining royalties?"* A gasp went round the audience. From his vantage point the Colliery Manager glared at Willie then turning to the platform made a sign that clearly promised, 'Sir I'll deal with him later!' The Candidate, his face almost as red as his hair answered, *"Abolition would be an illegal thing in the present state of law, Therefore I am not in favour of it!"*

*"Hear hear!"* echoed the Manager. This prompted a burst of loud clapping from the supporters, but before it had time to die down, Dave Young was on his feet and without waiting to be invited to speak, in a clear voice thundered, *"I'm Young, Niddrie Delegate to the Miners' Federation! Colonel Wauchope, wull ye state yer position in relation to the reform being put forrit by the Liberals, namely the legal enactment o' an eight hoor day?"* The audience held it's breath....Wauchope gasped! But before he had time to recover his composure, the room resounded with a long drawn out rattling snore. It came from the drunk, whose embarrassed neighbour was self-consciously digging him in the ribs. Opening his eyes, the unfortunate man looked towards his Laird, attempted to repeat his previous blessing, gave up, and went back to sleep.

When the Candidate's answer finally came it was loud, clear and emphatic.... *"I am opposed to such legalisation. In my opinion Young, it is an infringement of the individual liberty!"*

*"Wha's liberty?"* chorused young miners through their teeth.

But not all agreed! They were those who could be seen squirming in their seats, uncomfortable and embarrassed at the Laird being attacked thus. Looking towards the platform, hoping they would be identified, they shook their fists at the culprits and cheered as one of their number cried, *"Wha dae these twa ignorant louts think they are, speaking to their betters like that!"* Others although they said nothing, silently cheered Dave and Willie on.

Among the latter was the Dominie. Dave had not only been one of his best pupils but as his teacher he was proud of the fact that after leaving school at 12, using the Miners Library to read everything he could lay his hands, Dave had continued to educate himself.

Afraid things were getting out of hand, Sir Charles hastily closed the meeting. Together he and the Laird rose and marched back down the aisle to the accompaniment of their supporters chant, *"Gladstone Out- Wauchope In!"* But this was underpinned by a distinct hissing which gradually reached a crescendo as the two men reached the door. Hastily the front row rose and followed by the rest of the Unionist supporters hurried out. Only the Dominie remained behind. He hoped to speak to his former pupil. (This was the first time he had seen him since his family had been evicted for his father's Union activities and he had often wondered what had happened to his brothers).

Now there were only miners left in the Hall. Jumping on the platform, Dave yelled, *"Right men that's it! Ye've heard it frae the horse's mooth. Ye a' ken Broon the Miner's Agent went to Dalmeny Hoose where Gladstone is steying wi' Lord Roseberry. He sends you his assurance that the Liberals wull ficht fir an eight hoor day fir miners. Men, ye dinna need me tae tell ye tae vote wisely, the vote mony o' oor forebears gave their life fir. Vote Liberal! Aye oor vote can change history alricht- but no they wey the Laird wants it!"*

The election result was **Gladstone 5845 - Wauchope 5155.** Most miners were elated! But when Unionists learned from the newspapers that Wauchope had reduced Gladstone's majority from 4631 to 690, they claimed a moral victory. *"We should be congratulating the Colonel- it took courage to oppose the 'grand old man' of British politics and two years of dogged hard work to drastically cut his majority thus!"*

In the Miners Institute Reading Room Dave was studying the Newspapers. *"Listen to what the Scotsman is saying!"* he cried to the others. *"Remember this is the paper that has supported Wauchope thro' a' his campaign".*

*'If Colonel Wauchope had fallen and bowed before the eight hour idol, he would have been the Member of Parliament for Midlothian at this time!'*

*"Now lads there's a thocht! What was it oor Laird said about us influencing history? If only......"*

*"If nothing!"* interrupted Willie, *" The fact is, Wauchope didna win. Wauchope lost! and there's nane here wha's sorry. Three cheers .... hip, hip horray!"*

*"Talk fir yerself,"* yelled a wheezy middle aged miner sitting in the corner, *"Jist wait an' see what happens- I fir yin, trust the Laird tae ken better what's guid fir me an' mine, not the likes o' some o' ye!"*

*"Christ ye young yins, ye think ye ken it a'!"* shouted his angry companion as they made to leave. *"Ye open yer mooth an' let yer belly roar! Mark ma words, ye'll no get an eight hoor day. An' if Gladstone gets Hame Rule fir Ireland it wull be as the Laird says, the beginning o' the end o' the British Empire- then God help us a!"*

*"Dinna listen tae them!"* yelled Willie to the others *"They were not the only yins that did as*

the Menister telt them and voted fir their Laird- frightened Hell an' Damnation wid follow if they did'na!"

"An' what aboot the ithers, wha dinna fear fir their souls, but fir their jobs, an' did as the Colliery Manager telt them, an' voted fir their Laird!" asked another. "Weel, maybe that we can understand-especially men wi' families!" said Dave, "But maybe yin day even they'll see, that it disna mak sense tae form a Union tae fight the coal-owners, then send a coal-owner or yin o' his ilk tae Parliament tae mak the laws that governs oor lives and keep us where they want us!"

"Weel!" concluded Dave, "There's yin thing fir shair- frae noo on some o' us are marked men wi' the Company!"

Paraffin lamps flickering behind the curtains and smoke swirling from chimneys flung out a warm welcome, as families waited for the miners to come home from the pit. Down at the pit-head, the back shift, tired, wet and hungry, tramped up the incline and into the crisp moonlight night. But instead of the usual rush home to the hot bath waiting in front of the roaring fire and the supper simmering on the hob, they stopped to speak to the night shift, who were on their way down.

Sparra, a small nervous man, still panting from a fit of coughing, darted towards them and flinging wide his scrawny arms and appearing to cry to the moon, yelled excitedly, "God is guid. At last we've struck a Klondyke!" His voice trailed off as the effort proved too much and he doubled up coughing and spitting. "What the Hell's wrang wi' this gowk?" cried Lonie, a great, dim witted, hulk of a man. Stopping, he pushed back his bonnet, scratched his bald head, and looking down at Sparra, enquired of the others, "Is he fu' or something? Weel it maks a change, He's a greetin' face git at the best o' times!" Tam, Lonie's mate, shrugged his shoulders as he cried out laughingly, "It's the full moon Lonie! It affects some puir critures like that! They canna help it!"

Young Ginge, who fancied himself the village ram and was renowned for his one track mind, shouted, "Oh he's shairly on a promise- lucky him!" This was greeted with loud laughter by all except Lonie, who impatiently barked, "Will some bastard tell me what's gang on?"

"Aw, yer jealous!" retorted Ginge, "Yer luck's never in, is it Lonie?- yer arse is ei oot the winda!" Lonie, who by this time was purple with rage, angrily raised his fists and making a lunge at Ginge, yelled "Shut yer face- I've warned ye afore!" Tam in an effort to calm his mate, roughly pushed Ginge out of the way saying "Come on Lonie, he's nae worth it!... Look there's the Penny Lawyer- let's ask him. He has mare sense that the rest of these ignorant buggars pu' thegither!"

Dave Young, as well as being an active Trade Unionist, helped people with the reading and writing of their letters or deciphering and filling in official forms. When postage was required, a penny was left for the stamp- hence the nickname, 'The Penny Lawyer'. For three years after his family had been evicted for his father's part in a strike, Dave's family had been homeless. They were split up and lived with relatives and friends, or where they could. It nearly destroyed his mother and had a lasting effect on them all. As a result, Dave, the youngest member of the family, was the only brother to follow in his Father's footsteps and live out his life as a miner in Scotland. The others had had enough. They emigrated, taking their skills to the American coalfields. Dave stayed on to be with his mother who was by then a widow. For years now, he had followed in his father's footsteps, playing an active role in the local Trade Union Branch and when he was elected as their delegate to The Miners' Federation of Great Britain realised a life-long ambition. Now married to Kate, of late they had become increasingly interested in the fast growing Co-operative Movement and had been involved in establishing a Co-operative Store in the village. This was a great step forward, freeing the miner and his family from the claws of Company owned truck shops with their spiral of debts. People were now, not only able to buy the necessities of life at a fair price, but as shareholders they collected a twice yearly dividend. Surplus profits made by the Co-op after that were used for the benefit the community.

Down the pit Dave worked hard and became an efficient and committed miner. His average weekly wage at that time was four shillings a day. Through his Union he was involved in fighting for a better and a set wage, an eight hour day, proper compensation for injury, and much needed improved safety measures. In common with his brothers, he had been trained by his father to become a highly skilled picksman. As a result of his rigorous apprenticeship, he was ambidextrous, could shovel with either hand and use the pick, lying first on one shoulder then on the other. In was a pleasure to watch him working. The steady beat of his hand pick was a work of art. The skill and the pride Dave displayed in his craft, gained for him, not only the respect of his fellow miners, but grudgingly, of many of the Company bosses.

By now Dave was living with his wife and children in Third Avenue, Newcraighall- one of the dreary featureless two roomed houses built in monotonous rows by the Company a decade before. Each house had an outside dry lavatory and the family carried their water from a communal street tap. There were no roads or pathways. The result was the houses were more often than not marroned by a sea of mud. The other great passion in Dave and Willie's lives was studying the works of Robert Burns -'Scotland's People's Poet' he called him.

So on that moonlit night in 1897, when the rest of the men heard him about to answer Tam's enquiry they stopped and gathered round, anxious to hear his verdict on the first day's work in a new incline pit the Company had sunk at the west side of the village. In his usual quiet manner Dave was saying with a grin, *"Weel we a' ken that Sparra is given tae exaggeration, but this time he jist maun be richt! Wha kens! At first sicht it looks as if we micht- jist micht- in this the year o' the American Gold Rush hae struck oor ain Klondyke here in Newcraighall!"*

Willie, jumping on to the wall and hauling Dave up after him, yelled excitedly, *"Men jist wait till yer lamp lichts up the new seam fir the first time. Ye'll gawp! Its a sicht fir sair e'en!"* His eyes danced as he flung wide his arms proclaiming, *"Aye it's jist like an Aladdin's cave doon there in the bowels o' the earth. Black shinin' coal- the like ye've ne'er seen afore- sparklin' like diamonds in the pit dark. Black Band they ca' it".*

"Aye! an' grand coal it is at that!" shouted Doddie the boilerman "Burns tae a fine ash, wi' nae waste intae the bargain.....Bodes weel fir this village- oor troubles could weel be o'er- eh Dave?"

Dave paused for a minute before replying, "Weel, it could be a new era if the Company were tae play fair wi' us. An' why not?- they'll mak a fortune. Their markets are assured noo that Britain supplies nearly 80% o' the world's coal!"

"Aye" interjected Willie, "an' we a' ken fine they hav'na invested six thousand pounds in puttin' the biggest steam engine in Scotland in fir nae return!" "An'" said Dave, " they tell us this seam o' coal is the biggest and best in Scotland today and that it could last fir three hundred years an' mare!

"Three hundred years!" the cry went up. "Imagine that! That's work weel inta the 22nd Century!" As the excitement gathered momentum, comments from the crowd came fast and furious as they yelled, "It could mean nae mare short-time or gang idle fir want o' work!"

"An' maybe noo we'll be seen as craftsmen and get a set livin' wage!"

"Aye! an' maybe oor sons, wha hud tae leave hame tae find work, wull can come back!"

"Aye! an' idle miners no only in Niddry but elsewhere in Scotland where pits are closing doon, wull can come here an' join in Newcraighall's black gold rush!"

"Aye there'll be plenty work fir a'!"

"An' maybe noo, we'll be able tae gie oor bairns some o' the things we ne'er had!"

"Like a decent education fir a start! Not yin that fits them fir the pits an' nathin' else!"

Sparra now sitting on his hunkers, looked exhausted and drained under his grime, as he feebly piped up, "An' maybe there'll be something ither than the Puirhoose or the Parish fir oor wedows an' bairns, when they hae tae get oot their tied hooses when we dee!" Jock, proud Father of twelve, yelled "An' maybe noo we'll get decent hooses, big enough tae bring up oor families in!"

"Aye! wi' an inside tap maybe, an' an inside water closet as well yin day!" shouted another. "Aye wha kens! We micht e'en get gas in the hoose.

"Aye, an' that'll be the day!

"An' why naw? Aft'r a', fir years here in Newcraighall we've howked the cannel coal that maks the gas."

"Aye" retorted Dave, "An' noo when it looks as if the bottom's gang tae drop' oot o' the cannel market wi' the invention o' the incandescent mantle- this Klondyke could'na hae come at a better time!"

"Dave! Dae ye think the time has come, when the miner wull tak his richtfu' place in Society?" asked an old miner from the back of the crowd.

"Hud on- dinna get cerried awa!" cautioned Dave. "Dinna count yer chickens afore they're hatched. If the past is onything tae gang by then we'll hae tae ficht every inch o' the wey. We're still fichtin' fir the eight hoor day promised by Gladstone remember! Promises, promises! that is a' we e'er get so let's ca' canny! Let's wait an' see what promise the black band brings! Dinna forget that maist o' the progress made these last years, as been got by miners ain united efforts an' sacrifice, a' done in the name of brothering. The results are we noo hae oor Union, an' Federation,[5] Oor Miners' Club an' Library, Bowling Club and noo oor ain Co-operative Store".

"And" piped up a Kirk Elder, "Dinna forget that we noo hae a Kirk and a Church and Dalrymple frae Newhailes has promised us land fir a new bowling green!" With that, the voice of "Hallelujah Joe" cried, "Hallelujah. God is guid- his licht shines upon this village this nicht! We should a' get doon on oor knees and thank Him fir gieing' us a Klondyke! Hallelujah!" Geordie, making a move to go shouted, "Come on lads, its gettin' late- let's gang an' brek the guid news tae the wemoenfolk. I ken what ma Missus wull want frae a Klondyke- pit baths- then she'll no hae tae wash ma back or choke on stinking sulphur fumes frae wet pit claithes drying roond the fire!" As they reached the gate a startled cat darted across their path, dropping a mouse from its mouth as it ran.

"Look lads! A black cat!" yelled Geordie "A guid omen- its guid luck "

"A black cat promising luck- an' black gold promising what?" shouted Willie as he nimbly leapt from the wall. With that a spontaneous cheer went up from the Back Shift as the men followed Geordie through the gate into the incline. Few cast a backward glance at Sparra, who, by now was sitting holding his head between his knees. Dave jumped from the wall, bent down, picked up the frightened mouse and carrying it to where Sparra was now squatting and spitting up blood after a bout of coughing said, "Sparra! are ye a'richt? Jist tak yer time an' get yer breath back. We'll walk ye hame!"

Sparra nodded and with a grateful smile mumbled, "Ta!"

As Dave sat on his hunkers quietly waiting beside the sick man, he stared at the mouse now starting to recover from its ordeal. After a while he said "Willie remember what Robert Burns said aboot promised joy tae the wee moose he turned up with his plough?" Cupping the mouse in his hand he quietly recited to it.

> But mousie, thou art no they lane,
>
> In proving foresight may be vain
>
> The best laid schemes o' mice and men
>
> Gang aft agley
>
> An leave us nought but grief and pain
>
> For promised joy.

As he finished, gently he let it go and watched it scuttle into the dark as he helped Sparra to his feet. Taking an arm each as they said, "Tak yer time!" the two men, walking slowly, carefully propelled their friend through the gate, stopping every few minutes to rest, and all the time trying to distract Sparra by talking about the Bard, whom they knew he also greatly revered.

As they rested Sparra panted as he mumbled "Dave the Bard kent poverty, but he also telt us where tae look for the real gold!

"*Aye he did that Sparra!*" said Dave,

> *Is there fir honest poverty*
>
> *That things his head an a' that*
>
> *The coward slave, we pass him by*
>
> *We dare be puir fir a' that*
>
> *Our toils obscure an' a' that*
>
> *The rank is but the guinea stamp,*
>
> *The man's the gowd for a' that.*

"*An' Sparra,*" went on Dave, "*He also left us yesterday prayer fir tomorrow's dream!*"

> *Then let's us pray, that come it may*
>
> *(As come it will for a' that)*
>
> *That sense and worth o'er a' the earth*
>
> *Shall bear the gree an' a' that*
>
> *That man to man the world o'er*
>
> *Shall brithers be for a' that.*"

"*Aye*" said Dave, "*Withoot sic hope... an' vision, man must surly perish!*" After a pause he went on, "*An' wha kens- maybe the Guid Lord's promise o' 300 years o' Klondyke, is tae gie us time tae find oor ain gowd at the end o' oor rainboo!*"

"*Hame at last Sparra!*" they cried as they reached his house. They handed him over to his wife who helped him struggle up the outside staircase. Reaching the top step, while gasping for breath Sparra stopped and watching his two friends disappear into the shadows he smiled and murmured to the night, "*Guid Nicht.... Brithers!*"

## CHAPTER 15 **BUNS AND BROTHERHOOD**

The grim and hungry nineteen thirties arrived. Although Niddrie's ancient Mill had long since disappeared from the banks of the burn, a red-bricked school, proudly bearing its name, stood on the opposite bank.

It was autumn. In the Hall the school had assembled for a carefully rehearsed annual event. Excited pupils rose and stood to attention as the headmaster, followed by a sombre lady dressed from head to foot in black mounted the platform. This was Mrs Wauchope come on her annual pilgrimage.

Most of the children, though shabby, were neat and tidy. Closer inspection would have revealed that there were some with bow legs; others had the backside hanging out of their trousers and had no shoes on their feet. Others wore heavy 'Parish' boots punched with five holes, warning their parents not to pawn these boots! On receiving the customary bag of buns from their benefactor, as instructed the boys saluted smartly while the girls lowered their eyes and shyly curtsied as they said *"Thank you Mam!"*

But when it came to the turn of an auburn haired girl, dressed in a thin, shrunken woollen jumper, worn beneath a greying white cotton dress it seemed she was having difficulty getting her leg to bend and her head to bob. Instead she defiantly looked the old lady straight in the face, hesitated, then silently walked away.

Jessie Young came from Newcraighall. After just managing to scrape through her Qualifying Examination that year she had been transferred to Niddry Mill School to complete two years of secondary education. Originally pupils came from the Jewel and Newcraighall mining villages as well as Niddry Estate, but since 1931, there had been a growing number of children coming from a new Public Housing Estate, being built on what had been Niddrie Mains, the Wauchope Home Farm.

Jessie was happy at her new school and made many friends. Perhaps she did not learn as much as her grandfather, Dave Young, would have wished, but it was a caring school where her many absences were tolerated. As her mother was dead, Jessie was often kept from school to look after her brothers when they were ill or when she would take them with her to the "tattie howking" to help supplement the meagre family income. Her father was on short-time, working one day on, and one day off at the Klondyke, where he earned eight shillings and ninepence a shift. This meant his weekly wage was below what Public Assistance allowed as relief benefit. But as he was in work there was no way his wage would be supplemented, so the young Jessie knew what it meant to live from hand to mouth. Still, Jessie fancied herself too proud to accept a hand out of buns from the lady 'fra the big hoose'. But she knew only too well what retribution she would get from the Headmaster if she refused them!

Although she liked most of the teachers at school, there were some she feared, particularly those who enforced the rule of law by belting pupils on the palms of their hands with a vicious strip of narrow leather called the taws. Her other dread, was the Tartar~ a screaming female, whose screeching voice could be heard by passers-by outside the school, as she showered scorn on her pupils in an effort, as she put it *"To teach these children the Kings' English."* For years Jessie would blush with shame when she recalled the day she fell foul of that malicious tongue. Over the years, although her brain was to erase the question asked by the teacher, the answer she gave, was for all time, indelibly scratched on her memory. It was, *"Soor dook Miss!"*

*"Soor dook"!"* screeched the 'Tartar' with a sneer. *"S o o r  d o o k! What do you mean girl? Such words are not in the Oxford Dictionary! Say it in English!"* Jessie's mind went blank. Her heart raced as she stood frantically groping around in her mind to find the answer, but all she could think of, was the penny worth she bought daily from the "soor dook cairt" With every eye on the class focused on her, and wishing the floor would swallow her up, she cringed with shame, as the jeering voice demanded of the class. *"Boys and girls, tell this illiterate girl the words in English!"* Well aware of being one of the shabbiest in her class she was at that moment convinced she was the stupidest and bowed her head in shame as voices from the back row, without hesitation sang out the correct answer. For her sin, Jessie had

to stay behind after class and using slate-pencil scratch in capitals, one hundred times on her slate- *sour milk*.

But there were other teachers, like the gentle Mr. Brown, whose voice never rose in anger, yet who instilled in many a pupil a desire to learn and gave them more than he ever realised. His gifts to Jessie included a life long love of the works of Robert Burns. Indeed, Jessie's only claim to fame was that she won a Burns Prize, an award, the Newcraighall Miners' Poosie Nancy Club donated annually to the two village schools. Many of Mr. Brown's boys grew up to become enthusiastic and knowledgeable members of 'The Poosie Nancy'. But alas, Jessie was destined never to enter its hallowed doors. Since the Club's inception by the miners in 1920 its rule was- men only!

While at Niddrie Mill there was only one task Jessie ever coveted. At that time the school kept a Daily Weather Chart. Like many other pupils in the school, she longed to be a member of that elite league who occupied the back row in class and whose high marks, bestowed on them the honour of becoming a Weather Chart Recorder. Jessie's marks never merited such esteem. All her School Report ever showed was 'Good' adding, *'Jessie talks too much!'* When her granny read it, her only comment was, "*I'm nae surprised- vaccinated wi' the gramophone needle, wis oor Jessie- an' misses naethin' intae the bargain!*"

So each morning, her granddaughter would wistfully watch, as four of the 'top' pupils would take up their stance on the banks of Niddrie burn. There, looking and feeling extremely superior, they would solemnly study the shining old weather-cock on top of the school tower, then record on their slates the direction of the wind. Carefully using the school thermometer, they would proceed to record the temperature in the sun. After which they would vanish beneath the bridge- supposedly to take the temperature in the shade. Judging by the giggles, squeals of laughter and tales told afterwards in the playground, what went on was totally unrelated to any weather chart. But many a romance had its roots under that bridge. But for Jessie and other aspiring recorders, there was always playtime as consolation…

Now Niddrie Mill was unique among schools. It possessed something no other school had, or may ever have again. Standing just inside its gate, in all its glory, was a formidable iron cannon. Originally from Germany it had been captured during the Great War. So, rain, snow or shine Jessie would join the mad race to be first in the line forming up behind the cannon. Nimbly climbing on to its wheel, with arms flung wide, eyes closed tight, she would relax her body and with a squeal of pure delight and gay abandon, gracefully slide down the rim, which shone like silver, polished by the seats of countless children down the years. Reaching the ground, she'd race back to re-join the end of the fast moving line of yelling children as they sped up and over, up and over. Never mind what it did to the already threadbare trousers or navy blue school knickers- especially if it had been raining. Who cared, if it meant sitting shivering on a wet bum until dinner-time; a small price to pay for a taste of Heaven!

Now Jessie may not have shone at school, but she loved living. While her alert ears missed nothing, her twinkling brown eyes eagerly devoured the world around her, aided and abetted in no small measure, by her aging grandfather, Dave Young.

One of the great pleasures in her life was to accompany him as he tramped the countryside with his aged whippet, Jipp. She knew some folk said he lived in the past but she never tired of hearing of the days, when as a militant Trade Unionist, and later as a member of the Labour Party and the Co-operative Movement he battled with company bosses and politicians over pay, compensation and safety measures. A quiet spoken man most times, sometimes she found it hard to imagine him taking on these daunting giants.

*"Nae use saying ye hae principles lass,"* he would quietly tell her *"unless ye're prepared to live by them, ficht for them~ an' if necessary dee fir them!"* And she knew from the stories her granny told her of the past that in the end, he, and many other mining comrades who had lived by their brothering principles, paid dearly for them. By the time she was twelve she already knew that to be a militant Trade Unionist in the Klondyke, or in the Woolmet, the Company's other pit, was fraught with perils unconnected with digging coal. Miners who dared to stand and fight for their rights, did so in the knowledge that they put their families future in jeopardy.

She never tired of hearing the story of the three years of misery her grandfather's family had spent after they were evicted from Whitehill Street. She had also seen with her own eyes two families of active Trade Unionists suffer the same fate. She watched horrified as bailiffs and police flung their few sticks of furniture into the streets one frosty January day. As they did so one of the weeping wives, with five children at her skirts, clutched her howling month old baby to her bosum.

The two fathers, one of whom was a Workman's Inspector, were down the pit making an inspection. He had been appointed to the post by a ballot of the men, whose weekly subscriptions paid his wage. The campaign to appoint these Inspectors met with bitter opposition from the coal-owners, with police being brought in to intimidate the men. Two months before, the miners at Klondyke had staged a three day strike to prevent the victimisation of their Inspector who was being threatened with eviction. Now the threat had been carried out.

Sometimes when out walking along the dyke-side on the Wisp Brae, Jess and her Grandfather would come to No 12 and 13 pits lying dead and desolate. *"Aye!"* he would wistfully say, *"Here I met ma Waterloo!"*

He had worked at the Wisp Pit until the General Strike in 1926 when the miners came out protesting against a cut in their wages and the sweeping away of the minimum wage. The average earnings at that time was between £1. 8s to £2 a week. Although only six years of age at the time there were many things Jessie would remember all her life about the General Strike. Like watching her father, grandfather and others join Hunger Marchers, as they walked through the village on their way to London. Or the many times there was no food in the house and the family went to bed hungry. She would lie awake hearing her mother sob as she held a crying babe to her empty breast. It seemed to the six year old that the whole world was against them. Never more so than one summer evening when she and other children were happily sliding down the bing on a piece of old corrugated iron. Suddenly a group of Special Constables had swooped down on the village. A miner grabbed the terrified children, raced them up the road and bundled them into the first house they came to. He had to stay there: trapped. He was in danger of being arrested, as a curfew had been imposed on the village. During the seven months the miners were out, the Wisp pits flooded. The Strike ended with the men having to accept the wage cut and an increase in working hours. The Company took a decision not to re-open their Wisp pits. This left only two pits operating in the Niddrie area- the Woolmet and the Klondyke.

*"Alricht!"* Dave would say, *"I kent I had only a few workin' years left, but that was lang enough fir the Company tae get their revenge. Me an' ither strike leaders were telt 'Nae job fir ye in any o' oor pits!' Mind ye, I had worked o'er forty five years wi' them. Twenty five o' them in the Klondyke! Weel I suppose I should thank the Lord that at least I survived tae work that lang. No like young Tam, Willie's youngest!"* Tam, a young miner during the First World War, had taken the King's Shilling and gone to fight for his country. Gassed at the Somme he returned home to face years of ill health, resulting in him never being able to work in a pit again.

One wet afternoon Jessie stood with her grandfather and uncles outside a house in Niddrie Mains as Tam's coffin, draped in a Union Jack, was lifted on to a hand cart. His red eyed widow and four children stood weeping in the pouring rain, as they watched the body of the War Hero, being pushed through the streets, on his way to lie in a pauper's grave. As the cart moved off, men in the crowd removed their bonnets and bowed their heads. As it passed, someone cried out bitterly,

*Aye Tam,*

*Yer King an' country needed ye*

*Tae ficht on foreign soil,*

*But did yer King an' country need ye,*

*When they shared oot the spoil.*

So that autumn day in 1932, as Jessie stuffed the bag of buns into her tin case- the case her Grandfather had bought for sixpence from Woolworths for her twelfth birthday she thought of him and his "brothering principles". Then she thought about the old lady who had given her the buns and who somehow was not as she had imagined. Not that she ever thought Mrs Wauchope would look like a real Lady- Jessie knew better than that. Although most of the villagers referred to her as 'Lady Wauchope', she had heard her Grandfather quietly correct them many times saying, *"She's not Lady Wauchope, just plain Mrs, wedow o' Major General Andrew Wauchope!"* Depending on the mood he was in he would sometimes add, *"Aye!, and the last o' the line o' the coal oppressors o' Niddrie, wha even tae this day, get six pence royalties fir every ton of coal howked frae beneath her land!"* And if he happened to be near one of the many Miners' Union's 'Two Bob' posters displayed throughout the villages, he would point to it and say. *"Aye! six pennies fir every ton, at a time when the miner wha risks his life tae howk the coal, is fichtin' fir a rise o' twa shillings a day on his shift".*

As she left the school gate, Jessie thought to herself, 'Lady or Mrs- what's does it matter! She's jist a sad auld biddy wi' deed e'en! Then, for the first time since she had been at that school, she decided to stop and read the words on a monument which stood in front of the building. *'In memory of Major General Andrew Wauchope, killed at Magersfonteins in the Boer War in 1899- Erected by the tenants and miners.' "Aye!"* she thought, *"That's her man, puir auld soul, nae wonder she's sad. Its a lang time tae be a wedow- an her wi' nae bairns!"*

Acting on a sudden impulse, instead of going home, she crossed Niddrie Mains Road, ankle deep in fallen leaves from the estate trees. Haunted by the face of the old lady she wandered along the side of the estate dyke. Kicking the leaves as she walked, she thought of her own mother, dead these three years and her eyes filled with tears as she felt again the awful emptiness well up inside. She missed her so much! She thought of the terrible times she had during the General Strike. How with other women she had helped run the soup kitchen in the Church. How they pooled what little they had. Then when there was no money at all coming in and the family was destitute she, in desperation, had pawned everything, from her wedding china to her wedding ring. Saying as she pulled it from her finger, *"What dae I want wey a ring onywey, when I still hae ma man an' ma bairns!"*

Gazing up at the high wall as she walked along, Jessie was suddenly struck with a chilling thought, *"Maybe sometimes when I wake up in the night greetin' fir ma Mither, o'er this dyke in her big hoose this lonely auld biddy is lying greetin' tae. But I'm lucky I can cuddle intae ma brithers when the pain gets bad - what does she dae?"* Then she thought of her Granny, now bedridden, and of the women in the village who rallied round to help. Although worn out by hard work, poverty and suffering they could always be relied upon to help one another in time of need, to see a funny side to life and to make each other laugh.

At New Year the whole village would forget their worries. Going from house to house 'first footing', wishing each other *"A Guid New Year"* and then they would dance the whole night through- while some would dream the poor man's dream~ that this just might be the year the football coupon would come up and their troubles would be over. Thinking about the New Year, the annual Gala, the Penny Concerts and the Sunday School Treats, Jessie cheered up. Kicking the leaves in the air, she danced along pretending she was dancing in the streets, as she had done so often with her mother and others, to the music of the village accordion players. By the time she reached the massive iron gates of Niddrie Marischal Mansion they were securely locked for the night- Mrs Wauchope having returned from her annual visit to the school.

Jessie, thinking that she might get a glance of her, or the 'Big Hoose' she had heard so much aboot, but never seen, placed her tin case on the ground and standing on it, hoisted herself up on to the gate. Stretching her neck, she was disappointed. All she could see was trees. Then just as she was about to climb higher, something banged against the gate and she screamed as her face was licked by something wet, warm and panting. In her terror she let go and clattered to the ground to find herself looking up into the face of an enormous snarling dog, straining to get at her from the other side of the gate. Grabbing the case she made to run, but in her haste she fell. The case burst open, scattering the buns over the pavement. Quick as a flash she stooped down, picked them up, stuffed them back as best she could and fled across the road. Once safely on the other side, she fastened the case and as she looked down was horrified to see a trickle of blood running down her leg from a gaping hole in the knee of the black school stockings her granny had laboriously knitted for her. White faced, she stood staring down at the hole, muttering to herself, *"Oh, what wull I dae? Granny wull be mad!"* Deciding there was nothing she could do but cross that bridge when she came to it, she wiped the blood with the hem of her dress and quickly started off towards home.

First she had to pass the housing estate where only a week before her cousins had proudly moved into a brand new house and where already the groups of dejected looking unemployed men hanging aimlessly around the street corners were being accepted as part of everyday life. After leaving the now deserted school behind, crinkling her nose as she passed the piggery she stopped for a minute to talk to a friend who was filling a bucket at the communal street tap. Passing the joiner's yard she spied a piece of wood lying on the ground. Making sure no one saw her, she picked it up thinking it would kindle the fire when she got home. Up past the Quarry Cottages she hurried. She didn't mind having to wait at the level crossing till the coal train steamed passed; it meant she could swing on the gate as it slowly closed behind it. Rounding the corner at St Andrew's Church she put two fingers to her mouth to whistle to her cousin, Jim working in the busy brickworks opposite.

The road to the village now lay straight ahead. Beside it for almost an eighth of a mile stretched the bing- the burning bing. That long hillock of waste spewed up daily from the pit and now, an ever growing, festering carbuncle, blighting the face of the countryside. Reaching its end she stopped for breath at the pit gate and stood watching, fascinated as ever, by the great whirling pit wheel which drove the cage filled with miners deep down into the bowels of the earth. Its return brought up the tubs of coal. She thought of her father who that afternoon, after leaving the cage, would have walked two miles and would now be working at the 'sea dook' under the River Forth. Refreshed, she finished the last lap by running non-stop under the Railway Bridge, down Main Avenue, along Third Avenue then stopped. Pulling her dress over the hole in her stocking, she shuffled into her grandparents's house, where she knew her two brothers would be waiting for her to take them home.

There in the kitchen she found Jipp lying stretched out before the fire. Her eyes lit up when she saw her youngest brother sitting on the end of the box bed. Stretched tightly between his outstreched hands was the back of an old red jumper. Granny, propped up by pillows and obviously in pain was carefully unravelling the wool and winding it into a tight ball.

"Oh Granny!" she cried excitedly, "ye've got a red yin- its bonny- red's ma favourite colour!" Granny was putting into practise the message she was always ramming home to her family. "Use what ye hae and ye'll never want!" The jumper had been bought by her daughter at a jumble sale. Tonight she would take away the rolled up balls of wool, rewind them into loose skenes, wash them, then return them to Granny who would knit Jessie a jumper. "What's that I see?" asked Granny, glaring from behind her sixpenny Woolworth's glasses at the gaping hole in the stocking, which Jessie in her excitement was no longer hiding. "Richt ma lass, from noo on ye dae yer ain knitting. I'll show ye hoo. Then ye micht tak care o' what ye have!" Nonplused Jessie made to leave for home taking her brothers with her. Her head was in the clouds as already in her mind's eye she was sporting a new scarlet jumper at school. But the voice from the bed brought her back to earth, "Dinna forget to tak the marra bone frae the scullery, an' ye limmer- dinna burn the soup. Yer Faither micht hae vegetables in his allotment, but that's nae tae say ye can waste them!"

That night with her brothers in bed replete after having devoured the bag of buns with gusto and no inhibitions whatsoever, her father's supper simmering on the hob and two kettles of water ready for his bath boiling away, Jessie at last sat down to attempt to darn the stocking. She hated darning, or sewing for that matter, but knew needs must! Anyway this was Thursday, the night her Aunt came over from Niddrie to sit with Granny, and let Grandfather out for his weekly dram at the Miners Institute. On his way home he would look in to say goodnight. Jess loved these Thursday nights, especially when her father was on the Back Shift and she would get Grandfather all to herself. So she smiled at the sound of the latch being lifted and his cheery voice cry "Everything alricht lass?"

As usual, he first went into the bedroom to talk 'men's talk' with his grandsons. Like most of the young lads in the village they were 'Fitba' mad' and had only one real ambition in life. That was to grow up and play football for their village and be in a team that could repeat the famous and unforgettable win of 1927/28 when Newcraighall village team~ the famous Niddrie Thistle had won six cups and a shield as well as bringing home the East of Scotland Cup. Coming back into the kitchen, Dave said, "My, but that supper smells guid!" Lifting the lids he took a good sniff then grinned saying, "Dinna tell me ? Let me guess! Tattie Soup an' stovies!- weel stovies wi' an Oxo cube an' nae sausages. Jist the marrow scraped oot the bone tae gie some taste. But never mind! Granny and me wull enjoy oor share tomorra jist the same!" Turning the gas mantle down to a peep, he sat down in the old easy chair in front of the gentle fire, lay back and lazily lit his clay pipe.

Watching him, Jessie wondered how to begin telling him about her day. She knew he would understood why she could not bring herself to bend the knee, far less eat the buns. She was not so sure of his reaction to her feelings about the Lady Bountiful. She decided to omit that part, but somehow while telling the story of the buns, before she could stop herself, out it came. Her freckled face flushed scarlet, abruptly she stopped talking and pretending to concentrate on the darning, waited anxiously for his reaction. It was a long time coming. He just sat there sucking his clay pipe, keeping her in suspense.

"*Aye!*" he said at last, "*puir auld soul! Of course yer lassie's heert wid go oot tae her, and why no? She maun be lonely. O'er thirty years is a lang time tae live alane wi' neether her man nor a bairn!*" There was another long silence before he went on sadly, "*A'richt, God in His wisdom, saw fit tae tak oor dochter, yer mither frae us, but every time Granny an' me look at ye, ma bonny lass, we see oor Jean. The Guid Lord didna bestow on Jean Wauchope sic a blessin'!*" As he sat thinking and staring into the fire, his pipe went out. Taking his knife from his waistcoat pocket he scraped out the barrel, knocked the ash into the fire, filled the barrel with tobacco, relit it, sucked it, then went on. "*Aye I weel remember cousin Lizzie wha was 'in service' at the Big Hoose, tellin us, hoo she often heard her Mistress, Wauchope's second wife, jist married six years they were, greetin' as if her heert wid brek, an' talking to a faded red heckle she kept by her bed. They say, afore the Major General went awa tae the Boer War, he took it frae his Glengarry an' telt her tae keep it always, in memory of him. They say he kent he wid ne'er cam back! Oor Lizzie's heert went oot tae her- she wanted tae go in an' comfort her, as only anither wemen can, but she couldna, she wis jist the servant. Aye! Jist a servant!*"

Giving the fire a poke he lay back and after another long comfortable silence, relaxed by the baccy in his pipe, warmed by the fire and no doubt by the more than one 'wee dram' consumed earlier at the Institute, it was as if the fire in his belly rekindled. It was at times like these that, as his granddaughter watched and listened enthralled she would picture the fiery, red haired young miner, standing on his soap box at the pit head, urging his fellow miners to stand up and fight for their rights.

"*Aye!*" he said, addressing an imaginary audience in the flames, "*Today we're witnessing the end o' an era. Fir o'er six centuries, the star o' the Wauchopes, fuelled by wealth and power, soared thro' the heavens, lording it o'er the lands of Niddry, only tae burn itself' oot- leaving what? Scant trace of its once prood heritage! Ony street names, a graveyard, an' a monument, standing sentinel o'er his high stane dyke, the dyke built to keep their serfs at bay in their slave villages. And that monument erected, not by his Queen and Country, wha wi' sic pomp hailed him a national hero an' mourned him throughout the Kingdom, but by miners and tenants. Payin' their respects and leaving for posterity, a record of the place Major General Andrew Wauchope earned in history, as a soldier, defending the greatest Empire the world has ever known! The same Empire, whose rulers cares naught fir the lot of those wha labour produces the wealth and power that has made it, and him, great!*

*But in the end, like us a', Andrew Gilbert Wauchope was but mortal. He died leaving his young bairnless wedow to live out o'er thirty years o' solitude in their majestic mansion, kennin' fine that the Dynasty wis doomed tae dee. The only surviving bairn, by his first marriage, puir wee Andrew Wauchope, wis sick in the heed- an' could ne'er inherit. So what, ye may ask, will the House o' Wauchope bequeath to those o' us whas' toil an' sufferin' gave them an' their ilk vast riches an' power? Those whose blood watered the tree o' liberty. Naught! Naught but a legacy o' poverty an struggle, that's far frae o'er!*"

Then after another long pause, when his granddaughter seeing his eyes close assumed he had nodded off to sleep, he suddenly smiled and looking at her said, "*But never fear lass, the dyke, that great divide, like the walls of Jericho wull come tumbling doon, stormed by the descendants of his serfs. Wha, if they proodly cairry their mining banner an' live by its principles of brothering for yin inither in sickness and in health they could, yin day, recreate a Garden o' Eden fir a'!*"

## CHAPTER 16 **A RETURN**

Nearly a hundred years has come and gone since Wauchope's defeat at the hands of the Newcraighall miners. On the Village Green, where the youthful Dave Young stood on his soap-box rousing the miners to vote against their Laird, a crew-cut teenager wearing tartan trews and a teeshirt stands looking up at an eight foot high limestone sculpture. *"What's this Gran- a modern standing stone?"* he asks the smartly dressed, grey haired woman, climbing out of a car beside him. *"I guess you could call it that Andy!"* she replies, *"But this monument, dedicated to the community spirit of the mining families, takes no chances with it's message being lost in time. The carvings tell the social history of this part of the Lothians for over six centuries"*. A group of children playing on the Green heard them and promptly offered a running commentary. Starting with the fossil, they explained each relief in detail. The miner working in the narrow coal-seam; his house in the miners' row, the tools of his trade; the pick, shovel, water-bottle and coal-cutting machine, plus his hobbies; pigeons, greyhounds and fishing.

*"Why a ladder?"* enquired Andy. *"Because up until last century women and children used to carry coal*

in creels on their back up them. We can tell you some of the names who carried them here in 1842 - Janet and Agnes Moffat, Agnes Johnston..." chorused the girls. "And!" chimed in the boys "Robert Thomson drove the pit pony and Alexander Gray was the Pump Boy! We know because we played them in the village Historical Pageant!" All talking excitedly at once, they told how their school and youth club helped to fill a Time Capsule and bury it beneath the monument! How they helped collect everyday things in use today as well local mining history from mediaeval times to the victory that saved the village from the bull-dozer after the Klondyke Pit closed in 1968. "Hundreds and hundred of years from now, when it is dug up, we'll be remembered along with the lads and lassies o' long ago! Do you know how we know that? Because in it is the name of every single person living in the village the day it was buried!"

"Tell you what!" said the woman "Let me take a photograph of you standing with Andy beside the sculpture, then down under in Australia where we come from, you'll also be remembered!" What she did not add was that in her country she was a well-known TV journalist, broadcaster and writer.

As the couple left to stroll 'round the village and admire the modern houses, the lady was overheard to say "This must be a very desirable place to live and bring up a family! " Desirable it certainly is, but there is no mistaking it is still Newcraighall. The heart of the community is still there; The Kirk, the School, the Drinking Fountain, The Miners Club, the Bowling Club, the village Post Office/General Store, Park View and the old Whitehill Street cottages. Although the interiors are now modernised, outside they are as they were in 1828- traditional Scottish stone built cottages, with red pan-tiles, slatted doors and sash windows.

By now the couple were standing outside the cottage where Bess Young had started to write the story of the Niddrie coalbearers all those long years ago and where it is said, her spirit still lingers to this day. A sprightly silver haired man dressed in a white sweater and navy blazer, carrying a leather bowling bag, was coming towards them. In common with the villagers, he had become accustomed to visitors stopping to examine the sculpture and then walk round the village. About to give his usual welcoming nod and wish them "Guid day" he halted and stood open-mouthed as he heard the woman say, "Well Andy, this is it! This is the cottage from where, when he was your age, your great grandfather Dave Young's family was evicted for practising what he called 'their brothering principles'!'

An incredulous grin spread over the man's face as he exclaimed, "My God! The rusty pow micht hae lost its glow, but the e'en still glints an' ye're still vaccinated wi' the gramophone needle....Ye're Jessie Young!" For a moment Jessie was taken aback, then her eyes lit up in recognition as she cried "Oh Cousin Jim!." Hugging him tightly, then holding him at arm's length she laughed saying, "Let me look at you! Aye, still as good looking....and as gallus as ever!" Introducing her grandson, she told Jim "By a stroke of luck I was in Brussels when he 'phoned to say he was coming to Scotland to take part in a Folk Festival and could I meet up with him. So here I am proudly showing my grandson his Scottish heritage!"

"Having been brought up on a diet of Gran's Scottish politics, Scottish history and Robert Burns- I know a fair bit about it already!" retorted Andy. Jim suggested that they go to the Miners' Club, where they could meet some 'auld yins' who would help them catch up with the last 50 years of gossip. As they walked he pointed out old landmarks still there. Brunstane House and Walk-way, The old Wanton Wa's Farm House, the auld road and dyke, Newhailes Estate, the pigeon duckets and Kittle Macvie O'Bridge. Digging Andy in the ribs he sniggered as he said. "Aye Andy I bet yer Gran hasna' forgotten that brig- she used tae dae her coortin' there!"

Waiting to cross the busy main road Jim said with pride, "Nearly 20 years it has taken to get this village rebuilt as we wanted it. Talk aboot David taking on Goliath! It meant folk here takin' on the might o' Edinburgh Cooncil who had made up their minds there was no place for a working class village in their high falootin' cultural City. But nothing daunted we fought for the richt to hae a say in our future. Something unheard in snooty Edinburgh, until Jack Kane, a miner's son from these parts became the Corporation's one and only Labour Lord Provost ever! During Jack's four years in office we worked as partners wi' the authorities. For the ither years we had to fight every inch of the way, never letting up till we got the village the wey we wanted it. Mind ye- there are still folk wha are no pleased- but ye'll never please everybody!" As they approached the building which had once housed the Co-operative Store, Jessie's face fell as she exclaimed, "Oh Jim- where's the Store?".

"Gone!" he said, sadly shaking his head, "Today folk shop in the big supermarkets and ne'er stop tae think hoo that affects their community!... They've forgotten the power and benefits their Store gave them. So now there's nae profits tae recycle fir the good o' the community!"

"But," he went on, "the Miners' Social Club's profits still benefit the village. Aye withoot oor Club, there wid hae been nae heert tae ficht from. It wis the Club that paid fir the Feasibility Study for the Tenant's Association plans for redeveloping the village. Alricht, there are some wha say that now the Miners Club is only a social drinking club but they canna deny its profits are still used to promote village life. It helps the elderly, housebound, youth clubs, playschemes, holidays an a host o' ither activities as well." From the outside, the Club was just as Jessie remembered it- but inside it was transformed beyond recognition. No sawdust on the floor! No spittoons! Instead, wall to wall carpeting, a tastefully decorated function suite, a well equipped games room, a lounge, and around the walls of the modern dance hall a Scottish artist had created beautiful murals depicting the history of Coal Mining.

"And the Poosie Nancy Club?" enquired Jessie. "Still going strong!" said her cousin proudly "We celebrated oor half century in '71."

"Oor!" said Jessie with a grin "Dont tell me- still men only!"

Jim grinned, "Aye alricht! But nooadays the miner wears a collar and tie tae his Club and brings the wife. Many mining families wha left the village long ago, still come back regularly tae their Club. Miners visiting Edinburgh come here and only last weekend we had oor annual visit frae the Welsh Miners up for the Rugby at Murrayfield! In '84 the Club was a Strike Centre fir the members frae Monktonhall, one o' the few pits left in Scotland by then. You can see on this wall names of some o' the miners who suffered for their part in that Strike. Some went to jail, others lost their jobs. That strike was the worst in the mining history of this country. But it was also the strike where the miners' wives came into their own".

Leaving the Club, Jim invited Jessie and Andy to his home in Niddrie Marischal. With Jessie driving her hired car they left the village and as they drove through the tunnel she told her grandson how she used to walk that road to Niddrie Mill School. *"But now"* she sighed, *"no whirling wheels- no pit baths- all dead and gone!"* Unable to believe her eyes she cried out, **"No bing!"**

The burning bing of her childhood, that gigantic mountain of waste which had blighted the landscape- all gone- but where… and how? *"Aye Jessie, gone!"* said Jim *"But this is yin recycling job Grandfaither wid approve o'! Jist as Granny ripped doon auld jumpers tae knit us new yins - so, oor auld bing was ripped oot and carried, lorry load by lorry load, across the road, where modern technology used it tae build this great new motorway ye see there, that carries traffic hundreds o' miles doon tae the South of England into Europe and beyond!"*

As the car turned the corner Jim said with pride, *"See Jessie the brickworks may be away but oor St. Andrews' kirk lives on. It is noo an Arts Centre- where folk o' a' ages dae music, drama, art an' crafts, or as Granny wid say- were we can mak the most o' the gifts the guid Lord gies us a'"*

*"Aye Jim, but how she despaired o' me!"* said Jessie *"After a lot of sweat and tears she had to finally concede that the good Lord forgot me when he handed out knitting and needlework gifts!"* When they came to Niddrie Mill School Jessie stopped the car and stepping out, her face fell as she cried, *"Oh Jim! The Canon! It's gone!"*

*"Melted doon in 1940 tae help the War effort!"* was the reply. *"Aye"* she said wistfully, *"The war changed so many things for our generation Jim. Me! I was called up to the Forces and like thousands of other women was given responsibilities we would never have thought ourselves capable of. For the first time in our lives we found scope for the talents we never knew we had. Of course, it was in the forces that I met my Australian husband, after marrying him he took me back to his country, I had a son, went to college, was divorced, became a journalist, a granny and later a writer!"* Standing on the bridge looking down on the running stream she went on, *"Often Jim, on the other side of the world when my mining blood stirs in my veins and I feel the pull on my roots, I dream of this burn… the heart of auld Niddrie! Only it goes on forever! It was here long before the days when the Saxons came and marked the lands of Niddrey with their Standing Stone, whose message is long since forgotten. It has seen us all come and go. If it could talk, it would tell us, that things do not die, death just recycles and changes the nature of things!"*

Turning to her grandson she said *"Andy it is here that the roots of the Youngs and countless other collier families lie buried deep in the bowels of the land. Once this stream was the life blood of Niddrie, driving the two Mills which fed its hungry people- and providing water. Just look at it now, its no longer fit to drink but I'm sure it still gives pleasure to the few who make the time to stand and stare!*

*Alone it can bear witness to the long dark centuries when the lands of Niddrie shuddered as countless, powerless human beings, young and old, were forced underground to plunder Nature's bounty- for what Jim?"*

"To build a bastion of privilege for the few!" he replied without thinking. "And now," he went on, "the Wauchope Dynasty is no more! Their majestic Niddrie Marischal Mansion was burned to the ground by modern day vandals. The beautiful estate and gardens, is now a vast housing estate. Over 22,000 people live there, many struggling with all the social ills of modern life."

" I wonder Jim, how many among them know why parts of the estate bear the proud names of Cleekhim, Jewel, Hunters Hall and Niddrie? Few appreciate why it is that Newcraighall alone of all these old villages lives on. Or how it came about that in the barren coal-dust of centuries of suffering, sorrow and exploitation, a spirit of community flowered to spur the miner and his family to fight to preserve a living monument to the power of that spirit- their re-born village of Newcraighall!"

Returning to the car, before stepping in, Jessie gazed back once more at her old school as she said, "Oh well, this old red brick building, once our gateway of hope to a better life through education, still hugs the burn, and Major General Andrew Wauchope's Monument stands sentinel over what is left of his stane dyke- that great divide! But just as Grandfather said it would, in the fullness of time the great dyke too fell, stormed by descendants of the collier serf families and the countless other workers, who came from Edinburgh, bringing their culture, traditions, political beliefs and individual talents.

Take heed Andy, for here the spirit of community has re-emerged to embrace the whole community, as people learn to share and care for each other. Something you young folk need to be minded of".

"Jessie.....How do you know all this? asked Jim, who had stood open-mouthed listening to her.

"Fate I suppose!" she replied. " As a journalist and writer I became more and more frustrated at having to feed the public's appetite for sex, violence, greed and self-inflicted social destruction. I longed to write a screen-play showing the other side of life: survival through spiritual growth. I knew I could find financial backing. I suppose you could say I became obsessed with the idea, but I've been struggling to get a start on which to build a story. Then just as I was about to retire, an new director joined the Company and for the first time I found a soul-mate. He told me of an EEC Poverty Programme he had researched and suggested I go to Brussels to study it.

There I found what I had been looking for. Described as 'a real-life fairy story', the marvel was that it was happening in a most unlikely place- a deprived Scottish housing scheme suffering all the social ills of modern urban living. There, against great odds, for over twenty years, people had taken on the authorities and won the right to have a say in the shaping of their own destiny. Described as a marvelously eloquent hymn of hope, it gained world acclaim bringing people from many lands to study and take home a blueprint of what was being pioneered there. Fascinated I read on.

Then suddenly it rang a bell! Craigmillar! Was not that the name of housing estate built on the old Wauchope Estate, near the village where I grew up? I was amazed to read that one of the many successful campaigns was a twenty-year fight by Newcraighall villagers to keep their village alive. 'The village that refused to die' they called it! Isn't this a fine example of my grandparents brothering principles?"

"Before I had time to digest it fully, Andy phoned to say his band would now be touring Scotland. Could we meet up in Edinburgh? It was uncanny! Immediately I flew here and used the week before he arrived to visit newspaper and media offices checking facts!

I've found it! The story I had been searching for.

So Jim, now you see why I say it is Fate!"

"But Jess, Fate is fickle! Why did you have to leave Scotland and live on the other side of the world before you could appreciate the potential and power of the creative and caring spirit. Why could you not see that it had always been here in your ain kail-yard?"

"Why indeed Jim. When my childhood dream was to be the one that would set Bess Young's spirit free. And now by the magic of modern technology and the knowledge and experience I have gained I **can** tell on film the whole story that Bess began - the story of the Niddrie Coalbearers".

THE END

## ACKNOWLEDGEMENTS

### THANKS

A special thanks to Archibald Livingstone *(of the Edina Dance Band)*, who completed significant research, and wrote great text and verse.

Thanks also to the late David Spence *(ex-manager of Newcraighall Pit)*; Councillor David Brown; David Carson *(for his thesis on Wauchope)*; George Montgomery *(for poems 'The Arled Bairns' & 'The Lass o' Niddrey Mill')*; Newcraighall Miners Welfare Club; various Newcraighall Miners; The Craigmillar Festival Society; Irene Macdonald; Larry, Philip, Stephen and Andrew Crummy and Carmel Daly.

### BIBLIOGRAPHY

*The Barony Bard* by George Montgomery

*History of Newton Village* by George Montgomery

*General Wauchope* by William Bain

*Mine a Rich Vein* by Helen Crummy

### FOOTNOTES

1    1668

2    an ancient form of trial marriage

3    a union.

4    school teacher

5    friendly society